Get the full experience at:

PRAISE FOR

"I wish I had IGIST growing up as a young girl excited by science. IGIST is a thrilling read that will inspire future generations to change the world."

—McKenna Kardish
Harvard 2015, Astrophysics

"An exciting journey . . . part intergalactic adventure, part coming of age, and 100% inspiring for young girls interested in technology."

—Annie Pratt
Stanford 2014, Design

"The story is a rather breathless succession of escapes, intellectual pursuits, dangerous missions, unexpected encounters, with each one ending in some kind of defeat until the final one, making for an incredibly fun journey."

—Sarah Decker
Forks Junior High School, 7th Grade Teacher

"I first gave it to my son to read: He loved it! He actually likes to read but is a pretty picky reader. He texted me from school during the day to tell me how much he loved the book!"

—Science in the City

"A stellar futuristic tale with an exemplary heroine."

—Kirkus Reviews

L. S. Larson

IGIST Studios 2018

CONTENTS

Throughout the book you'll see black and white IGIST Sci-Fi photorealistic illustrations. Download the IGIST Experience app on iOS and use the Augmented Reality (AR) scanner to bring the illustrations to life.

For Kendall:
seek the best ideas to
build a better future.

PROLOGUE

Venter looked up at the Sappho of Oculus. The sun brightened the red sandstone statue of the supernal pioneer. Her gaze appeared warm and resolute, her arms outstretched, and her palms faced up. Standing two hundred meters tall, the tribute was built to pay homage to Sappho, whose inventions allowed Mars to be terraformed.

Venter's gaze shifted from the giant statue to the domed structure at the top of the arched stairway. He took a deep breath and started the ascent. His hands were clasped in front of him, holding his prized possession delicately.

As he climbed the stairs, Venter desperately hoped he would win. To win the ritual would be a dose of good luck that would increase his standing in the high council. Venter was superstitious and had decided he wouldn't utter his racer's name until the race was over.

When he reached the top of the stairs, Venter turned around and looked back over the Martian city. Arcing roads symmetrized seafoam-green grass stretching one hundred miles long and twenty miles wide. Towering structures stood on the sides glowing hues of lime green, orange, pink, purple, and sky blue. Venter loved Oculus. The Capital of the Galaxy was more than a city. Oculus was an idea.

Venter turned away from the panorama and entered the domed structure. The six other members of the high council stood around a circular table all wearing their ritual robes.

1 · THE ANCHOR

It had been fifty-four days since Emi submitted her application. Her mother had always hoped that Emi would one day attend IGIST, the Intergalactic Institute of Science and Technology. Every day that passed with her waiting to hear back about her admission became more and more unbearable.

The admission notification was legendary. If selected, the student would receive a miniature model of the space station. The model displayed a hologram image of the chancellor with a personalized message.

More than anything, she wanted to receive that notification. Emi was confident the package would be waiting when she got home, but first she had to endure a day of school at Rockland. Today was the last day that a model would arrive if she'd been accepted.

***

The teacher listed off the students as their names appeared on a leaderboard. He was old and gaunt with warm eyes. Although it seemed cruel to rank each student based upon secondary school, the list was a Rockland tradition. Mr. Lemore beamed with pride as he announced the placement of his students at top schools on Earth.

Two-thirds of Emi's class was already placed, leaving only the bottom group. She stared at her name near the bottom of the list with no school beside it. The lower her name fell, the smaller she felt. She never thought her name might end up in last place. Emi watched Mr. Lemore walk to the leaderboard. Several students snickered about the six names still not placed.

Mr. Lemore rattled off five placements. Now only one student did not have a school listed on the leaderboard. All eyes in the class turned to Emi. It was official: her name sat at the bottom of the list in the dreaded anchor position. She wished she could climb under a rock and disappear; she felt as small as a speck of dust. Several students whispered her name under their breath. The tone in the air had shifted from elementary meanness to one of universal pity.

There was a certain irony in less intelligent pupils calling Emi stupid. She didn't hate the other kids. She felt sorry for them. They would all be bygones. A few might make it to space, but the majority of her peers were destined to lead boring lives stuck on Earth. Emi's ambitions included getting off the planet.

Emi looked out the window. Usually an orangish-gray smog hung over the dreary city, making it hard to see the sky. Today a strong wind had opened up the clouds, creating a blue and orange sky-canyon that framed the moon and the space station.

Earlier that day she had read about solar-sailing: students of IGIST would sail between the moon and the space station, using the sun's light to propel them through space. She desperately wanted to be up in space and wondered how small Earth would look from the stars.

"Emi?"

Snapping out of her daydream, Emi noticed her peers filing out of the classroom.

"Come sit," said Mr. Lemore.

She sat down near him, their two chairs facing each other. Emi had always liked her eighth-grade math teacher. She assumed the girl in the picture on his desk was his daughter. There were rumors she had dropped out of school.

"You must pick a school," Mr. Lemore said. "You've received several acceptances. You are at risk of losing your spot if you don't choose one. Franklin, Verity, even your safeties fill up fast. I'd hate for you to end up out of the school system. Here, I've prepared this packet for you to review."

On the wall behind him hung a Legion poster. In the picture a teenager grimaced, wearing a drab gray jumpsuit and sitting behind a screen. For students who didn't have the grades to go to a secondary school, a tiny percentage would go into a government work program known as the Legion. The program used to train people in trades, but since the automation era, it had devolved into a forced work program. Legion members wore caps to keep themselves focused on the monotonous tasks required.

"I've already picked IGIST."

Mr. Lemore moved his chair closer to her and lowered his voice in a sympathetic tone. Emi could tell by the look in his eyes he cared about her.

"Emi, we've been over this. There are a million reasons you can't go to IGIST." He paused for a moment and looked back at the picture on his desk. He continued balancing a tone between parental sternness and sincere affection.

"There are countless odds stacked against you. In twenty years IGIST hasn't issued a single acceptance to someone on Earth. It's too expensive to get to space. You'd most likely get dropped from the probo screening. I'm not saying that you're not smart enough, but the reality is that you just didn't get accepted. We're running out of time, Emi. You must consider the alternatives."

Emi told herself to stay confident. After all, her parents raised her to be strong. "I should hear back today," she informed her teacher.

2 · LANDSLIDE

The first fifty days Max had been hopeful, but this week rumors were percolating that his daughter was the "anchor." The dreaded position was one no parent would want for their child.

Max scanned his incoming messages on his tablet. He deleted all the requests from headhunters and focused on one new message from an old friend:

I'm headed to Santiago.

The message contained a link to a developing story: "Landslide in Andes Reveals 68-Million-Year-Old Dinosaur Tracks."

Max smiled as he read about the tracks that had been discovered. As an astrogeologist, he was in high demand; many companies wanted him to leave Earth and work on projects in the asteroid field or on one of Jupiter's moons.

Most Earthlings flocked to study astrogeology because it was a ticket off Earth, but Max had studied the discipline because it was the only track that included Earth geology, a stepping-stone to a deserted field. He was not only an astrogeologist but also a paleontologist, someone very unique. The message from his old friend Chavez was a call to action.

Max slid away from his desk and took a moment to savor the second love of his life. Hanging from his ceiling, a pterodactyl skeleton spread its bone wings, covering nearly the entire space. A glass-framed baby plesiosaur fossil spanned the entire back wall of his office. The fossil showed the creature's four flippers, a rare find from the Triassic period. These were just a few of Max's prized possessions that kept him on Earth. Max was a digger. The little voice in his mind told him to dig—to look for things of the past.

Max was a bygone. He would never leave Earth. The vast majority of bygones did not want their children to pursue a life in space. Max was different. His wife, Maria, had been taken from them when Emi was five years old, and it had been her lifelong dream that their daughter would study and live among the stars.

Over the last nine years, Max had done his best as a single father, focusing on the paramount love of his life: Emi. In his gray and brown office of scattered papers and dinosaur bones, a bright arrangement of balloons stood out. He always thought Emi would get accepted into her first-choice school and wanted the day she received the announcement to be special. Now on the fifty-fourth day and counting, he was starting to get worried that he should have spent more time talking to her about alternatives.

3 · BYGONE

"Hurry up, Sadee," Emi called back to her drone.

Hovering above the sidewalk, the drone looked like a miniature flying saucer with an orb in the center. Two glowing lights on the orb above the saucer ring gave the drone the appearance of eyes. The orb section of the drone glowed green.

Emi and her dad had built Sadee from an old, unmanned aerial communication flyer. Her dad always told her that there is no such thing as an unachievable goal. Sadee was his favorite exhibit to remind Emi how she could engineer something. Sadee wasn't only a science project; she was Emi's best friend. When they arrived at their house, Emi burst through the door with Sadee hovering over her shoulder.

"Did it arrive?" asked Emi.

"Nothing yet, honey," replied her father. "You know, the last deliveries are usually the ones from space."

He winked and gave her a big hug. "Dinner's ready."

He was an awful cook but was diligent in making dinner every night for the two of them. Emi was still optimistic. The salmon looked bland, but the asparagus would suffice. He smiled and went on with their ritual.

"What did you learn today?"

"That there is a constant route between the moon and IGIST where the luminaries solar-sail back and forth," said Emi. "It sounds remarkable."

"Ahh, that's great, my dear," said her father. "I love that your passion for space is so contagious. I wish I had your confidence."

"What did you learn today, Dad?"

"There was a fossil discovery in the Andes."

"Dad, the only real discoveries are out there," said Emi, pointing to the sky.

"For you, that's probably right, my love."

Emi tucked her hair, black with blue highlights, behind her ear and looked over her shoulder at the balcony. "Can I wait outside?"

"Go for it."

Emi went out to the balcony with Sadee hovering along. She paced back and forth outside. Moments later, her father saw her shoulders drop. The delivery vehicle had passed their house. Emi came in from the balcony.

"Emi, I'm sorry, sweetie," said her father.

Emi ran to her room and slammed the door.

***

Stepping into his office, Max sighed. He opened the window and let the balloons float off into the night. He took the article about the Andes he'd tagged and deleted it.

"There has to be a way," he muttered to himself.

He thought for a moment before opening his inbox and scrolling through the requests to drop by the asteroid belt.

***

Emi's entire room was a shrine to IGIST. On her wall several thin screens projected images of space, the IGIST campus, and great scientists. On one monitor was a green radar display obscuring the stars. Its glowing radius spun around the center like a loading icon. *Why do I bother?* she couldn't help thinking. The sector scan had yet to identify a single trace of her mother's special plants. As Emi tapped the screen off, she broke into tears.

She did not belong here; she was certain of it. While Emi wiped her eyes, Sadee shut off the remaining screens.

"Thanks, Sadee."

Emi heard a knock on her door.

"Emi, can I come in?" asked her father.

"No," replied Emi. "I just need a few minutes."

After the screens were off, two items remained in her room, reminding her of her apparently unachievable goal. On her nightstand stood a model of IGIST that her dad had given her years ago. Sitting beside the model was her rose seed, a special gift from her mom. Emi had promised herself that she would plant the seed somewhere it could flourish, shining through the night, free from the plague.

There was another knock outside her room before a handwritten note from her father slid under the door. Emi picked it up. The note read:

The right idea can overcome seemingly overwhelming challenges.

Her dad loved reminding her of IGIST's ethos, but now it only magnified her disappointment. *Was it all a lie?* she wondered. She set the note down next to the model and then switched off the lights. In the dark, the model glowed. Emi closed her eyes and envisioned the illuminated hologram proclaiming her acceptance. She switched the lights back on. She had dreamed of her admission notification a million times, looking at this replica. Etched on the base of the model was the Institute's motto: *Intelligentia, Curiositas, Perseverantia.*

She set the model back on her nightstand and traced the last word, Latin for perseverance, then picked up a packet she'd set on the nightstand and flipped through it. A handwritten note from Mr. Lemore pleaded for her to pick a school. Emi appreciated the folder yet got the feeling it wasn't prepared for her. Confirming her suspicion, the form on the last page showed another person's name: Jacqueline "Jack" Lemore.

She threw the packet from Mr. Lemore in the wastebasket. Emi had read the admissions process so many times she knew it by heart. Her application to IGIST would have benefitted greatly from an interview, but the Institute only offered them to valedictorians. She grimaced with frustration. The only blemish on her transcript was her grade in English. She deeply regretted her last term paper. According to her English teacher, she had repackaged their class discussions in her paper, neglecting to add her own point of view. Emi emphasized the points they had discussed in class because she thought they were the right answers.

Emi had pleaded her case with the school administrators. She had asked her favorite teacher, Mr. Lemore, to intercede on her behalf. She had even started a student petition demanding that subjective courses like English be graded "Pass/Fail." Almost nobody signed her petition, and her English teacher dug in, leaving her grade as a B. Nobody understood why it mattered so much to her. It was the only B she had ever gotten. None of them even entertained the possibility of a student from Earth getting accepted to IGIST, so why would it matter if she was number one or not.

It would be pointless to explain all this to the admin bots at IGIST. They had been accommodating in giving exact info on the process, and that was it. She couldn't even get her favorite teacher on Earth to vouch for her. The IGIST bots would be of no help at this point. She would have to figure out a solution on her own.

Emi picked up the notecard from her father and paced around her room, reading the note out loud. "The right idea can overcome seemingly overwhelming challenges."

Sadee circled the room, following Emi's lead. Emi tapped on two screens. One showed the IGIST campus while the other portrayed a spaceship. Sadee pulled up the IGIST admission hologram.

"That's it. Sadee, give me the model!"

In a few minutes Emi disassembled the IGIST model. She had an idea to get the Institute's attention. She placed a small imager inside the model that could both record and project a hologram.

"Sadee, record."

Emi took a deep breath. "My name is Emi, and I was born to go to IGIST . . ."

The video was one minute and thirty seconds. IGIST hacks were legendary.

Emi ended the hologram by splicing in a two-second video of Sputnik. To be "Sputnik'd" meant someone had placed an unexpected appearance of Sputnik in a video. Over time, the satellite had become a symbol of all IGIST hacks. She screwed the model back together and tested out the button she'd added to initiate the hologram. It was sweet.

She looked over the model. To ensure the button on the base of the model would get pushed, she added a final touch, painting the button red.

"Perfect."

With her extension arm released from her orb, Sadee brought Emi an old, shabby certified box and painted over the original address so that Emi could fill in the new one. If they re-sent the box standard, it wouldn't arrive at IGIST for a month. This way, the model would reach the space station in just one week.

"Should I make it out to Florin or Archimedes?"

***

The next day, after class, Emi braced for her teacher's lecture on her lack of school choice.

"I pulled some strings. Pacifica Academy is holding a seat for you. Another student's family from Rockland is moving to Mars. This couldn't have worked out better," said Mr. Lemore.

"I appreciate everything you've done for me, Mr. Lemore, but I can't stay on Earth."

"There is no chance, Emi. If you don't take this slot, you'll have to join the Legion."

"I'm sorry."

"Darn it, Emi!" He slammed his fist down on the table. "Can anyone help you? I like you, kid, but this is an awful mistake. I've seen this before, and I don't want you to end up in a bad place. When an opportunity knocks, you must open the door."

Emi touched Mr. Lemore's arm. Her eyes said thank you. "This isn't my door."

***

"Peculiar."

Florin examined the certified package sitting on her desk. These were very rare in space. Her late aunt used to send her hand-painted landscapes of Earth, now enlivening the walls of her office. She hadn't received anything from home in more than a decade until now. This particular box looked battered. Tearing it open, she saw the model of IGIST and smiled. It reminded her of her own acceptance. She held up the model of the space station and examined it. On top of its base, someone had hacked a red button above the school's motto.

4 · TUSK

Celeste Tusk, twenty-eight, was CEO and founder of Tusk Enterprise. Ten years earlier no one had heard of her. Now every person in the solar system knew the name Celeste Tusk, and every home on Earth and in space used a Tusk Air Ionizer to purify the air from harmful particles. Celeste interviewed every critical hire that Tusk Enterprise had ever made. Her employees called her Wonder Woman.

It was very easy to video conference in for an interview, but Celeste insisted on hologramming in for every interaction. She knew that most people would brag about the interaction and further spread the myth of the space business mogul. She had a sip of her hot tea.

On the display Celeste saw Max yawning as the image came up. It was early in the morning on Earth.

"Max, it's nice to finally meet you," said Celeste.

In her room the slender, seven-foot-tall magnate stood, knowing her life-size hologram would be projected on the other end.

"We've hired every notable astrogeologist from Earth, but you're the one holdout."

"I'm also a paleontologist," replied Max.

"I doubt that will help much in the asteroid belt, but only Sappho knows," replied Celeste, referencing the supernal astrochemist and astrophysicist. Anyone who hadn't heard of Sappho must have lived under a rock.

In Max's room, Celeste could see a pterodactyl fossil in the background, an odd sight.

"Ms. Tusk, I've got some questions about the arrangement," said Max.

"Please, call me Celeste. I assume this is about your family situation. I've read your profile and agree the asteroid belt isn't really the ideal place for a fourteen-year-old girl."

"Is there something you've done for other families?"

Celeste clasped her hands together and grinned. She knew that by asking, Max was opening the door on a pact that would be her opportunity.

The Tusk empire needed workers to mine rare elements from the asteroid belt in between Mars and Jupiter. These materials were the key to Tusk's filters. Tusk's employees were quite loyal. Celeste prided herself on her one hundred percent retention rate.

"We normally let the families figure out their situations, but in this case, maybe we could amend the contract to provide accommodations for your daughter. Of course, we consider any requests during a negotiation to ensure we get to a beneficial outcome for both parties."

When the magazines and talk shows covered Celeste, they focused on her groundbreaking innovation with the air ionizer that she had invented at Apollo University two years before she graduated.

She and a select few knew an equally and potentially more important insight was how to get skilled employees to commit to work in the asteroid belt. Other space entrepreneurs had dabbled in ionized filters before, but no one could get the expert workforce needed to extract the materials in the difficult conditions of the asteroid belt until Celeste had come along.

Her biggest insight was that everyone had a price. She had been extremely successful in finding people who possessed the skills she needed but also had some big request they must have filled. She had a rare gift of being able to discover what any individual really wanted, and then she was able to package an answer for that desire in such a way that the individual left the conversation feeling like she was the only one who could give it to them.

She sipped her tea and regarded the glum bygone.

"What were you thinking, Max?"

"One of the prep schools for Marston, Apollo, Sp43, or Ganymede Tech."

"Ah, four of the five Star League schools, the best schools in space. Makes sense. Who wouldn't want their child to attend one? I noticed you didn't say IGIST."

"Emi applied there but was turned down. She's very bright, and I'm sure her scores will be adequate for the others."

Celeste positioned her hologram to appear to sit next to Max on his couch. Her wide grin turned to stone.

"How important is it to you that she gets into one of these schools?"

Through the image she saw Max staring at a photo of what she presumed to be his wife holding Emi as a baby.

"There is nothing I wouldn't give to make this happen."

Celeste smiled. She knew how to close this deal.

"I can help your daughter," said Celeste, a touch of hope gleaming in her violet eyes.

She gestured with her hand as she spoke.

"Max, usually the asks are quantified for a year of additional service. For a normal prep school, it might be four to five years on top of your normal contract. For what you're asking, it could be as high as fifty. I'd have to run it by my team to get the exact number."

"Fifty! I thought it would be ten. Can I have some time to think about it?"

Celeste's hologram stood up, looking down at Max.

"If you can commit to a twenty-year contract starting next week, I'll commit to the agreement now."

Max paced in front of the screen, considering his options.

"One month. Give me one month with Emi on Mars while we select her school, and I'll sign today."

"Deal," replied Celeste. "I'll have my people send over the arrangement within the hour."

Celeste bowed to Max, then her screen turned black.

5 · THE PLAGUE

Jack Lemore felt excited, exhausted, and on top of the world all at the same time. On the bow of the ship, she took a deep breath of ocean air. The sun warmed her face and shone on her dark eyeliner. She watched a pod of dolphins frolicking alongside the cruise ship and smiled, feeling pure bliss.

She had done it. It had taken Jack more than a decade to save up enough zurcon for the Helix Cells. It was highly illegal to be in possession of them, but it was worth the risk. After finally procuring her much needed Helix Cells, Jack was so ecstatic that she had her first procedure done immediately. Now she had to wait four painstaking weeks before she could arrange her second and final procedure. She was desperate to have her transition behind her.

Suddenly, a strong gust of wind pushed her from behind, and she grabbed the guardrail instinctively. It was worn and rusty, and the paint had all but crumbled off.

Jack looked around the ship deck's worn exterior. The only thing that looked to have been designed in the last five years were the alarm sirens. The two shiny glass bulbs flanking a black speaker were an eerie reminder that, at any moment, the plague could strike. On the speaker a platinum *T* stood out, with two vertical marks coming down from the horizontal line of the *T* to represent tusks. It was the logo for Tusk Enterprise.

Known as the *Orleans,* the ship had been the most luxurious vessel in the world at one point, but now it was a depressing shadow of its former self. Jack imagined what it might have been like to be one of the rich passengers indulging in the opulent suites and comforts on the maiden voyage one hundred years ago when the ship was first christened.

"Last call before passengers must go to their cabins for landing." The deck bot interrupted Jack's train of thought with the drink call announcement. The robot's rough appearance highlighted what everyone already knew: the security on the cheap barge was subpar. It was easy for people to smuggle contraband.

"I'll have a Venus Thirst," said Jack.

The robot signaled that drink wasn't available. Jack sighed in disappointment. "OK then. I'll have a grapefruit juice."

Out of the corner of her eye, Jack noticed a sinewy bald man glaring at her across the deck. She hadn't seen him in eleven years. His eyebrows were still shaved clean. He sipped his green drink. This fellow had not only hazed Jack but also swiped her zurcon when they were in the Legion together.

At the same time the cylindrical-shaped bot in front of Jack ejected a cup onto a small platform and sprayed the juice from a narrow tube. A small robotic arm emerged from the compartment and pressed salt onto the edge of the glass. Jack grabbed the drink and took a sip. It wasn't a Venus Thirst, but the tart, acidic taste of the grapefruit juice was better than nothing.

She looked up, and the bald man was gone. Jack spotted him jostling through the throngs of ne'er-do-wells with a disc-shaped, jagged-edged blade dangling from a chain at his waistline.

A forceful gust of wind blew Jack's long dirty blonde hair over her eyes. She brushed it to the side and stood tall as the waves thrashed the ship. From the bow she could see the space compound in the distance. She had worked her way up from the Legion to become a space transporter. Everyone looked down on the transporters, but Jack loved her job. She had been back and forth from Earth to the moon and the Earth to Mars more times than she could count. Seeing people who never thought they could leave Earth finally make it to space gave her life purpose.

"Greetings, non grata," said the man with no eyebrows, now standing by Jack's side. "It's been a minute." He was gazing at Torrance Compound.

"How's it going?" Jack asked him.

The man smiled and turned to Jack. "You got two choices. You give me all the zurcon you've saved up, or I take 'em. Your call."

A high-pitched mechanical wail stole their attention. Jack dropped her drink, the glass shattering on the deck.

"Lucky you," grouched the man before he bolted away.

The siren's wail sounded a distinctive pattern, notifying everyone of imminent danger.

Jack crouched down to get her bearings. As she placed her left hand on the ground, she cut two of her fingers on the broken glass. She wiped the blood on her pant leg and looked up. People were running in every direction. She looked at the flashing blue alarm lights and back along the side of the ship. It was easily one hundred yards to the stairwell to her cabin.

"Come with us!" yelled a couple. They pointed to a life raft on the corner of the ship.

"I can't," responded Jack. "I need to get to my cabin."

Jack turned away from the raft. Passengers were running toward the front of the ship. Jack sidestepped them, darting back and forth as the siren wailed. A man grabbed her with a look of panic on his face.

"You're going in the wrong direction!" he screamed. "I saw it. Back there. Run!"

The blue flash from the siren illuminated her face like a deer in headlights. Jack pushed the man aside and continued toward the back of the boat.

Suddenly, she heard it. A loud crack. She stopped dead. Her ears perked, and the hair on the back of her neck stood straight up. She heard it again over the siren and the screaming. It was an awful sound. *Wuh-PSSSH,* then a loud crack. Again, *Wuh-PSSSH,* crack!

Jack was still paralyzed. The sound of the plague burst repeatedly like a whip cracking. A hundred feet away she saw it. A dark cloud exploded from one of the cabin doors. The plague was regenerating, with long fractal tentacles shooting out, while multiple rapid explosions expanded the dark cloud. *Wuh-PSSSH,* crack! *Wuh-PSSSH,* crack! The dark cloud engulfed several people.

It was the blood-curdling screams in the cacophony of whipcracks and wailing sirens that broke Jack's paralyzed state. Sweating profusely, she ran back to the bow of the ship. She could hear the sound gaining on her. She grabbed the rail and yelled, "No!" then punched the rail with all her might.

She couldn't bear to look back. There was no way Jack could get to her precious Helix Cells that she so desperately needed. She had no choice but to abandon them. She climbed to the top bar of the rail, looking toward Torrance Compound in the distance and the breaking waves below.

Her left hand gripped the edge of the railing. She could feel her grip slipping from the blood spilling out of her cuts. She felt a searing pain in her left hand. Boy did it burn. The cloud was upon her. Jack held her breath.

Wuh-PSSSH, crack!

She jumped.

6 · MET

Relishing the photos of him and his wife on his tablet, Max replayed the words in his head. *I'll see you for breakfast.* Her voice was still as soft as ever. She had gone out for a routine jog along the lake, around the park, and then back home. Only this time there was a plague outbreak, and Maria never returned. He set the tablet on the kitchen counter.

Max felt guilty. He had always been totally forthright with Emi, but now he was intentionally misleading his daughter for what he felt was her own good. He told Emi he had sold the house to pay for the trip. He also told her his friend Celeste would help Emi get into a Star League school but failed to mention that he had just signed the next twenty years of his life away. He justified the decision by telling himself it was worth it to have one spectacular month on Mars before Emi would go off to school. He was proud that he could give her the future that she was meant for but dreaded being away from his little girl.

He looked at the framed family picture sitting on the counter. Maria would have never guessed Max would do it. *Today is the day,* he thought. He sent a B2B message to Emi, "The coach will be here in a few minutes."

***

Upstairs, Emi sat on her bed while Sadee sat docked on her charging station. Emi's eyes were shut. She appeared to be in a state of meditation, but she was actually deep in thought communication with Sadee.

Sadee was connected to her via a brain-to-brain link known as B2B, a streamlined messaging system enabling people and computers to share information instantly. B2B was run by a small black device called a MET (Mind Enhancing Technology), which had two components: a detachable minicomputer and a dock that was permanently placed on the back of Emi's occipital bone. Everyone wore a MET because it was the fastest way to connect with others and learn something new.

Two days earlier Emi had checked the site and found out that she had not been accepted to IGIST. She thought through her options as Sadee showed her an immersive 360-degree image of the solar system with all the Star League schools highlighted.

In Emi's mind she saw Apollo on Earth's moon. Next, she saw IGIST orbiting around the moon. Farther out in the solar system, she saw Marston on Mars. In between Mars and Jupiter, she saw the asteroid belt and studied an enormous planetoid known as Ceres. On Jupiter's largest moon, Ganymede, was Ganymede Tech. Rotating around Saturn's rings was Sp43, the last of the Star League schools. In a separate B2B image, Sadee showed a window listing out several famous scientists and alumni of the Star League schools.

Celeste Tusk had gone to Apollo University on the moon. Emi had watched some interviews with Celeste describing her mission to protect humanity from the deadly plague. Emi's father had said they might get to talk with Celeste one day via hologram.

An incoming B2B notification interrupted Emi's train of thought. A message from her father appeared.

7 · SPACE DELAY

It was the most beautiful thing Emi had ever seen. Rising from the ground, twenty stories of alternating dark blue and silver glass created the crescent sail-shaped launch structure that towered over the horizon. Positioned on a tiny island just off the coastline, a brilliant white rocket stood next to the launch tower.

In just a few hours, they'd be blasting off and starting their journey in space. Though their trip from Rockland to Manhattan Beach took only ninety minutes, it felt as if it had lasted a lifetime, but laying her eyes upon the glorious rocket, Emi had never felt so excited. Her cheeks hurt from smiling. Her father peered out the coach with his hands pressed on the window, beads of sweat rolling down the glass.

Across from the launchpad, a village stretched from the coastline a mile inland with a huge bazaar of shops and restaurants.

"Ms. Tusk has lined up your last Earth meal as requested," a calm voice announced from the speaker as the self-flying coach touched down.

A map lit up, highlighting a dotted route to the restaurant. A wind advisory message scrolled across the screen as well.

***

"Do we have to do this meal?" asked Emi, striding through the throngs of travelers under her father's arm.

They carried all the possessions they would need in their waist packs. Emi's dangled beneath her black coat and gray sweatshirt emblazoned with a dream catcher surrounded with hunter-green star fractals. This dual-ring design represented the Starcatchers, an astronomy club that Emi's dad had convinced her to start at Rockland.

"Can't we go straight to the launchpad?" she begged her father.

"I proposed to your mom in Morocco," he said. "That's why we're here." He then explained that the village was a replication of the Moroccan city of Marrakesh.

The lively market streets bustled with all different kinds of people. Colorful experience shops lined the walking streets, each claiming to be the last place a person could experience their favorite Earth pleasure.

Standing out from the line of shops was an Arabian palace with a wide dome and a ten-foot-tall mini minaret. Emi couldn't wait to get through this meal and be on her way at last.

She ambled through the arched entrance of the domed building, where an elderly Arabian man awaited them. Emi was surprised; she had never been to a restaurant with human servers before. The man wore a long white robe and a red upside-down cuplike hat with a black tassel.

"My name is Fez. Welcome to the Marrakesh."

***

Once they were seated and eating, Emi couldn't believe how much her appetite had swelled. The sweet couscous reminded her of the risotto her father had once attempted to make, albeit unsuccessfully. Compared to his chicken potpie, the *bastilla* was something else entirely. Emi pictured herself tearing through the flaky crust of the savory pie on Martian lands.

"This is the last time you will hear this on Earth," said her father, grinning as he carried out their ritual. "What did you learn today?"

"I learned that the Tower of Oculus on Mars is three thousand feet tall," said Emi. "That's more than double the size of the largest building here on Earth!"

"I would love to feel what you're feeling right now," said her father. "I think I may have felt it once."

He looked off into the distance, and his head dropped down for a second. His voice softened as he opened his heart to her. "It was on my first dig when I found my first fossil."

His face perked up, beaming as he finished his sentence. "Seeing you feel that now, Emi—learning as you explore your passions. That's what it's all about. I love that you're hungry for knowledge."

When they were done eating, Fez strolled over to their table. "After your last meal, it's customary to take a photo in the minaret."

Emi rolled her eyes. She was too anxious to stop for a picture.

"It'll be fun," her father said. His bubbly tone and smile added a sense of excitement to life's mundanities.

***

They looked up at the balcony in the minaret tower before entering a tiny two-person elevator. Inside the elevator a glass door shut, creating a small cylindrical tube. In less than a second, the tube shot up one story, and the door opened to the balcony. Outside on the second deck, Sadee hovered, waiting for them.

Emi and her father looked out in the distance and saw the sail-launch structure. The wind blew across Emi's face, and she smelled the ocean. In the distance a ship cruised in the direction of the launchpad. Fez pointed to a large camera on the tower. Next to the camera, two Tusk siren speakers stood out from the tower's worn mustard-yellowish limestone brick.

"Look at the camera," yelled Fez. "And smile in three, two . . ."

"Sadee, you take one too," said Emi's father. He pointed at the rocket. "The right idea can overcome anything!"

Her father tickled her at just the right time, and Emi smiled. His arm was around her, pointing in the distance. On the tower the large camera flashed.

Emi hugged her dad. He gave her hope. When her mother had disappeared, she hadn't thought she could go on. Building Sadee together was her father's way of getting her focused on something other than her grief. He had dedicated his life to raising her.

***

"It's not working," her father yelled down to Fez.

Emi and her father had returned to the elevator shaft. He pressed the elevator button again, yet nothing happened.

"Ah yes," said Fez, pacing at the bottom of the tower. "It does that sometimes. You can try to jiggle the cable inside the panel or you can take the ladder down."

The wooden ladder leaned against the parapet on the balcony. Fez held the ladder as if he had done this a million times. Emi gestured toward the panel, and her dad grabbed her shoulder.

"Let's take the ladder down. Probably the last time you'll ever use one of those."

Emi climbed down the ladder and felt the wind gust against her back.

"There's no rush," said Fez. "There's a severe wind advisory. The launch will be delayed at least twenty-four hours."

Emi's head dropped with disappointment.

"Is there any other way?" asked Emi.

"The Hyperloop would get you to Alexandria Compound on the East Coast by tomorrow morning," said Fez. "But by that time the delay will be over here."

Emi sighed.

"You've waited fourteen years, Emi. What's one more night?" said her father, wrapping his arm around her. "Come on. Let's see where we're staying tonight."

8 · CRASH

After learning of the wind delay, Emi and her father left the Marrakesh and walked through the narrow streets toward the ocean. There was still a lot of activity on the street despite the heavy winds, which made it hard for Sadee to keep up. On the seafront path the palm trees swayed in the wind as the ocean waves crashed onto the boardwalk. The promenade hotel sat about a block from the bridge that connected the main side of Torrance Compound to the launchpad.

It was starting to get dark, and white lights lit up the crescent launch structure, illuminating the sail shape and highlighting the rocket. Sadee finally caught up.

"A little wind got ya down?" messaged Emi, teasing her drone.

"Let's get a photo with the launchpad in the background," her father said.

"Sadee, stop screwing around," said Emi as Sadee weaved through the air.

Stabilizing herself in the wind, Sadee managed to get into a position to attempt a photo. The drone snapped a few shots and then B2B messaged Emi, "Too windy. Take a look."

Emi closed her eyes to focus on one of the images that Sadee had shared. In the photo she and her father were blurry, but the launch structure was lit up perfectly. Behind it, a fuzzy ship looked as if it were nearly on top of the launch structure. Emi opened her eyes and turned around. Her father was already looking in that direction.

The *Orleans* cruise ship swayed back and forth, rocking in the wind. Black clouds rose in plumes from the vessel.

"Is it on fire?" asked Emi.

"Oh no!" exclaimed her father.

The ship crashed into the structure, knocking over the rocket. Emi gasped. This couldn't be. The black cloud covering the ship engulfed the lower part of the launchpad. Emi could see people running off the bridge toward the mainland side. The white lights on the launchpad were promptly outshone by the pulse of blue warning lights. Soon the lights and accompanying warning sirens cascaded through the space compound.

Her father grabbed her, and they charged across the street to the promenade hotel. The building's safety doors were shut, and all the windows' emergency shutters were closed. The only activity at the building was the Tusk sirens' wailing and the blue lights flashing. Her father pounded on the door. Emi heard screams. The black cloud engulfed the bridge and spread up the coastline and through the streets.

"Dad?"

"Hurry, Emi."

He pulled her by the arm and headed toward the Marrakesh. Sadee struggled to keep up. The force of the wind made it hard to run or fly against. Over the sound of the screams and the sirens, Emi heard something she'd never heard before. An eerie sound made her skin crawl. In the distance it sounded like a whip cracking.

"No. No. No," muttered her father as they sprinted toward the Marrakesh. A glass door closed off the archway. He pounded on the glass.

"Let us in!"

Inside the restaurant the lights were out. A group of people huddled in the center. Fez slunk out of the shadows and came to the window.

"Sadee," yelled Emi. "Sadee!"

She couldn't see the drone. Emi looked behind her and saw every shop's doors and windows shut in lockdown mode. Panicked people ran from building to building.

Her father pounded on the glass. Fez shook his head no, then a look of terror came across his face. Emi heard a crash. A gust of wind knocked down the ladder next to the minaret tower, breaking it in half. Emi heard a loud crack.

The plague exploded onto the street. People screamed. From the black cloud, fractal tentacles shot out and expanded. Her father pulled her to the bottom of the minaret tower.

"Quick! Climb up!"

Emi stepped onto her father's hands, and he hoisted her up. She reached the parapet on the bottom of the one-story balcony and pulled herself up. She saw Sadee. The drone emerged from the plague cloud closing in on them. Suddenly, Sadee dropped to the ground. Like a bowling ball, Sadee rolled toward Emi's father.

He jumped and missed the balcony edge. He jumped again and missed. He looked up at Emi.

"Emi, get in the elevator. Shut the door."

Emi started to sob.

"Try again."

He took a running jump and missed again.

"Emi, listen to me."

"Try again. Please, Dad. Try!"

"Get in the elevator and shut the door. Now!"

The plague reached her father just as Sadee rolled up and hit his leg. He tossed Sadee in the air as the plague engulfed him. *Wuh-PSSSH,* crack! The plague's cloud crawled up the side of the tower. Emi looked over the balcony to see if she could see her father.

All she could see was the billowing form of the plague. A tentacle shot out from the cloud straight toward Emi. The tip of the tentacle hit Emi's left eye. Burning pain exploded through her skull. She screamed and grabbed her eye, crying hysterically, and fell back into the elevator compartment.

Her head smacked hard against the back wall, and darkness rolled over her. The plague crept up over the wall. Sadee stabilized herself and hovered onto the balcony. The drone managed to open the panel and jiggle the wire. *Wuh-PSSSH,* crack! The elevator door shut just in front of the outstretching plague.

9 · ESCAPE

Emi woke up in the hospital triage area with a bandage over her left eye. She looked around. Sadee was resting on the floor beside her bed. Her eyes glowed in the dark room.

The triage area housed hundreds of victims from the plague outbreak in quarantined rooms. Emi found herself in a double room with a sheet draped between her and another patient. On the wall in front of her, a small screen showed her name, room number, and the time. It was just past two in the morning.

She reached up and felt the bandage over her left eye. A wave of dread washed over her as she recalled the piercing *crack* of the plague cloud that had swallowed her father. She hadn't said goodbye. Tears streamed down her face, raining onto the thin covers. She took a deep breath, trying to fill her lungs, to quell whatever was burning inside her. It felt like a blinding rage. She opened her mouth to scream to let it out, but she was drowning in her tears. Both her eyes stung as she lay in the night.

***

Before dawn, the patient next to Emi climbed out of her bed and pulled the sheet divider open. She crouched down next to Sadee and gently patted her orb. Emi shut her eye, pretending to be sleeping.

"How do I get to the Hyperloop?" the woman asked Sadee.

Emi rolled over, startling the woman.

"She can't talk," said Emi, then she paused. The woman looked familiar, and her left hand was bandaged. The screen in her area read JACK LEMORE. "Wait, are you Mr. Lemore's daughter?"

"Yeah," she replied, scratching her head. "You go to Rockland?"

"Yeah," said Emi, "He was my favorite teacher."

"He's a good soul," she said. Jack seemed nice, but something was off about her. She looked to be in her midtwenties, tall and thin with especially pronounced eyebrows and cheekbones. But almost as if to rebel against her lovely features, she wore thick black eyeliner as well as a nose ring. Not just any nose ring, but a jade-green nose ring. This symbolized someone making a transition to a misfit. Misfits were humans who chose to make genetic modifications to themselves to take on animal attributes.

It was too dark to make out the charm on her nose ring. Despite Jack's unusual appearance, she felt familiar to Emi and emanated an air of sincere trustworthiness.

"Do you know how to get to the Hyperloop?" she asked Emi in a gentle, low tone.

Emi closed her eyes and asked for Sadee's help. Sadee beamed a map of the Hawthorne Hyperloop on the wall. Jack smiled, gave a nod of thanks to Emi, and traced her finger along the bicoastal route to Alexandria Compound.

"Why do you want to go to the Hyperloop?" asked Emi.

Jack stood up and looked around. She leaned over to Emi and whispered.

"It's the only way to get back to space."

Emi nodded. The night orderly bot started to open the door. Jack quickly jumped back into bed. When the robot passed into the next room, Jack got up quietly and snuck out the door.

***

Emi was too sad to eat when they brought her a tray of food. She looked up at the screen that said it was ten in the morning. Emi wished her dad could take her home.

She couldn't eat or sleep. She was so sad that she couldn't even cry any longer. She felt drained and empty inside. She couldn't stop thinking about her father. The whole thing was unbearable. Emi just wanted to sit in his office and stare at his fossils. She ached to have dinner with him and tell him what she'd learned that day. She was utterly alone in the world, except for her drone. Sadee glowed blue, echoing her sorrow.

"We'll be back to take you at noon," said the nurse.

"Where will I be going?" asked Emi.

"We'll operate today," said the nurse. "It's standard protocol to amputate or remove any infected area. Your roommate had her treatment yesterday."

Emi reached up and felt her eye. It had gone numb.

"My eye?"

"Yes," said the nurse, turning toward the door.

"Is there an alternative?" asked Emi, tapping her fingers on the bed.

The nurse stopped and turned back to her. "We used to let patients wait a few weeks to see if the plague had infected them," remarked the nurse. "If there's no pain, it's a fifty-fifty chance that you're actually infected. Given the recent breakouts, we now have a zero-risk policy that warrants treatment of any potentially infected areas."

"Treatment?" asked Emi.

"You don't get it, do you?" the nurse scoffed and rubbed his eyes. He had heavy bags under them. "If you are infected, your ocular immune system would prevent plague particles from spreading for about twelve weeks. At a certain point, it would expand uncontrollably and very quickly, causing you to suddenly blow up."

"And after the treatment?"

"You'll be taken to the nearest Legion center." He charged out.

Emi stared at the screen on the wall as she pressed the bandage over her left eye. What had the plague done to her? As each second passed, she became more dejected. She remembered the moment her dad had told her that they were going to space and started to cry.

***

When the clock struck noon, the nurse opened the door to the patient triage room. He looked around, surprised that it was empty.

10 · PLOY

It felt good to run. Emi followed Sadee as she hovered above the streets. It was hard to follow Sadee only seeing out of one eye. Emi reached up and felt the patch. Her left eye hurt a little, but she figured she could keep it closed if she needed, so she pulled off the patch. Her left eye was a little blurry, but the fresh air made it feel better.

Soon they arrived at the Hyperloop. Although it was Earth's most extensive transportation network, encompassing more than a million cities across the globe, the Hawthorne Hyperloop was now practically deserted with only three hundred million people left on the entire planet. Sadee ordered Emi a ticket. They just needed to get to platform 17.

"There it is, Sadee," said Emi.

As they approached platform 17, Emi heard shouts over the sound of the subterranean station's humming. When she approached, she saw a group of Terrans harassing someone.

The Terrans advocated extreme reactionary positions in support of Earth. They used physical assault and terrorism against groups, individual people, and ideas they considered anti-Earthling. Sadee sent Emi a message to avoid them, but Emi thought she recognized the victim.

"She's a space transporter," said a mohawked Terran with cutoff sleeves. He held Jack by the collar, having lifted her off the ground. "I bet we can get her transport badge."

"She's also a misfit," said the other Terran. She felt the charm on Jack's nose ring. "I bet this charm will go for a pretty penny."

Emi looked at Jack. She wasn't fighting back. She slumped down and sighed in despair. Emi could tell that Jack had been through this sort of torment before. She charged up to the man holding Jack and grabbed his arm.

"Leave her alone," yelled Emi.

The two Terrans turned and looked at Emi. Jack bit the thug's tree branch of an arm. The man screamed and let go. Jack started to run. A hefty Terran emerged from the shadows of the station and clotheslined Jack, knocking her to the ground. The obese man stomped his boot on Jack's chest.

"Grab the girl," barked the mohawked Terran. "And her drone too."

Sadee hovered up out of the man's reach, but the woman grabbed Emi. She messaged Sadee to send for help. The drone notified the security bots, but they were minutes away. They were certain to miss the Hyperloop and, worse, Emi couldn't imagine what these bandits would do to her.

The speaker barked, "Attention, passengers: the doors will be closing in one minute."

The woman patted down Emi. She grabbed her waist pack and opened it, and Emi's rose seed dropped to the ground.

The Terran with the mohawk breathed heavily as he knelt, his knee pressing down on Jack. Jack flung her arm up, trying to get the Terran off her, and scraped the man's face.

The Terran slammed Jack's arm back to the ground. The thug put his palm against Jack's face and grabbed the charm. Emi turned her head away and heard Jack scream.

She needed to do something. Emi struggled to break free, but the thug's grip was too strong. She squeezed Emi's shoulders more tightly the more she struggled. Emi looked around, but the platform was empty. Jack's face was bleeding profusely. Emi yelled, "Help! Help us!" Her heart ached as the woman covered her mouth. Emi closed her eyes. An idea came to her, and she sent an urgent message to Sadee.

Suddenly, a high-pitched sound wailed along with the flash of a blue light.

"Let's get out of here," yelled the mohawked Terran.

Emi grabbed Jack and pulled her into one of the cabins on the Hyperloop. Sadee followed close behind. The drone pulsed blue and her speaker wailed the distinctive alarm siren, a sound that had been drilled into every Earthling's psyche through fear of the plague. Leaving Jack and Emi, the Terrans scrammed from the tunnel.

The door would close any second. Emi scanned the ground, saw the rose seed, and grabbed it just before the door shut. Emi breathed a sigh of relief. "OK, Sadee, OK."

11 · HYPERLOOP

The cabin went dark except for the floor lights as the Hyperloop jolted into motion. Emi felt her body press against the seat from the g-force of the first few seconds of acceleration. Once in motion, the ride smoothed out and the overhead lights came on.

There were two pod seats with white synthetic leather that could recline into a sleeping station. Each seat had its own screen, showing that they were just five minutes into their three-hour, cross-country trip. In the center console was a machine called a rator, which could create any dish or drink one desired.

Jack reached up and turned the lights back to dim. As they faded down, the pressurized tube became silent. Emi looked at her travel companion in the low light and handed her a tissue from her waist pack. Jack held the tissue to her nose to absorb the blood. The cabin's silence broke with sobs of despair.

Mascara ran down Jack's cheeks. After a few moments, the tears and the eyeliner formed a black line from her eye to the bottom of her face. The muddled line told the story of her life.

Her parents' formula for success, combined with her schoolmates' bullying her to conform, had pushed Jack to a dark place. At a young age she rejected the pressure to be pretty and the need to live up to plastic standards.

Following her own path had a cost. She became the schoolgirl who was teased and punched. Unable to find fulfillment, she searched for answers and found addiction. Then came a purgatory of being an outcast, followed by a deeper dive into addiction before detox and rehabilitation.

All the anxiety and stress had melted away once she had accepted the truth—she had never looked the way she felt inside. Her transformation would be her only shot at fulfillment. Her jade nose ring and charm showed the world that the misfit didn't care about societal norms or what other people thought. She had decided to be herself. The thugs in the station had taken that from Jack. She bawled.

The sight and sound of Jack hit Emi with a pang of sorrow. She turned away, trying to fight her own emotions. Even when it seemed Jack could cry no longer, the flow of tears continued. Emi felt sorry for herself but even sorrier for Jack. After an exhaustive and desperate final outpouring, she stopped crying, and the cabin fell into an awkward silence.

Jack hit the lights, illuminating the cabin again.

"My name's Jacqueline. You can call me Jack."

She sniffled and wiped the mascara lines from her face. The bleeding had ceased at last. She pressed the rator and said, "Two Venus Thirsts." Two glass bottles appeared, and the rator hissed and dispensed a glowing purple liquid into the bottles. Jack smiled and handed one to Emi.

Unsure of what to say, she stammered, "You are—forgive me—you are what they call a . . ."

"Misfit," said Jack, finishing her sentence. "To be sure of it."

"How rude of me," said Emi. "I'm sorry. I've never met a misfit before. Thank you for the drink. My name is Emi."

"Very pleased to meet you, Emi," said Jack. "Thanks for helping me back there. Normally I just run away." The misfit looked down for a second and sighed. "You know, there's no shame in running."

She turned her head and pointed to Sadee. "And what's this doll's name?"

"That's Sadee."

Sadee glowed green.

"Thank you, Sadee. You're quite the hero. Emi, you said you were from Rockland, right?"

"Yes," replied Emi, "You said you were from there too?"

"Oh yeah . . ."

And so Emi found herself riding in the Hyperloop with Jack Lemore. They made the Rockland connection and continued talking as if they had known one another for their entire lives. The Venus Thirsts kept coming and were a sweet and fizzy way to liven up the cabin's sorrow, packing a jolt of energy with each drink.

Jack told Emi about her journey from the Legion to becoming a space transporter. She loved helping people get to space but never ventured farther than Mars. She felt a connection to Earth and needed to stay close enough to return. Jack ordered them some comet cake—a confection of ice cream and cake drizzled with caramel sauce and peppermint flakes—from the rator.

As they ate the comet cake, Jack told Emi about how she had lost her Helix Cells on the *Orleans* and dived into the bay. She awoke in the hospital room where she first saw Emi. Jack explained misfits were people who desired to transition permanently to a form other than strictly human, most commonly an animal and human combination. Misfits could achieve their goals through genome editing, modifying their bodies permanently.

Jack was on her way to Alexandria Compound. She was hoping that she could catch a ride back to the moon, where she kept a flat. She'd have to work for a while, but she was determined to recoup enough zurcon so that she could afford more Helix Cells. After they finished their third bottle of Venus Thirst and second piece of comet cake, Emi thought she had never met someone nicer than Jack Lemore.

After a couple of hours talking with Jack, Emi got up and went to the restroom. In the small bathroom she studied her left eye in the mirror. It had turned from blue, the same color both her parents' eyes had been, to a topaz-brown color.

Suddenly, Sadee pinged her with a new video message from Celeste Tusk. Emi shut her eyes and hit play.

"Emi, I just heard the news. I'm so sorry for your loss," lamented Celeste, seated on the sofa in her office. "Your father was a good man, and he loved you very much. I promised him that I would provide you with a first-rate education, and I intend to honor our arrangement. You can return to Torrance Compound. It's safe there. I'll have a coach meet you. Let me know of any issues. I look forward to speaking with you, Emi." Celeste bowed gracefully at the end.

Opening her eyes, Emi stared in the mirror. Her left eye didn't hurt. She touched it but couldn't feel anything at all. If the plague had infected her, wouldn't it hurt? She was so overwhelmed that she couldn't remember what the nurse had said. She felt the skin surrounding her eye and wondered if her iris would ever turn back to blue.

Emi reentered the main cabin and took her seat next to Jack.

Jack turned to her fretfully. "Emi, is your eye all right?"

"I might be infected."

"Well, if I had a choice, I certainly would have kept my fingers." Jack grinned, fidgeting with the bandage over her left hand. "I'm sure someone much smarter than I am will figure out a cure."

Emi gritted her teeth and nodded.

"Where are you and Sadee headed?" asked Jack.

"I don't know," said Emi, shaking her head. "I was thinking I'd go to the offices of Tusk Enterprise—"

"Ugh," Jack interjected. "Tusk Enterprise isn't what I'd picture for someone as bright as you. That can't be what you really want to do. What's your real dream?"

"I've always wanted to go to IGIST," said Emi. "Now, with the plague, I just want to get off Earth."

"Why have you given up?" asked Jack.

"I haven't," said Emi. "I just need to find another way."

Emi was convinced that Celeste would help her, but upon losing both her parents, she could not settle for any other Star League school. Her mind was set on IGIST. That was what her mother had wanted, and Emi was determined to make her dream a reality no matter the cost.

Jack looked hopeful. "There has to be a way, Emi," she said. "If this is what you want, never ever give up."

"How?"

Jack touched her nose and pondered.

"What about the League?"

12 · THE LEAGUE

The Star League, more commonly referred to as the League, was an interstellar federal republic composed of planetary governments based on the principles of universal liberty, rights, and equality. People could enlist in the League and sign up to explore deep space.

"I would never join the League," said Emi. "I want to be a scientist, not a deep-space explorer."

"Emi, don't you know that IGIST was originally filled with the top candidates from the League? I'm certain it still works that way. If you score well enough on the League entrance test, you can be admitted to IGIST. Why do you think it's called the Star League?"

Sadee beamed an article on the League as Jack explained that the League still placed one or two top candidates into IGIST every year, in addition to the other Star League schools. Over time, IGIST and the other Star League schools had become more focused on scientific research than space exploration, although they still sent a small percentage of people into the League as space officers. Emi thought through the probabilities and worried about getting her hopes up again. She changed the subject.

"What was on your charm, Jack?"

She smiled. "You know Polar?"

Emi nodded. This was a rhetorical question. Polar, also known as the "Lord of Song," was the most famous singer, songwriter, and dancer in the galaxy. His music had reached unprecedented popularity, and he had sold more records than the rest of the top ten artists combined. At the peak of his career, Polar revealed that he was a misfit and then made his transformation into a lionlike being.

Jack continued. "Up until his announcement Polar was very eccentric but never openly declared that he was a misfit. His lyrics often alluded to him being one, though. There is one in particular that rang true to me:

Different don't you fear it
Panthera not beasts but magnificent spirits
Nothing stays the same, don't pass
No static, don't falter
Phases of matter. Solid, liquid, gas.
Look at yourself, and alter.

Emi nodded. She knew the song.

"When I heard those lines, I knew what I must become," said Jack.

The intercom interrupted them with an announcement that they had reached Manhattan, New York.

13 · QUOTA

Hannah Dern entered the recruiting station and navigated her wheelchair to her desk. As a recruiter, Hannah was tasked with signing people up for the League. At sixty-six her authentic grandmotherly appeal helped her persuade people into certain League Occupational Specialties, known as LOS jobs, which had a shortage of applicants.

Decades ago, the League discovered that having a recruiter who was paid a bonus when they signed up recruits for shortage areas drastically improved conversion rates, filling critical roles.

Hannah had crafted her technique to perfection over the years. She never just regurgitated the League's slogans like Aim High or Explore the Galaxy. Her approach was much more personal and subtle. She'd listen to the candidate, understand what they wanted, and then describe a fantastic journey the League could provide specific to that candidate's needs and dreams.

A certain sting hit her every time she signed someone up. Forty years ago, her husband left her alone with three kids to take a League assignment. He was supposed to send back for them. He never had.

On her desk was a picture of her youngest grandchild, Lily, who lived on the moon. Hannah had funded five out of her six grandkids' educations with her League recruiting commissions. *Just one more,* she thought. Lily was the last. She assured her grandchild she could pay the tuition for Apollo. Lily wasn't only her favorite grandchild; she was also the brightest, excelling in school. Hannah's heart swelled with pride at the thought of one of her grandkids studying at a Star League school.

The tuition payment was due in one day, and Hannah was short by five thousand zurcon. She'd been in binds like this before and had been able to *sell* her way out of them. A bonus for a specific LOS job would cover it, and she was confident that if someone walked through that door, her problem would be solved.

14 · GENERAL TEST

Emi looked out the window of the coach she and Sadee had taken from the Manhattan Hyperloop station. Across from the Statue of Liberty, an enormous white dome stood atop the League recruiting center, casting a shadow over the Hudson River.

Emi and Sadee got out of the coach and traveled down a black pathway intersecting a sprawling lawn. On the lawn, sixty-foot-tall holograms of League cadets glowed. One of the holograms displayed a space station rotating. The displays also showed images of doctors treating patients and explorers jumping out of space vehicles.

Sadee signaled to Emi to look back at the holograms. The holograms changed from random images of strangers to actually showing Emi's face as the medic, explorer, and engineer. One even showed Sadee. Of course she snapped a photo of it.

Emi walked under the last hologram, a giant glowing arch that read AIM HIGH, EXPLORE THE GALAXY. At the top of the stairs, a tall steel door automatically opened as she approached.

When she entered the building, she saw a huge circular fountain with an air rise, which sat in the middle of the lobby. The air rise shot illuminated air up into the dome, creating a cool visual and audible effect that made it look like a gateway to the future.

Inside the building an intuitive touch screen welcomed Emi. The display menu listed:

· Joining the League

· What we do

· Who we are

Emi tapped the "Joining the League" tab and read about two tests an applicant could take: either a general test or a specific LOS job test.

The general test would allow someone to take the test and then see their available options based on their aptitude. She couldn't believe her eyes. There it was. IGIST. If someone scored high enough on the general test, they could win a scholarship to a Star League school, such as IGIST.

The next section explained the League's shortage of key LOS jobs and that by signing up for a specific test, if the candidate passed, they would be given a bonus. Emi tried to click back to the general test, but the screen wouldn't let her leave the specific test portion.

As she tapped the screen, trying to get it to return to the previous page, an old lady in a wheelchair rolled up and smiled at Emi.

"You doing OK?"

"I'd like to see about taking the general test," Emi responded.

"I can certainly assist you with that. I'm Hannah and I help people navigate the process. How old are you, sweetie?"

"Fourteen."

"Hmm." Hannah looked worried for a second.

"I'm not a runaway," choked Emi in response. She paused, holding back the tears, and regained her confidence. "I'm an orphan."

"OK. OK. We'll get to all that. First, tell me what you'd like to do," said Hannah.

Emi explained her love of science and how she wanted to take the general test for a shot at getting into IGIST. She finished by saying, "I don't really picture myself as a space explorer. I see myself in a lab or an electronics shop, solving problems and inventing things."

"Oh, that's wonderful," said Hannah. "You remind me of my granddaughter, Lily. She's your age and hopes to go to Apollo."

Hannah touched Emi's hand.

"Have you heard of the Kapteyn solar system?"

Emi nodded. Kapteyn b and Kapteyn c were the first two planets out of the Earth's solar system that had been pioneered and homesteaded during the age of discovery, spanning the first fifty years of the Spacefaring era.

"It's about thirteen light years away," explained Hannah. "They've got a massive project underway where the League is building a huge space station called Stellar Jacobus. Once complete, this space station will be pushed from the Kapteyn solar system to be a scientific research center."

A hologram of the Kapteyn solar system with the planets and the space station illuminated as Hannah explained.

"Right now, they are in need of medical techs," said Hannah. "There's a fantastic LOS job specialty program in which you would take courses on the thirteen-year journey to Kapteyn. By the time you get there, you'll be a leading expert in your field."

"Can you give me a minute?" asked Emi.

Emi closed her eyes, and Sadee sent her an image of the distance between the solar systems. The Kapteyn solar system looked pretty underwhelming, but the station appeared magnificent. It was going to push out of the solar system and explore deep space. What did she have to lose?

Sadee B2B messaged her, "It could be cool. But it's a one-way ticket."

Emi pondered. No one ever traveled back; it would take too long. If she signed up for Kapteyn, it would be to go farther into space. Emi asked herself what she really wanted. She didn't envision herself traveling on a station, but in a lab. She was meant to invent things, not discover an exoplanet. She couldn't be more certain. Her destiny was to make an impact and it would be as a scientist, not an explorer. She opened her eyes.

"What about the general test?" asked Emi.

"Well, you can certainly take that. They're both four-hour tests administered right here, but you'll be losing out on a bonus. The assignments in this solar system are all focused on mining the asteroid belt or sun studies. Are you interested in that?"

"On the memo here, it says if you score high enough, you can get placed into a Star League school."

Hannah laughed out loud.

"In my twenty years working here, I haven't seen a single person from Earth do that," said Hannah. "I've read of recruiting stations on Mars and the moon that have placed people, but I've never seen it."

"But it is possible?"

"Yes, I suppose it is," replied Hannah.

Just then two teenagers sauntered in.

"We're here to take the LOS job test."

"Yes, please wait over there. I'll be with you in a minute."

She turned back to Emi. It was rare to have a same-day sign-up. A minor, no less, claiming to be an orphan and not a runaway. Still, if she signed up for a Kapteyn slot, that would seem plausible.

"If you'd like to take one of the afternoon tests today, we need to get moving. The morning tests are finishing now," said Hannah. "It will take forty-five minutes to get the paperwork done. After you sign the paperwork, you take the elevator up to the testing deck."

Emi looked around the wide-open atrium up to the dome. Elevators lined the outer edges that led up to a mezzanine level with clear glass testing rooms. In a few of the rooms, some test takers wore augmented reality headsets and interacted with floating objects. Emi looked back at Hannah.

"I'd like to take the general test."

15 · SPKPT459

Emi looked around the recruiting station, waiting for a response from the old lady. Hannah smiled. "OK then. I'll have you sit over here and enter your info. We'll need to check your identification and some other items. Once that is complete, I'll hand you your test tab, and you'll take the elevator up and begin. It usually takes about four hours."

Emi and Sadee headed to the table that Hannah had indicated and filled out the fields on the tablet. Hannah handed the other two test takers their test tabs with large designation numbers on the top and rolled back to her desk.

Hannah monitored Emi's information as it came in. Once complete, she would program it into a test tab that the candidate would take up to one of the testing rooms. They'd enter the tab into the computer and go through the program that evaluated them. The tests conformed to the candidates based on their inputs, with no test being the same.

The two key inputs were the candidate's information and the type of test. The code for the general test was GEN00001. There were thousands of codes for the specific LOS job tracks, ranging anywhere from SPAAT001 to SPKAST999. The code for the Kapteyn job was SPKPT459.

A notification light blinked when Emi completed her form. Hannah scanned it. It was common for the recruiter to receive the form from the candidate and then change the test code to the correct LOS job designation if something had changed. Hannah rolled up to Emi and Sadee beside the two teenage boys.

"You all will take elevator three up to the testing level," said Hannah. "Pick one of the three rooms and insert your test tab into the computer. Your drone can wait down here in the lobby. During the instructions they'll have you shut off your METs. No connectedness during the tests. I'll be down here monitoring. If you need anything, just hit the help button."

Hannah handed Emi her test tab and pointed to the elevators. Emi examined the test tab as she walked over. The tab was a thin black piece of plastic about the size of a sheet of paper. One side was black with four copper tabs and a white arrow pointing in the direction it was to be inserted.

Inside the elevator Emi looked down at Sadee. The drone messaged her, "Good Luck," before disconnecting. Riding the elevator, Emi examined her test tab. On the top of the test tab, white letters spelled out *SPKPT459*.

16 · GEN0001

"What test are you taking?" Emi asked one of the older boys.

He smiled proudly, clutching his test tab.

"The LOS job test for Kapteyn medical tech," he replied. "It's going to be incredible. Get schooled on the way out and then get a sweet gig on Stellar Jacobus exploring space."

She studied the teenager's test tab. His designation code read SPKPT459. She looked down at her tab. It had the same designation code.

"Are you still connected?" Emi asked.

"Yes. They don't cut off connection until you're in the test room."

The elevator reached the test level. Emi quickly reconnected to Sadee and messaged, "Need help ASAP. How does a test tab work?"

Sadee sent her a summary showing how the copper connections would transfer the data into the computer. They used test tabs to ensure an audit trail between key operations.

The other test takers filed into their rooms. Emi followed them, observing the test level. There were individual rooms surrounded by an indoor track that rested on the second level, above the main lobby. Emi reached the door to test room 3. Her connection to Sadee went dark.

Emi sat down in the room and read the instructions. *Insert the test tab, then put on the augmented reality set to be guided through several tests.* There was a final section of the test that was a physical obstacle course. The applicants would run it, and then the test would be over.

Through the glass Emi noticed that the two other test takers had already put on their headsets, inserted their tabs, and begun their tests.

Emi was about to insert her test tab when she got the feeling someone was watching her. She turned around and saw Hannah staring up at her from the atrium. Something didn't feel right.

Emi pushed the call button. "I just wanted to confirm I'm taking the general test before I start."

Silence. Emi reexamined the test tab and traced the designation code.

"Um, excuse me. Are you there?"

"I'm down here, yes. You are taking the general test. Just insert the tab and put on the AR headset to get started."

Emi suspected that Hannah was lying to her. She took a deep breath and considered her options. She could confront the lady. She suspected that if she did, Hannah would not help her take the general test. She could have Emi quarantined and then sent into the Legion. If the lady had gone so far as to lie to her and manipulate her test, she clearly wasn't a good person. Emi could leave, but then what? Where would she go? Neither option was good. Was there a third option?

"Is there a problem?" squawked the speaker.

Now it was Emi's turn to be silent. No MET, no Sadee. Emi would have to figure this out on her own. She closed her eyes and focused. The League's test program was a computer. If there was a way to enter the right code, maybe she could override the test designation. Emi eyed the test tab. There was no way she could reprogram this without Sadee.

She traced the copper connections. Bingo. She pressed the tab facedown on the table and scraped a line on one of the copper connections. She did it again, three more times, scraping a line on each of the four copper points. Emi put on the AR headset and pushed the test tab into the computer. An error message popped up on the display, just as she had anticipated.

"Is there a problem?" repeated the speaker.

"Yes," said Emi. "There's an error message."

"OK," said Hannah. "I'll have you manually reenter all your data and then we'll restart."

On the AR screen the display showed the initial forms that Emi had filled out. She raced through them. Finally, she got to the last page. Type of test. There was an open field.

"All right," said Hannah. "For the test code, enter SPKPT459."

Emi wondered what the letter part of the designation code indicated. KPT was certainly Kapteyn. SP probably meant specialized test. The 459 designators were probably for the specific role they needed to fill. What could the general test code be?

She typed in *G* and two letters—*E* and *N*—auto-populated the next two fields. She typed in *GENERAL* and submitted. Nothing.

"Excuse me, is everything OK?" asked Hannah. "The code for the test is SPKPT459."

Emi didn't respond. She tried typing *GEN11111* into the display.

"If the manual part is confusing, why don't you come down, and I'll get you another test tab," said Hannah through the speaker.

Ignoring Hannah, Emi tried everything she could think of. She entered ten entries with no success. On her eleventh try she typed in GEN00001.

In her augmented reality headset, the test sequence went live. Emi glanced at Hannah, who was examining her monitor. The old lady pounded her fist on her wheelchair.

Emi turned back to the desk and filled out a few more fields on the display. The last question was assignment preference for the general test. Emi scrolled through the options. Sparks flew in her mind when she saw it. There it was! Star League School: IGIST. She would need a perfect score of 500. She clicked "Submit."

17 · EXAM

On to the test, thought Emi. She took a deep breath. Her finger tapped her knee furiously. A friendly video image of a woman League representative played in augmented reality and described the test. Bullet points emerged next to the speaker as the lady listed out each of the five sections of the test: Coding Speed, Integrated Reasoning, Space Perception, Numerical Operations, and Candidate Stress Test.

Emi gestured in AR to start the first section of the test. In her display forty balls emerged, each marked with a number, in no particular order or structure. Emi found she could put the balls into a triangle formation, square formation, or circle formation. One ball was missing a number.

Emi quickly moved the balls into the triangle formation. What was the pattern? Her first idea was to add up the numbers and see if it was a missing-number sequence. That wasn't it.

Her next approach was to see what they all had in common. Square roots? They were all perfect squares: 1, 4, 9, **?**, 25, 36, 49, 64, 81. The number that was missing from the sequence was 16. Emi's confidence skyrocketed.

She quickly moved on to the next question. She kept the same approach for every section of the test. Emi would quickly make an assumption and go right for the answer. Before submitting, she'd check her mental model. After three exhausting hours, she had completed ninety questions and four sections of the test.

When she finished the last question of the numerical operations section, a status update showed how she was doing. She was in the ninetieth percentile, meaning she had scored better than 90 percent of the other candidates who had taken the test. Her heart sank.

Comprised of timed fitness and logic tests, the final section was worth one hundred points. The screen displayed the options that would be available to Emi with a passing score of 70 on the test. There were many Kapteyn assignments, including medical tech and solar power researcher.

In fuzzy, barely legible letters at the bottom of the screen, there was another category: Star League Schools: 490–500 points. She had 380 points. Even if she scored perfectly on the candidate stress test, she would still be shy of getting into IGIST by twenty points.

A pit formed in her stomach, and she felt nauseous. What had she done? The next message directed her to the track loop for the last section.

The teenage boys were already waiting by the time Emi had left the test room. She struggled to pay attention to the hologram instructor explaining the final test. She would have to run around the inner circle of the track loop and navigate six stations of obstacles and performance tests.

At each station she would earn points for completing the tasks. The instructor explained they could skip stations and make up points for speed. If she skipped every station and made it in less than a minute around the four-hundred-meter loop, she would pass with the minimum score.

The last leg of the test was to run up a flight of glass stairs and pull a finish rope that appeared to hang down from the top of the dome. However, the optimal strategy was to finish in under eight minutes, completing every obstacle or logic test. If she aced every obstacle and test, she would get a score of 100.

Emi scanned the course and looked down into the lobby. Hannah glared up at her. Sadee glowed green in an attempt to show her support. The other two boys stretched and jumped around.

"We just need to pass this test and we're off to Kapteyn!" exclaimed one of the boys.

Emi looked across the opening that extended down to the lobby. The air rise blew lightly up to the top of the dome. It looked like it went directly to where the test ended on the glass platform suspended in the middle of the open area below the dome.

Disappointed in herself, Emi debated walking out. She vaguely remembered signing something that had committed her to the League. The test would start in two minutes. A timer started to count down. Maybe she could find work in the asteroid belt and then transfer into a Star League school. She sighed, knowing that it was probably a pipe dream.

Emi took a deep breath and loosened her neck, bending right to left. Sadee flew over to the air rise, and the pressure pushed the drone back. Emi squinted at the air rise. The light bursts seemed to be forming some code or signal.

The countdown timer was at twenty-five seconds and going down. The boys both knelt in sprinters' starting positions. Emi squinted again at the air rise. The light appeared to spell *jump*.

A loud bell rang, and the two boys took off to the first station. Emi's instincts told her to race after them, yet she stood still. The hologram reminded her that the race had begun.

Emi was frozen. A clock at the top platform showed the time passing. She picked up her waist pack. The three-foot gap between the rail edge and the air rise looked farther from the second floor. The air rise shot out from a fountain of water. If she was wrong, the water would break her fall. To be sure, Emi picked up her pack and threw it over the edge toward the air rise. Her waist pack shot up toward the platform with the rope and hovered from the upward air pressure.

She squinted one last time. She was sure that the light spelled *jump*. The boys had arrived at the first station. The clock showed that five seconds had passed. Emi backed up from the rail and aimed toward the air rise. *Are you mad?* she wondered.

She ran toward the rail and leaped.

18 · WELCOME

Emi dived over the rail and spread her arms like the wings of an osprey. For a moment she felt the sensation of falling until she reached the air rise, which thrust her up briskly. She leaned toward the glass platform elevated in the middle of the atrium near the dome.

Emi glided through the air and pulled herself over the rail. She was so excited that she almost forgot to pull the rope. She grabbed the rope with both hands and gave it a vigorous pull. The clock read nine seconds.

In her AR display a message popped up: Bonus Score. For the candidate stress test, she earned 120 points. Emi's total score read 500. Flying up to her, Sadee glowed green, spinning with joy.

A door from the top of the dome opened, and a hydraulic arm lowered down with a bucket to the platform.

She climbed in, holding Sadee, and the hydraulic arm pulled her up to a secret room. As she rose, Emi looked down. Hannah's mouth hung open, shocked that an Earthling had found a way to gain entrance to IGIST.

In the room a screen displayed the following message:

> The Star League is delighted to inform you of your acceptance to IGIST under the Star League commissioning program, pending successful completion of the probo. The League congratulates you, for this is an outstanding achievement. Please open the admission notification.

The screen flickered and turned off. Emi gasped. On the edge of the table, a small compartment opened, revealing an IGIST miniature model.

She pulled it out and set it on the table. The model was more glorious than she could have imagined. The detail and brilliance of the finish were breathtaking. She looked at the base and traced the letters of the school's motto. She'd dreamed of this moment. A wave of pride swept over her as she pressed the button on the base.

A life-size hologram of Archimedes appeared from the model and spoke.

"Congratulations. Each year more than one hundred thousand candidates apply for a few hundred coveted slots to enter the IGIST probo period. The selected candidates are evaluated and screened at the probo, resulting in one hundred finalists who matriculate into the IGIST Class of 160 S.E.

"We take great care to ensure that every student will not only thrive in our competitive academic environment but also embody the IGIST motto of intelligence, curiosity, and perseverance. You are one of four 'plicants who will enter the probo through League recruiting. Passing the stress test with an air rise bonus is a testament to your curiosity and willingness to take confident risks. Such a proclivity has produced some of our finest alumni.

"I hope this notification brings you the exhilaration that you deserve. IGIST is the perfect place to prepare you for your future role as a scientist in a galaxy that needs you. Congratulations to the IGIST probo class of Delta Dragon Oh-Seven. As the chancellor of IGIST, I wish you good luck and many eureka moments. Yours sincerely, Archimedes."

19 · TAKEOFF

"All systems go," squawked the speakers next to the display. "T minus fifteen seconds and counting."

Everyone in the rocket ship cheered. The display showed a spanning image of the rocket from the nose down to the thrusters. White smoke gushed from the boosters.

Emi clutched Sadee on her lap as her heartbeat raced. They had finally made it to Alexandria Compound.

"T minus ten seconds. Nine. Eight. Seven." The rocket rumbled loudly, and Emi's seat shook as the engines pushed the seven million pounds of thrust required for liftoff.

"Three. Two. One. Blastoff!" yelled Emi with all the other passengers. Her heart was pumping so hard she thought it would burst.

The rocket boosters blasted massive smoke clouds. Out of the smoke and fire emerged the rocket, pushing off the launchpad and propelling the spaceship into the sky.

Out the window, the blue sky gradually turned to black as the rocket exited Earth's atmosphere. Emi couldn't contain her excitement. She grinned ear to ear. Her hand pressed against the window. Despite the glass barrier, it felt like she was touching the sky.

As they reached space and the shuttle stabilized, an announcement broadcast that it was safe to get up. Several passengers unbuckled and started to walk around the shuttle.

Gazing out the window, Emi saw a section of the Earth's blue sphere that was covered in hoary clouds with bursts of bright white light. She wondered if she would ever see lightning again. She reached inside her waist pack and felt the rose seed. It would take her some time to adjust to the realization that she was in space. Sadee observed Emi looking out the window.

"How are you feeling?" Sadee messaged.

Emi closed her eyes and asked Sadee to show her pictures of her family. Memories flashed of her mother. There was her favorite picture of her mom holding the glowing rose. Behind her mother stood her father, holding the microscope that he had bought Emi's mother. Emi remembered her mother's excitement when she had finally figured out how to create a glowing rose.

For months her mother had been experimenting with single-celled organisms, such as bacteria and yeast. Others had tried and failed to infuse the genetic properties that made certain animals and plants, such as fireflies and rare mushrooms, glow. If Emi's father's mantra was that the right idea can overcome seemingly overwhelming challenges, her mother's was that a solo inventor can generate magical breakthroughs.

People often told Emi that she was her mother's child. They shared certain extreme traits, such as unwavering determination to do things their own way. She remembered when her mother woke her up in the middle of the night to show her that she'd done it. Instead of focusing on the plant, she'd focused on the bacteria that had a symbiotic relationship with the plant. The result was a bacteria bio film that accomplished something that was a bit of a holy grail in synthetic biology. It made the plant glow.

Sitting in Emi's room, her mom described the science, but what Emi heard was her mother's passion for inventing things. Emi envisioned the glowing rose. In her head she heard her mother's voice: "There is no other thrill that hits the human heart like an inventor seeing her creation unfold from her brain and come to life."

And so Emi's mother planted the seed in Emi's heart that great scientists are solo heroes who toil away at tough technical problems, only to emerge through independent thought and resilient intellectual exertion with a brilliant insight that pushes the boundaries of what is possible.

Whenever she revisited memories of her parents, Emi couldn't avoid reliving that tragedy that took her mother from her. Emi opened her eyes and observed Earth's blue sphere as it shrank.

"This is my door," messaged Emi to Sadee.

Some of the travelers never wished to return. Emi was unsure if she'd ever be back.

Suddenly, she felt a tap on her shoulder and turned.

"Jack!"

She jumped out of her seat and gave Jack Lemore a big hug. Sadee glowed green, and Jack gave the drone a knuckle bump. Sadee changed her appearance to glowing tiger stripes as they approached a little galley.

"Jack, I did it! I aced the test!"

"Well then, we must celebrate."

Jack tapped the rator and ordered them two Venus Thirsts, along with comet cake.

Emi explained how she had made it into IGIST by jumping over the rail during the fitness test. She was very curious about the probo and how long it would take her to get to IGIST.

"It will take forty-eight hours to get to the moon," said Jack.

Pulling up a hologram display of Earth and the moon, she traced a line around Earth's orbit.

"We'll make a translunar injection here," she explained. "It's a propulsive maneuver that will set us on the right trajectory to the moon."

She drew an S-curve in the air from Earth's orbit out to the moon that illustrated how they would target where the moon was heading and end up in the moon's trajectory.

"You'll spend about five hours on the moon before you take a little shuttle ship over to IGIST."

"What about the probo?" asked Emi.

"I don't know much about it," said Jack. "I know that it's a few weeks long and involves a series of tests. You can't take this gal, unfortunately."

She nodded at Sadee.

"At the end of every week, they transport the dropouts off IGIST. I heard seventy percent of the kids don't finish."

"What about the wardens?"

"Ahh, the wardens of IGIST. Yes, they're quite renowned, aren't they? In some ways they were the first misfits, although they reject that notion. The wardens are mystic heroes in the misfit community. We celebrate them as early transhuman figures. The warden company was created by the League one hundred and fifty years ago as an experimental group to test becoming transhuman. During the last wars on Earth, the League had experimented with more aggressive animals.

"The wardens were the first large-scale successful test group, resulting in a little more than two hundred volunteers turning into half-man, half-yak beings imbued with superhuman characteristics of the animal as well as the first radical life-extension capabilities. The yak was chosen as the ideal animal for space exploration because it possesses several physiological characteristics that optimize energy consumption. They can survive on very little oxygen and consume a very small amount of food yet keep their astonishing strength and endurance. The majority of the group was sent out for deep-space exploration missions. The few who stayed back became the wardens of IGIST, where they've run the probo since the Institute was founded in the fifty-first year of the Spacefaring era."

***

Over the next two days, Emi and Jack met for all their meals. Jack shared with Emi that she had come up with another plan to obtain her Helix Cells. Over the course of the trip, they became even better friends. On the last night Jack informed Emi that when they woke up they'd be in the moon's orbit.

"Jack, I've got a favor to ask."

"Yes, Emi?"

"Will you watch Sadee while I go through the probo?"

"You bet."

***

Emi fell into a deep sleep that night and dreamed of solar sailing at IGIST. When she awoke, she heard an announcement.

"Landing on the moon in thirty minutes."

20 · LUNAR PARK

Emi hurried along the path surrounding Lunar Park. She thought checking out the park might ease her anxiety. There was just enough time to see the flag and make her next flight. Apollo University sat on the edge of the park. Emi chuckled looking at an Apollo sign where someone had scrawled underneath, "Because not everyone can go to IGIST."

A memorial path led out from the main walkway, looping around where the first humans had landed on the moon. On the way to the memorial, Emi saw several Apollo students milling about in their white uniforms, intermingled with obvious tourists.

Two girls stood out from the crowd. They looked like students but sported sleek black suits instead of Apollo uniforms. Everyone else hurried along the path. The two stood still, gazing out into Lunar Park. One of them held binoculars. The other's eyes were glued to her remote-control tablet. Emi wondered what they were doing but continued on to the memorial.

Looking up, Emi mulled over the technological marvel that was Sappho's membrane. Covering the moon completely, the transparent membrane was thinner than a nanometer and contained retractable "S-Zones" for spacecrafts to travel through. The combination of Sappho's electromagnetic membrane and her chlorofluorocarbon formula enabled humankind to terraform Mars and then the moon and much of the solar system.

During the colonization of the moon, in partnership with the citizens of Earth, the moon's founding pioneers set aside Lunar Park. Known throughout the solar system for its size and depth of landscape, the park stretched seventeen miles long and five hundred miles wide, preserving the moon's pristine nickel glow. From Earth, Lunar Park looked like a huge glowing rectangle—a preservation symbol that represented the four and a half billion years of its barren existence. City structures now brightened the whole sphere in the night sky, though the park was the only segment that still glowed purely.

Something caught Emi's eye as she walked by a crater. She peaked in and observed a beaded name bracelet spelling "Karen." Flashing bright yellow, Sadee flew ahead and curled around the US flag that had been planted more than two centuries ago. Next to the flag were several footprints and a plaque that read: "Here men from the planet Earth first set foot upon the moon. July 1969 A. D. We came in peace for all mankind."

Next to the footprint monument was a pillar with the face of Yve. One hundred years after the first man stepped on the moon, the first human, a girl named Yve, was born in space on September 30, 2069. The statue of Yve represented the dawn of the Spacefaring era and the end of the AD era.

Emi looked back to Earth. Half the Earth showed, while the other half appeared consumed by black space. Sadee messaged her. They needed to get back to the shuttle.

On the main path Emi looked down and saw a Sputnik. The IGIST space station shape glowed on the path. An IGIST student had placed the glowing symbol on Apollo's turf. Emi smiled. As she glanced down at the Sputnik, Sadee messaged, "Wow!" Suddenly, Emi heard a clang and then jumped as a drone struck the ground beside her.

"Shoot!" shouted the girl holding the remote-control tablet as she rushed over. The girl clutching the binos lagged behind.

Sadee spun in circles in the air before she got her bearings. Emi messaged her, "Are you OK?"

Sadee quickly replied, "Minor collision."

"Be extra careful up here!" Emi warned Sadee. Eyeing the girls who were crouched over their drone, Emi blurted, "I'm sorry!"

"It's fine," said the girl with the binos. "That thing is cheap."

"Come on!" exclaimed the other girl as she held a button on the bottom of the drone. Its lights began to blink. "And we're live." The two girls looked like they were up to something.

The girl stood as her drone ascended. Her friend dropped her binos and looked Emi and Sadee up and down. Both girls were very tall and lanky, indicating that they were spaceborn.

"Do you go to Apollo?" Emi asked them.

"No, we're surveying the park for a school project," said the taller girl with the binos. Her friend turned and glared at her. "What? This kid's not going to tell anyone."

A few hundred feet away, Emi made out a robot rover equipped with what looked like a surveying pole. It seemed to have stopped moving. She noticed the arrow buttons on the taller girl's binos and figured she must have been controlling it.

"We go to IGIST," the girl said to Emi. "My name's Ripley. This is Gal."

Emi's mouth dropped open.

"My name's Emi," she said, trying to hide her excitement. "I'm from Earth and attending the probo. I leave in a few hours."

Both of the girls laughed.

"Wow, a real-life bygone," muttered Gal. "I've never met anyone from Earth."

Ripley gave her a look.

"What's the probo like?" asked Emi. "What's IGIST like?"

"The probo pretty much embodies TPFS," said Gal.

"TPFS?" replied Emi.

"'The 'Plicants Failed Space,'" retorted Ripley.

"TPFS is 'This Place Flipping Sucks,'" said Gal. "It's an unofficial IGIST motto that luminaries use to describe the essence of IGIST."

"I figured the probo isn't fun, but IGIST sucks?" asked Emi.

"Well, it can be hard, but that's a good thing. To me the saying means I'd rather hate being here than love being anyplace else. Being tough is what makes it special. But yeah, the probo really sucks and is TPFS on a whole other level," said Gal.

Emi nodded, following along.

"It's really intense and the wardens—they're going to push you," continued Gal. "IGIST, though, is incredible! There isn't a better place in the universe for scientists. What you can learn and do there is amazing."

"Why do so many people drop out?" asked Emi.

"The probo is a crucible," said Gal. "You have to do a million things right."

The girl started to list off items. "Get into the first probo tube. That's the most important thing you can do. It will save you fifteen minutes each day because you'll live closest to all the facilities. That fifteen minutes is the difference between life and death at the probo. You pick up study time and sleep time. Both are essential. Make sure you go to sleep on time, eat quickly and maximize your study time, study like crazy before each task, check your work, don't stick out, don't challenge the wardens . . ."

Emi's eyes grew wide as Gal continued to rattle off what seemed like a thousand items. She signaled to Sadee to start recording and specifically made a mental note of getting into the first probo tube. Ripley looked Emi up and down.

"Gal, shut up. Emi, let me give you the only advice you need," said Ripley. "If you made it into the probo, you're smart enough to pass. Here's the most important thing you need to do. Remain calm and think your way through each problem. That's it."

The older girl smiled in a comforting way.

"Remain calm," said Emi.

"Yup," said Ripley. "It's that simple. Just remember to think and spend your time wisely. There's no limit to what you can achieve out here."

Emi nodded.

"You'll do great, I know it," said Ripley, tilting her head toward Gal. "We need an Earthling at IGIST. Too many Martians there these days . . ."

"Thanks so much," said Emi.

"Good luck," said Gal. "When you pass the probo, look us up. We're seniors in the prep tube. We're looking for some smart young talent to help us with our robot project."

21 · SCOUT

Emi and Sadee approached the loading dock. When she arrived at the edge of the dock, several parents from the moon were saying goodbye to their kids. She overheard one parent saying, "Calm down! There's nothing to be nervous about."

Emi took a little comfort in knowing she wasn't the only one who was nervous. Who wouldn't be? For her there was no turning back. If she dropped out of the probo, where would she go? What would she do?

Seeing these kids say goodbye, she desperately wished she could see her own parents. She remembered her father sliding her the note the day she had created the IGIST model. Even now she felt that her father was still in her corner. Her mother would have told her, "Somewhere, something incredible is waiting to be created by an inventor."

Emi tried to channel her confidence to get ready for the probo but felt something that she couldn't get over. At first, she thought it might be nervousness, but she came to realize that it was something different. The strongest feeling in her bones was not a nervous presence but self-pity. It hung over Emi like a dark cloud, overshadowing the amazing journey she was about to embark on. Having no one to say goodbye to hurt.

Across the platform Emi saw two scouts, explorers who were present via hologram. The scouts' holograms beamed from a small drone that gave them the appearance of a real human, showcasing a glowing three-dimensional avatar. The two hologram 'plicants stood facing each other and made a gesture of recognition. The scouts simultaneously bumped their fists against their own chests then made the signal and motion of an archer shooting an arrow out of a bow, an homage to the constellation of Orion.

The scouts were part of the federation's deep-space exploration mission. They were shipped out into the galaxy on large spaceships destined to find and explore habitable planets.

All scouts started off life as a chilled human embryo that remained in a frozen state until their spaceship was roughly twenty-five years out from a likely habitable planet. At that point the embryo, along with several other scouts making up a reconnaissance team, would be raised and trained by humanoid robots. Several scouts enrolled in Star League schools and attended as hologram avatars, beaming in from light years away using a quantum entanglement data transfer for instant communication.

There were three scouts entering Emi's probo class. She had spotted two of them so far. They looked about her age and the two she saw were introducing themselves to other 'plicants. The scouts started the probo on the moon and had to pass the entire course or they'd be dropped like any other 'plicant.

Seeing the scouts, Emi realized she did have someone to say goodbye to, even if it wasn't her real family. She saw Jack Lemore and hurried over to her. As she got closer, she saw two 'plicants near Jack. They were both tall and fit and had dark skin and black hair. She guessed they were Martian boy-girl twins. They were pointing at Jack.

"What is this thing?" laughed the boy.

The girl with him laughed louder. "Look at those clothes," she said.

"Misfit, why don't you go back to Earth?"

As Emi approached the taunters, the last scout emerged. The first two scouts appeared fit and lean, but this scout looked different. He had shaggy hair and freckles and looked plump compared to the other 'plicants.

"Hey, guys, leave her alone," said the scout.

"Who are you to tell me what to do?" said the Martian boy. "Do you know who I am?"

"I presume you're Ankor," replied the round scout. "I'd expect more from the top prospect entering the probo."

The boy scoffed and turned to his sister. "I didn't expect a scout to be a misfit lover. Let's go, Achimi. We don't need to waste our time with these freaks."

The two Martians headed toward the space shuttle. Emi walked up and hugged Jack.

"Jack, I'm so sorry," said Emi.

Unfazed, Jack smiled at Emi. She turned to the scout.

"I'm Jack Lemore. I'm a space transporter. This is Emi. She'll be joining you at the probo."

"Nice to meet you," said the scout. "My name's Hans."

A loudspeaker called, "Last call to IGIST. Five minutes."

The 'plicants started filing toward the space shuttle.

"It was nice to meet you both. I'll see you at the probo, Emi," said Hans. "I'm going to head to the shuttle."

Emi nodded at Hans and then turned back to Jack and gave her another big hug.

"Jack, thank you for everything," said Emi. "Please take care of Sadee."

Jack smiled, and Emi gestured for Sadee to come to her. She grabbed her drone pal and squeezed her tight. "I'm going to miss you," said Emi. Sadee turned blue.

Emi let go, and Sadee hovered above Jack's shoulder. "One last thing," said Jack.

Emi turned to her, and Jack offered some words of wisdom. "Don't be intimidated by anyone. You have a lot to offer."

Emi smiled. "Thanks, Jack. I'll miss you."

"Miss you too," said Jack.

Emi turned and walked toward the shuttle. Her mouth was dry. She'd never felt so homesick in her whole life. When she got to the shuttle door, she paused for a second and looked back. Jack waved. Sadee glowed green and messaged, "You can!"

22 · PROBO

Emi looked out the window and saw IGIST. For years she had dreamed of seeing the space station. Seeing it in person in space exceeded her wildest dreams. It was magnificent. The torus ring contrasted against space like a silver donut floating in a black sky. The circular tube's silver bottom half shone in the reflected light, and the top half was illuminated by the lights of the buildings, showcasing the lush green plants and trees on campus.

As the shuttle approached, she saw the fountains of IGIST on the four main catwalks leading from the outer tube to the center of Snow Tower. The obelisk tower shot out from the center of the station, piercing space. The tall, four-sided narrow tapering monument had a pyramid on the top that gave off a vivid, greenish-blue, nickel glow. The exterior of the tower was made of polished moon rock known as lunar basalt. The shuttle dropped below the space station and headed toward the landing dock.

"'Plicants, follow me," boomed the warden.

At the bottom of the ramp from the shuttle door, five of the strange man-beasts stood. The Martian twins hustled to the front of the pack.

"Four lines," bellowed one of the wardens.

Everyone quickly filed out of the shuttle and formed four lines following the wardens. Emi peered around the people in front of her and tried to catch a glimpse of the warden leading her line. His shaggy, yak-like hair poked out from the teal tunic he wore. On his head two horns shot out from his ruffled hair.

The 'plicants marched swiftly down a small catwalk from the loading station to the main outer tube. The glass ceiling created a tunnel that was barely illuminated. Emi looked back at the obelisk tower and then at the long line of 'plicants behind her. The scout Hans was a couple of 'plicants ahead of her in line.

When they reached the end of the catwalk, they moved through a large arch onto a field where more wardens shuffled them into formation. At the front of the field, a warden in a white tunic stood on top of a large platform. Emi scanned the layout. On each side of the field were buildings. She wondered how they assigned tubes and how she might get into the first one.

The warden in the white tunic spoke in a majestic tone. "Attention, 'plicants." His gravelly voice commanded authority. "We have a greeting message."

Behind the platform a projection of the chancellor glowed in the air.

"'Plicants, welcome to the probo. I am Archimedes, the chancellor of IGIST. The probo's mission is to screen, evaluate, and qualify only the best for entrance into IGIST. The wardens are charged with keeping the bar high.

"Throughout the next two months, you'll be put through a crucible of mental tests. I assure you, those who pass the probo will have earned a coveted seat at the best science Institute in the universe. 'Plicants, as you go through the probo, let me encourage you to embrace our motto: Intelligentia, Curiositas, Perseverantia."

The chancellor paused for a moment and brought the palms of his hands in front of his heart in a prayerlike position.

"As old stars die," said the chancellor, "new stars are born."

All the wardens and several of the 'plicants familiar with IGIST's distinguished phrase yelled the second line, "New stars are born," simultaneously with the chancellor. The unified response created an air of camaraderie that Emi hadn't felt before.

When the projected image faded away, the warden on the platform pounded his scepter.

"My name is Yash. I am the head warden of the probo. 'Plicants, look to your left. Now look to your right. Only one-third of you will pass the probo. For the next eight weeks, you will be put through a series of tests in order to gain acceptance to IGIST.

"There are four phases to the probo. In the first phase you'll be put through aptitude tests. In the second phase you'll be exposed to a combination of virtual and substance indulgences to ensure you can rise above the lure of these distractions. In the third phase you'll be exposed to abstract problem sets, and in the final phase we will test your persistence."

He paused for what seemed like an eternity.

"The wardens will collect your METs. The probo is a MET-free zone. Once you've turned in your MET, proceed to the changing area to get your probo uniform. Bring your old clothes back for the renewal ceremony, and we'll file into tubes."

Yash pointed his scepter at an enormous, bowl-shaped pit in front of the platform. A few of the 'plicants darted off the field immediately after he stopped speaking, but the rest hesitated.

"Move!" yelled Yash.

All the 'plicants scrambled toward the changing area behind the field. Realizing that the 'plicants who moved immediately had an edge, Emi charged ahead and ripped off her MET. When she reached the building, two wardens pointed to containers. A few of the 'plicants in front of her were taking off their METs. She tossed hers in the bin and rushed into the changing room. On her way in, she saw Ankor running out, wearing a gray probo uniform.

Emi now understood she wasn't the only one who knew about the benefits of getting into the first tube. In the changing room, behind a window, sat a warden. Emi ran to the window.

"Size?" asked the warden.

"Small," replied Emi.

The warden handed her a folded uniform jumpsuit. Several 'plicants were already changing. She darted out of the room with the uniform under her left arm. As she ran toward the platform, there were only a few 'plicants ahead of her. She slipped her right arm out of her shirt and then juggled the uniform over to her right arm and slipped her shirt off her left arm and over her head.

When she arrived at the burn pit, 'plicants were lining up in front of two wardens. They bowed before hurling their old clothes into the pit.

Emi saw four 'plicants who were already standing in the first row in front of the platform: the three scouts and Ankor. There were four 'plicants in each line, but several others ran toward the pit. Achimi ran up behind Emi then stepped around her and ran to the front of the pit. The wardens turned a blind eye.

Following her lead, Emi avoided the line and ran to the pit. Achimi threw her clothes in. Emi slipped off her pants and threw her old clothes into the burn pit too. The flames felt warm on her face, and it was odd to see a fire in space.

One of the wardens yelled, "Get in your uniform."

Emi resisted the urge to listen to him and sprinted toward where the other 'plicants were lining up. Though Achimi was ahead of her initially, Emi quickly caught up and passed her. Emi sensed she had a running advantage. Growing up with Earth's gravity had made her legs stronger than the space-born 'plicants. Emi ran up and took the twelfth and last spot in the line.

All the 'plicants stared at her. She stood in line in just her underwear and shook out her jumpsuit. Achimi ran up behind her and said, "What are you doing?"

Emi stepped into her jumpsuit and slipped her arms through.

"Putting on my jumpsuit," replied Emi. She eyed Achimi's bronze necklace, which had a trinket with the word *Paris* on it and the shape of the Eiffel Tower.

A warden counted off the line, starting with Ankor and the scouts.

"One. Two," said the warden.

He pointed to Achimi.

"Pick a line."

The warden continued to count.

"Three. Four. Pod one. One. Two. Three. Four. Pod two . . ."

"No fair," said Achimi.

"Next tube," grunted the warden, pointing his scepter to the sixth row of 'plicants. Now the rows were filling up fast as the 'plicants came running back in their jumpsuits.

Ankor stepped forward.

"Warden," said Ankor, "I need to stay with my sister—"

"Silence," grunted the warden, interrupting Ankor. He pointed his scepter at Achimi, then at the eighth row of 'plicants.

Achimi ran to the eighth row, shaking her head. In a few minutes the entire field filled up with all the entrants in their gray uniforms. Six distinct groups formed with four rows of twelve 'plicants.

Yash stood atop the platform.

"During the probo and throughout your time at IGIST, you'll be part of a team of teams," said Yash. "Four 'plicants make up a pod. Three pods make up a tube. Four tubes make up a tetra. For this probo class we have six tetras. Each tetra will have two wardens during the probo."

He pointed his scepter to the front line with Emi, Ankor, Hans, and the other 'plicants.

"You'll live with your pods and your tubes in the same building. You'll have a choice to help each other or study alone. I can't tell you which strategy is better. Burning your clothes represents leaving your past behind. The cold reality is seventy-five percent of you won't make it."

Emi looked down the line, pleased she had made it into the first tube. The warden brought his scepter to his chest and bellowed, "As old stars die."

As all the 'plicants responded in unison, Emi yelled the loudest, "New stars are born!"

Yash tapped his scepter, releasing some sort of element next to the fire pit, and the flames shot up even higher, turning from orange to blue. As the clothes burned, the wardens lined up their tetras.

Emi looked down the line at her tube. All but two of the 'plicants gazed into the fire. Hans smiled at Emi, while another 'plicant looked her way. It was Ankor, and he wasn't smiling.

23 · BALiN

"If you don't get a score of 90 percent on the pretest, you should hit the gong," Ankor told five 'plicants sitting at his study table. His firm, loud voice carried throughout the room.

On the tenth day of the probo, Emi's tube had split into three study groups. Each tube's common area contained one large round study table, a couch with a low square table, and several desks with individual workspaces in the back of the room. At the large study table, four Martians and one scout surrounded Ankor. Martians stood out, with their tall, elongated physiques and long fingers wrapped with sensor tape.

'Plicants could choose to wear sensor tape during the probo. These were four long strips of tape that would monitor the person's biometrics like breathing rate, heart rate, and others. Emi opted not to do it because it seemed unnecessary. She should be focused on the material, not her biometrics.

Led by Hans, the second study group included two 'plicants from the moon. They sat on the couch in the middle of the room. The third group, if you could call it that, consisted of three loners: Emi, a 'plicant named Najaa from the asteroid belt, and the final scout, Sloan. Each one studied alone at an individual desk.

During the first nine days, the 'plicants had two days of orientation, five days on the aptitude test content, and two days dedicated to final preparations. Several times Emi realized how much of a difference being in the first tube made. At each meal she picked up precious time to study and review the material. On the third day it became evident to her how much she needed the extra time. Each day she felt like she was slipping further and further behind.

In the coming days the 'plicants would take two prep tests and then have a day off prior to the aptitude final. To pass the final aptitude test, 'plicants had to have a score of at least 95 percent or they would be dropped.

"Would any of you like to join our study group?" asked Hans. His avatar glowed as he gestured to all three of the loners. All three, including Emi, shook their heads no. Hans returned to the couch. Emi got up from the desk and walked outside.

"Emi."

Next to the door stood Balin, her tube sponsor. Of all the wardens Balin seemed the most human. It was his eyes. He looked as if he was there to help. Despite his warm eyes, the rest of his chiseled face was adorned with a wild mane of hair. It was said that Balin had previously been a fierce warrior before transferring to the League and becoming a warden. Emi listened to the other 'plicants warn each other to steer clear of him with rumors that the primitive warden sometimes placed his knife in his teeth when he was done eating.

"Need a study break?" Balin said in a gruff voice.

"Yeah."

"Let's go for a star stroll."

***

Walking around the field, Emi and Balin passed the probo gong. From the field they could see Snow Tower looming above the space station. Looking out from the space station, they could also see a half-lit Earth and moon. The stars created an enchanting backdrop.

"How are your studies going?" asked the warden.

"Good," said Emi.

She squirmed a little, showing the pressure she felt. She was struggling to keep up on the sections of the aptitude phase.

"Let me guess, back there"—Balin gestured his scepter toward Earth—"you were always the fastest, smartest student, but up here, well . . ."

Emi nodded.

"Have you joined a study group?" asked Balin.

"No. I learn best alone. My mother taught me that to do great things, all you need is a mentor."

They rounded the corner of the field and walked a length in silence. Across the field Emi saw Sloan's avatar emerge from the building, heading toward the gong. When they reached the corner of the field, the sound of the gong echoed throughout the probo compound.

Across the campus several screens showed Sloan's picture with the number twenty-two. Twenty-two 'plicants had already dropped out of the probo before the first prep test. Sloan's avatar flickered, and she disappeared. Hovering in front of the gong, her avatar drone retracted its extension component before another warden emerged from the living quarters and grabbed it.

Emi looked up at Balin and blurted out, "I'm behind the other 'plicants. They all seem to be picking up the material so quickly. I'm really good at sections A and B but am struggling on C, D, and E. I'm really worried about the test tomorrow. I'm overwhelmed. I don't even know where to start."

Balin put his hand on Emi's shoulder. "Listen, Emi, just stick with it. All these 'plicants who have dropped aren't meant for IGIST if they can't even make it to the first test."

"I'm not worried about making it to the first test," said Emi. "I'm worried about the three sections that I'm not grasping."

"Recognizing where you're struggling is important. That means you can focus on your weaknesses."

Balin pulled two threads from his tunic and smiled.

"The obstacle is the way," he said in a gruff tone.

He stretched the threads apart between his hands and quickly tied a very complicated knot, then handed the knotted thread to Emi.

"When I was in the League Academy, there was a requirement to tie one hundred different knots. It was an overwhelming challenge. Worse, several of these were very complicated, multistep knots. Two days before the final test, I locked myself in my room and focused on the knots giving me the hardest problems. Starting with the knots I struggled with, I was able to build a base of critical thinking on how the knots were constructed. I would break down each knot. I'd deconstruct it and master the concept of how to tie the knot; step by step."

Balin pulled a few more threads from his tunic as he talked and stretched them out again between his hands. He moved more slowly, folding the threads at each step.

"Emi, identify the areas giving you problems and deconstruct them. Take the time to understand the principles and master them."

He handed her the second knot, and Emi felt she could probably tie the same knot after seeing him do the steps in slow motion.

"Now, Emi, if a beastly being like me can pass a hundred-knot test by locking himself in his room for two days, a magnificent girl like you can ace the aptitude test. I'm sure of it."

As they rounded the field, Balin pointed to the time dial on the tower. Only a few minutes until lights out.

24 · HiT THE GONG

Silence hung in the probo chow hall the following day. All the 'plicants had taken the first prep test in the morning, and in seconds they would find out their scores. Each tube sat at a table, above which a virtual bulletin board listed their names. On the board above Emi's table, Sloan's name sat at the bottom with a line through it.

They heard a soft chime, and the screen lit up with the results. Ankor received a score of 100 percent, as did every other 'plicant in his study group. Hans had also scored 100 percent. The moon-born 'plicants scored in the mid-90s. Emi's score read 80 percent, while Najaa's score read 75 percent. Ankor looked down the table and laughed in Emi's direction. The Martians high-fived.

Following the presentation of the results, several 'plicants with low scores ran out of the chow hall. Soon after, the screens lit up with gong hitters. Twenty-three, twenty-four, twenty-five . . . The screen showed the faces of ten gong hitters. Emi assumed they had all scored below 90 percent on their prep test.

Across the table from Emi, Najaa looked like she was going to cry. Najaa's face turned from one of sadness to disgust, and she ran out of the chow hall. Emi followed after her onto the field.

"Najaa."

"It's unfair," yelled Najaa.

"What do you mean?"

"Oh, come on, Emi. Even as a bygone you can't be that dumb. You think it's a coincidence that all the 'plicants from Mars aced the aptitude test? The Martians, scouts, and moon 'plicants don't just have an edge—the system is rigged in their favor. Not a single Martian has hit the gong."

"I don't understand."

"Emi, to think entrance to IGIST is merit-based is a joke. These other 'plicants have a leg up. They've been given years to study essentially the exact questions that will be on the test and are encouraged to do so. I bet the first time you'd even heard of section E was at the beginning of the probo."

"But everyone can get the prep tests," replied Emi.

"They're not tutored for hours and hours on how to master them."

Emi looked up. They were at the gong.

"Don't do it, Najaa. Stick it out till the final test, then at least you know you will have given it your best shot."

Najaa picked up the mallet next to the gong.

"Emi, don't you get it? Your best isn't going to be good enough."

Najaa hit the gong, and her face immediately lit up on the screens around campus.

***

The next morning the remaining 'plicants left in Emi's tube lined up to walk to the test center for the second prep test. Emi was last in line as they filed out. She couldn't get Najaa's comments out of her mind. *Your best isn't going to be good enough. The system is rigged.*

It was obvious now to Emi. She wasn't like the other 'plicants. As they walked across the field, Emi stopped.

Hans's avatar turned around. "Emi, don't do it."

"It's unfair," yelled Emi. "The whole thing is unfair."

She turned around and headed across the field. Her tube kept walking toward the test center.

Ankor turned to the group. "I knew she was going to hit the gong."

25 · OWN WAY

Emi walked along the edge of the field toward the gong. As she approached, she shifted from a walk and started to run. She ran right by the gong and back to the building. She paced around her tube's common area by her lonesome.

"It's unfair. So, what can you do about it? Quit? Not going to happen. Be upset? Not productive. Resent the other 'plicants?" She laughed to herself. "Not productive."

She would rather die than give up. The entrance to IGIST was unfair. She was not like the other 'plicants. In order to pass, she'd have to operate differently.

"Keep going. I'm going to keep going till I can't go any further."

Emi remembered Ripley's advice: *if you're smart enough to get into the probo, you're smart enough to pass.* Emi believed the older girl, but she couldn't pass if she was stuck in a prep test session for two mornings. She needed to focus on the areas that she struggled on, like Balin said.

She thought to herself, *Maybe the system is rigged. Maybe it is unfair. Of course the Martians have a leg up. What can you do?*

Emi sat down at the big study table and mapped out the three areas of the test she needed to focus on. Only forty-eight hours until the final aptitude test. There was no time for self-doubt or self-pity; she would have to focus all her energy on the challenge that lay ahead. She charted out a plan to divide her time on each relevant area.

Emi wondered if they would let her skip the routines and meals. She'd have to eat something, but maybe she could do one meal a day and bring something back. She didn't care. *They can drag me back to the chow hall,* she thought. *I'm going to keep going till I can't go any further.*

***

Five hours later Emi felt good about her progress. She worked through lunch and tackled one of her weakest sections in its entirety. She took something unattainable and broke it down into bite-size chunks. She could pass section C. She understood the material.

She got up to stretch her legs. She needed a break and would need something to eat at some point. She peered out the door. Her tube walked back from lunch.

"Ah, spend the morning crying?" asked Ankor as he opened the door.

"Leave her alone," replied Hans.

The 'plicants filed into the room. They sorted into their normal study groups. Emi moved over to her desk and started on section D.

***

Emi's stamina waned after not eating for almost two days. Emi planned to dedicate an entire day to section E. She skipped the final practice test and breakfast that day as well. Getting into the first tube saved her hours of time, but even with the shorter distance, she skipped lunch. It would take too much time to walk to the chow hall. She also wanted to avoid Ankor and his crew gloating over their scores. Her stomach groaned. If she was going to have the energy to focus and be ready for tomorrow's final test, she needed to eat something.

Emi had mastered sections C and D but still had a way to go on section E. She also knew that she would need a good night's sleep prior to the test. She just needed more time. A couple of hours didn't seem like much, but it could be the difference between her taking a lucky chance or going in knowing the material for every section.

She desperately wished for a Venus Thirst and some comet cake. The other 'plicants filed back into the common area. A few gong hits occurred, but it was clear the majority of the 'plicants felt confident and ready for tomorrow's test. Emi continued to focus on section E and worked her way through the material.

***

When the dinner chime struck, Emi gave one last thought to staying but knew it would be no use if she was weak and couldn't focus. To the shock of most of her tube, she lined up and followed them out the door.

"Emi," said Balin.

He tapped her on the shoulder.

"Please come back to the common area."

The other 'plicants snickered. Ankor had started a rumor the wardens were going to drop Emi for missing the pretests. The other 'plicants paused for a moment and then turned and walked across the field toward the chow hall.

Emi opened the door to the tube. Balin held a bag of food in his arms.

"For the other 'plicants, the hay is in the barn," said Balin. "But I figured you could use the study time."

Emi's mouth watered from the smell of the food. She threw her arms around Balin and smiled.

"Now don't waste any time," he said.

26 · GET UP EIGHT

Emi remembered the relief and joy she felt passing the first probo test more than a month ago. To her surprise, the aptitude test had been the easiest of the tests so far. The next tests had focused on measuring their ability to avoid temptation, their mental resilience, and their creativity. Now on the fifty-sixth day of the probo, only one final test stood between Emi and formal entrance to IGIST.

"Fall seven times," said Yash.

The head warden of the probo looked majestic the morning of the final test. Holding his scepter high, he boomed, "Get up eight."

It felt like a lifetime since Emi had started the probo. She felt more sure of herself than ever, but with every day that passed, the weight pressing down on her became heavier and heavier. A looming despair hung in her mind that, despite how much she had overcome, she still might fail.

"Here are the directions," Yash bellowed.

Emi shook her head and focused. The final test consisted of manually calculating the coordinates from IGIST to the moon and then piloting a shuttle with the plan. A child could fly the route using a joystick with integrated flight software. The purpose of the test was to ensure that the 'plicants could do the basic arithmetic to plot the course under pressure and pilot the ship with no assistance.

In the training, Yash and the wardens explained that civilizations in the Spacefaring era must never lose sight of the foundational concepts that had unlocked the cosmos for them. In class they had studied how ancient civilizations had mastered concepts that in turn effected extraordinary feats. The Romans built the world's most advanced aqueduct system. The engineering marvel allowed them to move water vast distances using only gravity. The Egyptians built magnificent pyramid structures that stood for centuries. After accomplishing those technological triumphs, these civilizations forgot the foundational concepts that allowed them to create their masterpieces and sowed the seeds of their own decline.

Throughout the prep they had been drilled that the key was not only to be able to do the calculations but to be able to do them under pressure when real stakes were on the line. In this case, if they messed up the calculations, they would not make it into IGIST. Without the guided autopilot corrections, they could literally crash and die or be flung off into space on a random trajectory.

Yash issued the directions and called for the 'plicants to collect their flight and shuttle assignments. Emi grabbed her mission assignment and read it as she strode toward the launchpad. She was assigned to Z-Shuttle.

Traversing the long catwalk, Emi looked down and savored the greenish-blue hue of the moon-brick path bisecting the fountains shooting out on both sides. The giant pools of water had glass floors and stretched hundreds of yards in length. Emi was anxious. It was the first time the 'plicants had been out of the probo section of the space station. Gazing at the fountains, Emi had never felt more certain she belonged at IGIST.

She was the first 'plicant to arrive at the Z-Shuttle, a little spaceship from the lander series. It was metallic black, with falcon doors and three cockpits separated by clear glass panels. Emi climbed into the central cockpit. There were two other pilot cockpits in the front of the shuttle. To her left through the glass, she saw Ankor climbing into that cockpit. He glanced at her and rolled his eyes. To her right Hans's glowing image floated in. He smiled and flashed her a peace sign. His drone plugged into the ship.

Their three cockpit sections were each soundproof, but they could see each other through the glass. A screen in each pilot compartment lit up, showing Balin's face.

"All right, pilots. This is your final test. Each 'plicant will have to navigate for a section of the course. We'll fly you to the starting point, then give you the starting and ending coordinates. At the end of each person's section, we'll pause the flight to give the new coordinates so you can plot your course from start to finish based on the latest information. This is the applied section. Oftentimes we see brilliant candidates get in the cockpit who can't tie their shoes once the pressure is on. Now listen to me. Please pay attention. This could save your life. If something goes wrong up there, keep calm and remember your training during the probo."

The screen then showed the order of who would be plotting: Ankor first, then Emi, and last Hans. Ankor looked through the glass and gave a thumbs-up with a big grin. Emi looked at her tools. They each had a whiteboard with a black pen. On the board was their flight plan. They would receive the starting coordinates and then have fifteen minutes to plot the course and do the math on the board. Then they would enter the coordinates. They could do one course correction. If they thought they plotted wrong, they could check and redo the calculation one time. If they corrected their mistake and reached the final plot point, they would pass.

"All right, pilots. Prepare for takeoff."

27 · CRACK

The Z-Shuttle, *Black 7*, containing Emi, Ankor, and Hans, gently lifted off and started to float into black space. Behind the shuttle, IGIST gleamed brilliantly. Looking down, Emi could see the fountains becoming smaller and the shadow of Snow Tower change as they pulled away. In front of them on the moon, Lunar Park glowed magnificently.

They would travel nearly an hour into outer space and then navigate back. Once they arrived at their starting point, a message on the screen appeared:

> The first 'plicant is in their session. Please stand by for your plot points once they are finished.

Emi looked over and watched Ankor plotting his section. Watching Ankor was like watching a lion or an eagle in the wild. There was something instinctual about his stunning capabilities. As a Martian, he displayed all the qualities of someone evolved to be a great scientist. His skills came so effortlessly to him. While others struggled to keep up, Ankor glided through any challenge with no appearance of facing any obstacle at all.

It often seemed that the tougher the cerebral challenge, the easier the material became for Ankor, creating a powerful cumulative effect to his advantage, pushing him to the inevitability that he would be right, be first, and always be the best. Ankor didn't hesitate; he acted. His thinking was clear and forceful, and others were attracted to his impressive intellect.

Even his biometrics were perfect. Ankor's sensor tape symbolized the Martian's dedication to being the best.

As Ankor worked through his calculation, his heart rate remained normal, showcasing his ability to remain calm in what should be a stressful situation.

In just a few minutes, Ankor had quickly calculated his course and entered it into the control panel. The shuttle started its route.

As the shuttle pushed on, Emi wondered how she ended up next to Ankor. He was someone destined to make it into IGIST. Contrasted with Ankor's ease and grace, Emi felt like an asteroid burning up in the atmosphere. Instead of acting instinctively, she needed to dig deep and give every task at the probo her all. The effort she put forth was superhuman. Why did she keep striving in the face of what appeared to be inevitable failure? What drove her? And yet she persisted. She had stayed in the race longer than others who had come better prepared. Emi had endeared herself to the other 'plicants and to the wardens.

During the probo Emi's struggle turned into something of a symbol for all the other 'plicants. If this Earthling, without a chance in hell, was continuing to take the next step, so could they. Every minor victory for Emi further infuriated Ankor. It wasn't her accomplishments or that she was making progress in the probo. It was something else.

As Emi persisted, her reputation in the probo had grown. The other 'plicants nodded when she walked by as if to say to her, *Keep going*. The wardens, while not outright favoring her, would give her words of encouragement that they rarely, if ever, gave to the other 'plicants.

***

Ankor could see the smiles and giggles of the other 'plicants in class when Emi fearlessly raised her hand, asking for clarification or more information to better understand a concept. Frankly, he couldn't understand why seemingly everyone who came into contact with this Earthling bestowed such an unspoken respect upon her. This small girl had started the probo with no chance of succeeding and here she was in the final test with the best of the best. *How had she done it?* he wondered.

***

The shuttle flawlessly reached the final plot point that Ankor had entered and came to a stop. Emi's screen shone with her directions, giving her the two data points.

Emi looked toward the moon. She took a deep breath, rubbed her hands together, and closed her eyes, visualizing the path to get to the final coordinates. She took her pen and started to plot the course on her whiteboard.

Everything was going great. Her thinking was crisp and clear. She got the first portion of the formula down, and then she heard a noise.

A crack in the front glass window of Emi's cockpit started to spread. Emi looked at the clock. She had ten minutes left. For a second she wondered if this was something normal. She wanted to believe this was a minor thing and resume her calculation. The crack continued to spread. Emi dropped her whiteboard and unbuckled from the pilot's seat. She stood up and observed the glass, which was cracking before her eyes.

She looked over to Ankor. He was out of his seat as well, looking at the glass in his cockpit area. Hans's window was also cracked. Her time was halfway up. Emi pressed the call button to IGIST.

"Balin, this is *Black 7*. We're experiencing an issue here," said Emi. "The front glass window has cracked."

"*Black 7*, this is Balin. Say again?"

"Balin, this is Emi. Listen, our glass is cracking. I think we're in serious trouble here."

The entire glass spiderwebbed out, splintering nearly the whole surface. The centers of the cracks were also becoming denser.

"Emi, roger. Stay calm. We're sending up a recovery ship. You're forty-five minutes away. You guys need to hang tight. Have your oxygen masks ready if it does break."

Emi opened a glove box compartment. As a cruiser meant for short trips, the shuttle was only equipped with light masks that would provide oxygen for ten minutes. If the glass did break, well, she didn't want to think about that.

Emi looked over at Ankor. He was holding his mask. Hans projected the breach protocol on the window separating them. If they could cover and cordon off the cracks prior to a breach occurring, it would be a nonevent. The thinnest membrane could stop the damage, but if the breach did occur, stopping it would be much harder and potentially impossible due to the rapid pressure drop.

Emi looked at the clock. Fifteen minutes had passed; her time was up. She searched the cabin. In the glove box beside the mask was a space blanket. It was a metallized thermal blanket that could be folded up to the size of a deck of cards.

She could cover the cracked area with the thin-sheet blanket. The airtight foil would stop the convection if the glass cracked, keeping the seal between the shuttle and space. She quickly searched for anything to seal the blanket. Besides the mask, blanket, and the whiteboard, the only other item was a flashlight. There was nothing else in her compartment.

Ankor was searching his area as well. Hans was running probability calculations on the likelihood the glass would crack.

Through the divider Emi could sense the hissing. Hans's front shield had cracked open.

28 · COVER

Red warning lights flashed in the three cabins. As a scout, Hans wasn't in the same danger that Ankor and Emi were. He could simply disengage his hologram avatar.

"We need to lock down the compartments," said Hans. "The stress on the entire shuttle will only accelerate if we don't do it now."

Hans engaged the compartment lockdown. The back of the shuttle connected the three spaces. Once the compartments had been locked, each area was quarantined with a mechanical safety door that slid over the regular door and sealed off each cockpit. Several clinking sounds announced that the safety doors had latched.

Locking down Hans's section was only a temporary solution. Whatever was causing the front glass window's destruction would soon do the same to Emi's and Ankor's sections.

Emi unfolded the space blanket and held it up. It was shiny, silver, and more than double the size of her window. She would need something to affix the blanket to the window, but there was nothing in her area.

Emi looked through the window at Ankor. He had opened his section, which appeared empty. From across the way Hans broadcast inside the cabin.

"We must work together to prevent the windows from cracking open in the remaining two sections. We can cover the window with the space blanket. We need to find an adhesive."

Emi responded, "There's nothing here."

Ankor chimed in. "Nothing except the mask."

He showed the calculations he had been running. "A breach is imminent in less than ten minutes, maybe sooner."

Emi looked at the clock. The rescue squad was still thirty-five minutes out. The oxygen mask was only good for ten minutes. She didn't know about Martians, but she knew she could only hold her breath for about two minutes. Emi could tell she was getting stressed and tried to slow her breathing.

She noticed Ankor had gone into near-robot mode. He was deep in thought, and despite the situation, his display showed his heart rate was still hovering around normal. Emi noticed the sensor tape connected to Ankor. *That's it!*

Emi broadcast, "Sensor tape. We could use Ankor's sensor tape to affix the space blanket."

"We can't reverse the compartment lock," said Hans. "The only way to get between cabins is through the escape exits."

"No," said Ankor. "If we open the escape hatch, the pressure release will be too much."

Ankor stripped off his flight suit and held it up to the front glass window. The shape and material weren't big enough to cover the crack. The red warning lights lit up his spacesuit reflectors as he held it up.

"OK, listen," said Hans over the intercom. "I've found the schematic of the Z-Shuttle. There's a way to get through the separate compartments. The two of you will have to each unscrew the cover above the partition, and you'll need to work together to hand the space blankets and tape through."

The clock read thirty minutes. It reminded Emi of the general test she had taken. She looked at the cracking glass. It would certainly break completely soon. The red warning lights lit up all three cockpit sections. She looked over at Ankor, who had already started to unscrew the cover portal. She studied her side of the portal. There were sixteen screws. This would take forever to manually unscrew.

"Emi, get started," said Ankor. "We're counting on you."

Emi snapped back, "We don't have time."

"Emi, you need to work with Ankor. It's your only hope," said Hans.

Emi studied the cabin. She felt there wasn't enough time. Trying to work together was just going to make the problem worse. They needed a bolder action.

"Emi, come on," said Ankor.

Emi had an idea.

"I don't need anyone's help. I can do this alone!" replied Emi.

"Emi, please," pleaded Hans.

"I said, I don't need anyone's help," repeated Emi. She knew what she had to do. "I can do this alone."

She grabbed the flashlight.

"Duck, Ankor!"

"Huh?"

"Duck!" yelled Emi.

Ankor knelt down in his cockpit. Emi slammed the back of the flashlight on the window partition separating the cabin. It cracked. She hit it again, and it cracked even wider. She lifted herself up onto the edge of her seat and kicked the window through. It shattered.

Emi climbed through the empty pane into Ankor's cockpit. She grabbed a piece of the glass, cut the space blanket in two, and held it up to his front window. Emi could hear the glass cracking. She ripped the sensor tape off Ankor's fingers and sealed the blanket to his section. She scrambled over to her own cockpit and repeated the process. As soon as she covered the crack, the red lights stopped flashing. Ankor and Hans looked stunned.

Balin's face came onto the screens in the cockpits. "Congratulations, Hans, Emi, and Ankor. You've passed the final test! Please proceed to the cruiser."

Suddenly, the escape hatches opened in the back of the shuttle. Emi, Ankor, and Hans went through the hatch and into the cruiser. Balin was grinning.

As the 'plicants lined up for the matriculation ceremony, Emi felt a rush of positive emotions ranging between joy, pride, and excitement, but joy stood out as the strongest. In the face of disappointment, sadness, loss, frustration, and failure, she had persevered.

All the 'plicants wore elaborate ceremonial dress. It felt good to wear something other than the drab probo uniforms. Their bright teal and white dress uniforms added to the energy of the event. The 'plicants' faces were also filled with excitement and relief upon making it through the probo. They all held their luminary hats, tall caps that shone brightly when worn. The 'plicants would hold these until they were formally announced as luminaries, official students of IGIST, during the matriculation. The final test proved to be the hardest, and several 'plicants had failed, leaving only the best to become luminaries.

"Forward, march," bellowed Yash as the wardens led the parade out of the probo area. Emi held her hat tightly. Of the nearly three hundred 'plicants who started the probo, only ninety made it through the final test. Balin had explained during the final debrief that the real test was not plotting the points but working as a team to solve the window crack. Hans's approach had been correct, and every other group that passed had figured out they needed to unscrew the panels and work together to solve the problem.

It was never discussed how Emi's group had solved the problem, only that they solved it. No one formally mentioned the broken glass, but the tale spread through the campus. Of Emi's tube, only half had passed. Emi, Hans, and Ankor marched in the front row as the 'plicants walked across the catwalks from the probo area, around Snow Tower, and down the other catwalk. The fountains of IGIST shot their names and pictures from the water into space, honoring their celebration day.

Emi looked up at three grand structures marking the entrance to IGIST from the catwalk. Three memorial spires made of platinum shot up into the sky, evoking a sense of exploration. Each spire represented the trajectory of a rocket launching into space, with each one individually representing the three most important launches from Earth: the first rocket in space, the rocket that launched the moon landing, and the rocket that launched the first manned Mars landing.

Emi looked into the space auditorium at the crowd. The entire staff and student body of IGIST as well as friends and family had come out for the ceremony. The matriculation ceremony at IGIST was an even bigger deal than the graduation ceremony.

The 'plicants lined up in the center of the auditorium, facing the stage. A glint of light shone across Emi's face. Sadee! She saw Sadee in the crowd. The signal from Sadee eased the anxiety she felt. The drone floated in the stands next to Jack Lemore.

When Emi looked at Sadee, she went black and made a sign of fireworks exploding. Emi grinned, excited to reconnect with her friends and tell them about the probo. Silence fell across the crowd as Archimedes walked up to the podium.

"Welcome to IGIST!" said Archimedes. "Today you are joining an elite scientific community. You are now part of something bigger than yourself. I want to start by thanking the wardens of IGIST. Yash, your teams have done it again. This class is particularly interesting and impressive, yielding students from across the solar system and our first Earthling in twenty years.

"All you incredible young scientists and explorers are joining something special. This unique school, the oldest and brightest of all the Star League academies, was created to educate those who wish to colonize space. We needed a school where the best scientific minds could be trained to tackle the most challenging problems in the universe.

"At IGIST, our philosophy is that we can overcome the most complex scientific challenges in the cosmos by believing that no matter what problems we face, the right idea can prevail. We're focused on creating an environment where you can envision a better future and then bring it to fruition. We believe that, as creators, inventors, builders, and explorers, inspiration is a key ingredient in the scientific process. To be truly inspired, you must find out what you love and what your purpose is. Your curiosity is the fuel that will motivate you to master the scientific method by asking questions and creating hypotheses. The purpose I speak of is a tailwind pushing you in a general direction of progress, not a defined endpoint.

"Here at IGIST, we want to impart to you the importance of intelligence, curiosity, and perseverance so that you not only understand how to find inspiration and stay curious but also have the tools to bring those ideas to life.

"The probo may have seemed harsh, but it is a necessary filter to ensure that we're creating an environment for the most resilient scientists in the cosmos. We do that by constantly failing. Failing, you ask, isn't that the opposite of success? What is the opposite of success? Think about it for a moment.

"Most people say failure. We know at IGIST that failure is not the opposite of success but part of it. The opposite of success is not trying.

"So, knowing that you will fail, and that failure is a part of succeeding, aim far in your ambitions. We want you to find the central question of your life. What is your purpose? Several luminaries are examples of people who have found their 'why' and been able to overcome endless obstacles. The right why will provide the fuel to bear the pain of what will appear to be never-ending challenges. There is a great need for the minds that are molded and sharpened at IGIST.

"The galaxy needs thinkers who have interdisciplinary skills and the IGIST mind-set. An IGIST scientist and founder, Berlin Snow, created the air distributor, which can send out an ever-evolving formula that enables bacteria to survive in space, allowing humans to explore new worlds and further colonize the galaxy.

"Just now, Fortna,. an IGIST grad, is leading an exploration in search of a habitable planet in deep space. On Earth the plague is spreading and is in need of a cure. I'm certain an IGIST grad will solve it."

Emi stood even taller and leaned forward as Archimedes spoke. Her focus was interrupted by Ankor scoffing at the comment. Emi shot Ankor an annoyed look and turned back to the podium to listen to Archimedes.

"Science can be an extreme power for good, but it can also be used in less than honorable ways. I've thought deeply about this, about the risks of advancing science, and am confident that it is our collective responsibility to ensure that those whom we empower to create understand that power must be used wisely.

"At IGIST, we want technology and science to advance humanity to even higher vistas. It takes our values and commitment to ensure we use these capabilities as a force for good. I believe in each and every one of you and your ability to make an impact. We're counting on you. Now, face Snow Tower to be crowned as luminaries."

The students turned away from the podium and faced Snow Tower. Out of the top a bright beam of light shot into space. This was the signal for 'plicants to put on their luminary hats. In unison the students put on their hats, and a uniform pattern of light shot into the sky with each hat glowing up into space. The stands erupted into applause.

"You are all now luminaries and officially members of IGIST. Congratulations!"

The chancellor paused as the clapping died down.

"As old stars die," said the chancellor.

The new luminaries and the audience cheered, "New stars are born!"

Everyone continued to cheer, and thousands of small lighted drones performed a choreographed show in the space sky. The drones' show consisted of several amazing shapes and formations. The final maneuver was to simulate the three significant historical rocket launches, with the drones lighting up a stunning image in space almost identical to the IGIST three grand arches.

Immediately following the show, the luminaries ran to the stands and embraced their loved ones. Jack Lemore and Sadee were waiting for Emi. She ran up and hugged Jack. She still looked like a human, but her appearance was starting to change. Her teeth were more fang-like, and her ears pointed up, stiff like a cat's. Sadee swirled around Emi, glowing green.

"Emi, we're so proud of you," said Jack. "I've gotten you a gift so you can remember your misfit friend."

Emi opened up the package, revealing a mask of Yve. It was a stylized portrayal of the beautiful woman's face.

"It's a token of our friendship," said Jack. "This fall, you'll get to celebrate your first Genesis, something that's not done on Earth. On the birth date of Yve, every human in space partakes in this celebration to honor the birth of the Spacefaring era."

"Thank you so much, Jack."

Emi had plugged her MET back in and was excited to reconnect with Sadee. Her flying droid companion sent her images of the parade coming in, the drone light show, and a shot of Archimedes speaking to the group.

"I loved Archimedes's speech so much," said Emi. "It felt like he was talking directly to me."

"Who are you going to impact?" Sadee messaged. "And what's your purpose?"

30 · FLORiN

"Imagine being introduced in front of thousands of spectators to reveal your scientific discoveries."

The tall moon-born man thrust his arm in the air, pointing to the stands of the Coliseum. The P-lumins gasped. The professor, Volta, possessed a childlike quality that so few adults had. His wavy blond hair bounced as he became ever more excited.

The morning after the matriculation ceremony, sunlight shone through the pillars of the space structure. The group of first-year students lined up on the platform, looking down into the amphitheater, which was located across the catwalk from the parade deck where the matriculation ceremony had been held.

"P-lumins," said Volta, addressing the first-year prep students by their common group name, "this Coliseum is the pride of IGIST. It is constructed from moon rock, and home to the Agon. The IGIST Agon is the most renowned science competition in the galaxy."

Next to Volta stood another professor. She wasn't as flashy as Volta. Compared to the other professors, Florin was short—a sign that she was an Earthling. Her short, jet-black hair framed her stern face. Despite her understated look, Florin portrayed the resolute strength of someone who had, by sheer force of will, made it off Earth and into IGIST. Emi couldn't wait to hear Florin give the tour of the Bio Center and was eager to meet her. She wondered if Florin had ever received her package.

At the end of the tour, the P-lumins would be assigned to their pods, tubes, and tetras, similar to the probo. A dedicated professor served each tube as their mentor. As the P-lumins filed out of the Coliseum, Emi noticed a plaque of Agon winners from previous competitions. Volta's name was on the list. Emi was certain she wanted Florin as her mentor, but Volta's energy and excitement were captivating.

The P-lumins climbed into the space gondolas. An inner loop at IGIST contained a cable system with gondolas for the IGIST students and professors to get around campus.

Emi climbed into a gondola with Sadee. Ankor and his sister joined them. The gondola shot up high, overlooking all of IGIST.

"It's beautiful," said Emi, pointing down to the campus.

The combination of classical and modern space design created a distinct look and feel. The futuristic elements shone black and silver, representing a space station with features to run the resource-intensive structure. Interwoven with the high-tech design stood Roman-inspired statues, fountains, and pillars, all made from moon rock. Encircled by four teal gimbals, platinum sculptures of animals stood atop every building. Dubbed "spacevanes," these instruments used cardinal directions to depict other Star League schools' positions in the solar system. Spacevanes also displayed the location of IGIST relative to the sun, moon, and Earth.

"You probably wouldn't know this, but it's called ancient future," said Ankor's sister, Achimi. "This architecture is inspired by 'where the past meets the future.'"

The gondola passed over the probo area, which looked dull compared to the rest of the IGIST campus.

"Congrats on passing the probo," said Emi.

"It was harder than I thought," said Ankor. "I didn't expect the final test. It was a bold move breaking that glass, Emi."

"Who do you want as your mentor, Emi?" asked Achimi.

"Florin, but I'm so intrigued by Volta. He's amazing, and I saw he won the Agon."

"I'd never heard of Florin till today," replied Ankor. "Volta is the best. You want to study under someone like him, whose accomplishments are unparalleled. To the scientific community and the public at large, Volta is synonymous with genius. He also has an eye for emerging talent, which is why he mentors P-lumins. He was an early prodigy himself."

Emi closed her eyes briefly as Sadee sent her the two bios. Volta's contained eleven sections listing his awards and honors, an entire section on his Agon prize, and several on his published theories. Florin's bio consisted of one paragraph, showing she had attended IGIST and now taught biology and chemistry.

Emi looked at the twins and wondered what it must have been like to grow up on Mars. They weren't that bad after all, just different. In the end, they all loved science. Maybe they could become friends.

The gondola passed over the parade deck, where the matriculation ceremony had been, and the IGIST Mausoleum before lowering down at the Bio Center.

"This is one of the galaxy's most unique facilities, dedicated to the research and understanding of multiple model ecosystems," said Florin.

The P-lumins followed Florin as she took them on a tour of the different ecosystems: an ocean area, a forested swamp filled with mangrove trees, a savanna grassland, and a desert region.

Florin's monotone delivery of the tour undermined the beauty of the Bio Center. Emi's mother had made science exotic and exciting. Florin possessed the curse of describing something that should be magical, like a biosphere in space, and somehow managing to make it sound soul-crushingly boring. Compared to Volta's contagious energy, Florin's delivery was quiet and jumped straight to terms the first-years had never heard, like *ceiba pentandra* and *syngonium podophyllum*.

The last leg of the rather vapid biosphere tour was a rainforest with thousands of tropical trees and plants. Drawing in the herby fragrance through the thick air, Emi messaged Sadee, "Even Florin can't make this place suck." Sadee snaked around the trees with her eyes glued to the frogs scaling the leaves. Ankor and the other P-lumins were walking slowly, barely awake. Emi recognized a palm tree from a painting in her mother's room and pointed. "Oh my, is that an 'ah-kah-eye' palm?"

"A what?" Ankor asked.

"An akai palm." She pointed again up to the dark berries dangling from the palm tree.

The P-lumins burst out laughing.

"An 'ah-sigh-ee' palm," Ankor clarified. He turned to Achimi and bent over laughing, nearly biting the big one.

"She can't pronounce açaí," joked Achimi, cackling with glee. "What a dumb as—"

"OK," said Florin, interrupting Achimi as the Martians lost it. "Settle down, everyone."

Emi felt embarrassed. "Just laugh it off," messaged Sadee.

Emi messaged back, "So what I can't pronounce it? That's what we're here for."

***

After the biosphere tour, the students headed back to the gondolas. A little ahead of Emi, Ankor and Achimi and a third Martian, Vega, climbed into their gondola.

Emi and Sadee stepped into the gondola behind Ankor's crew. Achimi and Vega looked back at Emi and appeared to laugh. Emi had Sadee aim her directional microphone toward them so she could hear what they said.

"How did that bygone make it through the probo? I hope they pair her up with Florin. That was the worst tour I've ever seen. They should send them both back to Earth," said Vega. "And why were all the other 'plicants rooting for her?"

"The wardens practically carried her through the probo," said Achimi. "The other 'plicants weren't rooting for her, Vega. It's called pity."

Both Achimi and Vega looked at Ankor. Ankor and Emi had been in the final test together. He might not have passed without her breaking the window. Emi hoped he would stick up for her. Ankor sighed. "She's pretty pathetic. Did you notice her eyes? One is blue and one is . . . well, the color of something you'd see in a space toilet."

Emi signaled to Sadee to shut off her mic. She'd heard enough. These people were not her friends and never would be. Despite Florin's lackluster tour, Emi still wanted her as her mentor. She'd show these Martians.

The gondolas dropped the P-lumins off in the courtyard where a large display showed mentor assignments. At the edge of the courtyard, the professors lined up to meet their groups. Emi read the board. Ankor, Achimi, Vega, and one other Martian had all been assigned to Volta. The Martian students ran over to meet him, clearly thrilled.

Emi looked at the board. She and Hans had both been assigned Florin. Emi walked over to Florin with the other P-lumins assigned to her. Florin handed each of her mentees their new carbon-fiber backpack. They were glossy, silver, and black. Emi ripped hers out of the cellophane wrap and felt the teal monogram with her initials, EHS. Her mother's maiden name was Hayden, and her father's surname was Swift.

"Let's get started," said Florin. "In my group we adhere to the rules of the road. First, we have a mantra that hard work, done right, feels good. My expectations are high. I'm going to push you harder here than you've ever been pushed.

"This is not going to be easy, but you will succeed. In order to be successful at IGIST, you must show up and do the work. We share the same goal. You want to learn as much as you can and pass the first year, and no one wants that for you more than I do."

Florin paused, looking at the group.

"The one thing that I will need from you in order to make that happen is drive. I can't give you inspiration. You must find your own motivation that will burn past the thousands of hours of hard work required to become a great scientist."

***

At the end of the gathering, Emi approached Florin.

"Florin, I wanted to introduce myself. My name is Emi."

"Yes," replied Florin.

"I'm also from Earth," said Emi. "I always dreamed of coming to IGIST, and you were my inspiration." She blushed. "I even sent you a mocked-up hologram. Did you receive it?"

Florin stared back at Emi with an emotionless face for what seemed like an eternity. The professor leaned down.

"Emi, I'm not your friend," said Florin in a firm tone. "I'm your professor."

***

Stargazing, Emi stood over a small hole she had dug in the savanna grassland. She clutched something special in her fingers. Hovering over her shoulder, Sadee glowed red. They hadn't crossed paths with anyone on their way back to the biosphere. All the lumins were at the dining hall, but Emi didn't have much of an appetite. She felt a bit nauseous. She'd never missed her mother so much. Wishing she could celebrate her matriculation with both her parents, she imagined them holding her, all smiling. She brought the rose seed to her lips and gave it a kiss before she placed it in the soil. She pledged to herself that she would cure the plague to honor her mother's legacy.

31 · AGON

Emi walked underneath the IGIST entryway monument, looking up at the spires shooting into space. She could have taken the gondola but wanted to walk across the catwalks.

"Sadee, take an immersive shot."

Emi posed, her arm pointing toward Snow Tower. She took several more photos and sent them to Jack. She sent back a picture of a neon sign that said HIGH HIDEAWAY. As Emi crossed the catwalk, some of the other P-lumins were walking toward her. Emi overheard them. "Can you believe he meets with every first-year? He knew all about me too. It was a great session . . ."

Emi tried not to get her hopes up. Florin and Archimedes were giants in her mind. Her follow-up exchange with Florin had disappointed Emi even more than the professor's tour of the Bio Center. Demanding and strict, Florin lacked any appreciation for creating a motivating environment. Emi hoped her meeting with Archimedes would be different. She had imagined the chancellor on the welcome hologram a million times, and his matriculation speech had exceeded her expectations.

Archimedes's office sat next to the Coliseum. As she waited to be called in, Emi studied the list of award winners on the Agon Science Competition plaque. In addition to Volta, the vast majority of winners were from IGIST and had won as part of a team rather than as individual competitors. On the list, one name stood out from the non-IGIST winners. The plaque listed the solo participant: Celeste Tusk—Apollo.

Emi's name was called to meet with the chancellor.

***

Archimedes's office was a large, circular room that was all white, representing the future-design element. It was completely empty except for two chairs. He was sitting in one with his legs crossed. His chocolate-brown hair was parted down the middle, and his pencil-thin mustache curled ever so slightly at the ends.

"Chancellor." Her voice sounded shrill.

"Please, call me Archimedes."

"My name is Emi."

"Good day, Emi. Yes, of course, our first Earthling in many years. Please have a seat."

Emi sat down across from him. Archimedes held his hand up to his face, adjusting a monocle in front of his right eye and leaning in to examine her. He smiled, putting her at ease.

"Welcome to IGIST. I like to meet with all the P-lumins to ensure we get them started with the right mind-set. The most important thing I can impart to you is to encourage you to ask 'why' and to think for yourself. Be a nonconformist."

Emi nodded.

"Emi, you in particular should know that greatness can come from anywhere. I grew up in the asteroid belt. If I believed the Martian tutors I had studied under, I would have thought that it was impossible for someone like me to get into

IGIST. In my opinion, the best scientists do not always come from places like Mars. In the laboratory of life, only on rare occasions do gold-minted backgrounds produce the really innovative, impressive breakthroughs.

"Real breakthroughs come from the edge. I've always believed one should have a healthy disregard for what everyone else is doing and instead try to do the impossible. If you want to create something great, you can't be afraid to challenge the status quo. To ascend to greatness, you must break the rules. This terrifies most Martians, and that's why most of them will never be that interesting. A few are but most, not really . . ."

The chancellor winked and smiled. Emi took a mental note about challenging the status quo and breaking the rules. She felt comfortable with the chancellor. His presence was quite inspiring. Talking with him, Emi felt she could do anything.

Archimedes continued. "The key is to find something you're excited about, then go for it."

"I'm very excited about engineering and biology," said Emi.

"Excellent. I encourage P-lumins to study a range of sciences. The really interesting stuff usually doesn't happen in the depth of one field but rather at the intersection of two. Also, there is much value in taking your ideas out of just writing papers and making something of them."

"I'd like to learn more about the Agon."

"The Agon is the most prestigious science competition in the galaxy, hosted by IGIST. It's held as a competition to solve the galaxy's grandest challenges. It embodies the ethos of IGIST that powerful curiosity, compelling ideas, and dogged persistence are the keys to overcoming any problem. The winners go on to do great things."

"Can P-lumins enter?"

Archimedes chuckled.

"I recommend waiting a few years before entering the Agon. No first-year has ever won, and very few even enter. I'd encourage you to focus your first year on developing your learning skills."

"If I've got a compelling idea, waiting until after my first year doesn't sound like exploring curiosity or being persistent."

Archimedes leaned back in his chair, surprised at her response.

"Fair point, Emi. Maybe you should enter. If you do, you'd be wise to have a partner. Who knows, with the right help you might even win."

***

"Hello, Florin," said Hans, his avatar floating into her office.

Florin looked up from the screens glowing above her desk. "Hey, Hans."

Hans was infatuated with one of the landscapes of Earth on the wall. It showed a lighthouse at sunset.

"That's my favorite one," said Florin. "My aunt made them all. Hans, I wanted to talk to you about one of your classmates: the Earthling, Emi. The wardens informed me that she can be quite stubborn. As a P-lumin, it's imperative that she grows. From my experience the best way for a P-lumin to grow is by collaborating with their classmates."

"I can see that," added Hans.

"I think, because she's an Earthling, Emi feels disconnected from her classmates. I fear that she'll dig herself into a hole. I'm sure you've felt alone as a scout and can relate?"

Hans nodded.

Florin continued. "There's a great opportunity for you guys to help each other. Can you be her friend?"

Five hours later Emi had lost track of time. In a private room in the library, she brainstormed ideas for the Agon. The walls in the room were white, but some equations were written on them. Her initial interest had transformed from intense curiosity to her being fully possessed with the idea. Emi stood in front of the idea board where Sadee beamed a mind map of how they structured the problem. One idea stood out.

"I've been looking all over for you, Emi," said Hans. His avatar hologram entered the room. "I thought you'd be studying for our upcoming quiz. What are you up to?"

"I'm going to enter the Agon," replied Emi.

Hans laughed.

"No first-year has ever won. Why in space would you want to distract yourself with the Agon in your first year?"

"Ever since Archimedes's speech, I knew I had to find a way to prevent the plague."

"Emi, we just started here. The competition is only two months away."

"Yes, October fifth."

"Yeah, it's a Sunday," Hans quipped back. He possessed a unique gift for being able to say what day of the week any date would land on. He continued. "Still, several of these luminaries have been preparing for months, and even years in some cases, for the Agon. Entering as a first-year seems like you would be setting yourself up for failure."

"I've already decided I'm going to enter," replied Emi.

"Why is this so important to you?" asked Hans.

Sadee beamed the picture of Emi and her father at the Marrakesh the day they were supposed to go to space.

"Hans, my father was killed by the plague."

The scout nodded his head in respect. It would be lying to say the only thing driving Emi's desire was to avenge her dad's death. Since her meeting with Archimedes, she'd only thought about winning the science competition. As a first-year, winning would be a glorious way to show those Martians what she was capable of doing.

"I won't be able to rest until I've discovered a way to stop it."

"I see. What are you thinking?"

Sadee highlighted the areas of the mind map on the idea board.

"I've jotted down several ideas and have two finalists," explained Emi. "There may be a way to kill the pathogen outright, but it would be very difficult to find an effective option, and I'm not really pumped to explore something where I would need help from Florin. My favorite idea is to create a wearable filter or device that could block the plague from entering the mouth and nose."

"A mask?"

"Exactly!"

Hans examined the idea board. He wasn't just smart—he was brilliant. As a scout, he had been trained since birth for space exploration. The scouts were educated using the

Maximilian system, focusing on mathematics and applied science. Like the Martians, Hans and the other scouts had been born, bred, and trained for IGIST, yet they carried themselves without the arrogance and elitism displayed by the Mars-born luminaries. The scouts radiated a sense of service and optimism that made them great explorers and problem solvers.

"I retraced some of your thought process," said Hans. "It has some limitations as a cure to eradicate the plague. But if your goal is to stop it in live situations, I think a mask blocking the plague is a viable option."

Hans quickly beamed several different images of functional masks on the idea board.

"These are great! Thanks so much, Hans."

"It's so simple," said Hans. "We just need a form factor that can house something to block the plague. I wonder why this hasn't been done."

"Because no one cares about Earth or bygones," said Emi.

Hans's contagious enthusiasm excited Emi. She quickly scanned the different masks he had presented. Hans would be a perfect partner with his training, and he was so easy to get along with. They spent the next hour evaluating and brainstorming form factors for the masks.

After they vetted the masks, Hans pulled up the Agon's competition guidelines, which stated that they needed to submit an application by September 10. He also outlined a quick prototype development path with five iterative phases.

Emi looked at the application projected next to the idea board. The field showed a checkbox to enter as an individual or a team. Hans filled in both their names and checked the team box.

"Hans, let's take a break," said Emi brusquely.

***

Outside the library Emi beheld Snow Tower. She was torn inside. If she worked with Hans, he could certainly help, but how much difference would he ultimately make? She'd already come up with the idea. Emi messaged Sadee, "Team or partners for Agon?" Sadee listed out the winners of past Agons, which provided a unique insight.

Emi studied the list. She had heard of all the individual winners, like Volta, Snow, and Celeste. Teams had won more often, but for whatever reason their contributions weren't as memorable. Emi looked back at Snow Tower. She had heard Berlin Snow's name mentioned several times. When people talked about Berlin Snow or Snow Tower, they didn't mention any partners he had worked with, only him.

Emi walked back into the library.

"Hans."

The scout studied the board.

"Hans."

He continued to map out a process to develop the mask and homed in on the biggest challenge. They would need to find or develop a filter. Hans looked up.

"Yes, Emi?"

Emi looked at the scout. Hans was pudgy, and his hair was constantly a mess. As an avatar, Hans could have altered his projected image to make him look better than he actually did. He didn't care. He didn't care what other people thought, and here he was trying to help Emi on something that was so important to her. It pained her to say it, but she couldn't do it any other way. It was her nature.

"I'm going to work alone."

33 · PALCERIUM

Two and a half months had passed since Celeste last thought about Max and his daughter. Since her profits had stagnated, she was under pressure from her board to regain her momentum. With the thought of losing her empire, she would do anything to protect what she had built. She had attempted to reach out to Emi once and never heard back.

She remembered Max diligently negotiating for his daughter's Star League school to be paid for in exchange for his service to Tusk Enterprise. As a woman of her word, Celeste would follow through on the deal. Max had signed the contract. Celeste was optimistic that she would eventually employ his daughter. When she received the notification, she assumed the girl was looking to collect what was owed to her.

***

A chime started the call. A hologram of Celeste projected into Emi's room. Celeste brushed her hair back. At first, Emi was a little intimidated by Celeste's larger-than-life hologram. Emi got the feeling the egotistical reputation of the tech titan might be accurate, judging just by Celeste's posture. Emi took a deep breath. She didn't have time to be intimidated, so she jumped straight to the point.

"Thanks for meeting with me, Ms. Tusk. I've got an idea to win the Agon, and I'd like your support."

Emi held up her mask prototype. The mask contained glass openings in the eyes and a curved beak shaped like that of a bird. Two straps on the back held the beak appendage in front of the person's nose.

"What if we could shrink the Tusk Air Ionizers into a smaller form factor, one that could be worn?"

"Yes, the thought has occurred to me," said Celeste, intrigued by Emi's prototype. She sipped her tea. "Please go on."

"I've studied the filter and think if we could shrink the device to something that could fit over someone's face, it would be a huge breakthrough. Ms. Tusk, I was hoping you would consider supporting my project by providing an ionizer air filter that I could reengineer for my mask. The project will fail without one. I need to understand how you've designed the system. I only have two months until the Agon."

This was not a small request. The filters contained an extremely rare substance known as palcerium, which made them exceptionally expensive, especially on Earth.

"Emi, you're a first-year, correct?"

"Yes, a P-lumin."

"I admire your boldness, but I want to be candid with you. Your idea is a long shot. Air filters are in short supply right now. I just learned one of our spaceships carrying palcerium will be delayed due to a malfunction, and it will take six months to a year to get it back on track. No one knows this, but it will make even one extra air filter for something simple like you're proposing very difficult to spare."

Emi's shoulders dropped a little as Celeste continued.

"Even if we could get you air filters, the approach you've laid out, while plausible, has some real challenges."

Emi thought for a second, then responded.

"If it were straightforward, it wouldn't be worthy of winning. I'm sure plenty of people said a non-IGIST person couldn't win the Agon and that the first air ionizer wouldn't work."

Celeste laughed out loud, emanating an aura of power and confidence.

"Emi, what you are proposing is very interesting. You know Volta?"

Emi nodded yes as Sadee showed her the time. Emi was going to be late for her meeting with Florin, but this was the only time Celeste could do the call.

"As I was saying, the key to the air ionizer is palcerium. This is what your father was going to help mine in the asteroid belt for Tusk Enterprise. Volta has done some initial work on increasing the concentration of ions using smaller amounts of palcerium, which would be a breakthrough . . ."

Celeste paused midsentence and for a second appeared excited.

"Not only in making the size small enough to fit in a mask but by . . ."

She paused again and brought her hand up to her face, pushing her long violet hair over her ear, and then regained her calm, confident image.

"Look, Emi, if you can get Volta to sign off on your project's direction, I will send you an air ionizer. I believe in you." Celeste paused, then she smiled. "I remember the first time I chased the light. My motivation is to help other great scientific minds reach their potential."

Emi's eyes lit up, and she exclaimed, "Thank you! Thank you, Ms. Tusk."

Sadee changed her appearance to a black sphere with fireworks exploding then back to a silver orb showing the digital time. Emi's heart raced at the possibility of Celeste providing an air ionizer. The mogul certainly exuded confidence and a larger-than-life appeal, but she also made Emi feel like she could do this thing. Celeste's tone was uplifting and even encouraging. Emi couldn't stop smiling as she continued. "Thank you so much. I'll talk to Volta and be in touch."

"Thanks for reaching out to me, Emi," said Celeste in a motivating tone. "Remember, I can help—if Volta signs off."

34 · DEMERIT

Emi switched off the hologram projector and ran out of the room, sprinting to the gondola. By the time it touched down, she was already fifteen minutes late for her meeting with Florin. As she approached the meeting room, Volta walked around the corner.

Emi stopped for a second, debating whether to continue on and meet with Florin. She was already late and would certainly get a demerit for missing a one-on-one session with her mentor, but Emi wasn't at IGIST to be the number-one student. She didn't care about that; she wanted to make an impact. She also knew she couldn't be the best at everything; that's what the Martians were at IGIST for. She called out, "Professor Volta!"

"Yes, Emi, can I help you with something?"

"Can I run an idea by you?"

"Is it an inspiring idea?"

"I think so."

"Then by all means, please tell me."

"I'd like to create a mask that would contain a small air ionizer to protect people from the plague."

Volta scratched his beard and thought for a moment.

"That *is* inspiring."

He locked eyes with Emi.

"It is possible," he said. "You'd need to shrink the footprint of the ionizer by increasing the concentration of ions to use smaller amounts of palcerium."

"How might one do that?"

Volta pulled out his tablet and started writing out an equation.

"Let me explain. You see, ions are defined as atoms or molecules that have lost or gained electrons."

As Volta talked, another professor interrupted.

"Excuse me?"

Emi and Volta looked up. It was Florin.

"Yes. Florin, I'm teaching young Emi the basics of air ionization. I couldn't miss an opportunity to add fuel to the fire of one of our P-lumins' curiosity."

Florin looked annoyed.

"I'll take it from here, Volta."

"On air ionization?"

"No. Emi missed our one-on-one. She skirfed me. She must be distracted by whatever fire you're fanning."

"Oh dear. Emi, I'm happy to continue our conversation, but please attend to your obligations first."

Volta smiled at Emi, nodded at Florin, and walked away.

"You skirfed," said Florin in a stern voice. The teacher's tone shifted from anger back to her normal monotone as she continued. "You missed a commitment. Commitments make things work, Emi. Commitment to study is how you become a great scientist. Commitment to people is how you make a great relationship. Commitment to a group effort is what makes a team work, an organization work, a society work."

Emi nodded.

"Curiosity isn't enough. If you only follow your curiosity, you'll deprive yourself of a more fulfilling discovery that requires dedication and discipline as well."

"I'm sorry for missing our meeting."

"Don't say you're sorry, Emi. Just don't let it happen again. There's an opportunity here for you to learn. A Spacefaring civilization depends on commitments, which is why we must have consequences. If I don't issue you a demerit for this, I fear you'll believe that missing a commitment has no consequences. If you don't get your homework in tonight, I'll issue you another."

Emi nodded to Florin, then walked back to her room. Emi made a mental commitment to wait to fill out the Agon application until her homework was finished, but by the time she finished her homework she was exhausted. She started to fill out the application but only got her name down before she fell asleep.

35 · HIGH HIDEAWAY

The dealer blew smoke in Jack's face. The harsh wisps of silver and gray smoke wrapped around her head. She waved away the hazy air and coughed. *One more roll,* thought Jack. Smoke filled the chamber.

Not since the *Orleans,* when she had finally obtained the Helix Cells, had Jack felt so alive. She sat at the Wagers table with the bones in her hand. The game was simple. The bones had an even number of ones and zeros. To win, the thrower needed a pair.

It had taken her ten years to save up enough zurcon to pay for her first batch of Helix Cells. If she was going to have her transition completely done in time for the Esteem celebration, she would need to get ten thousand zurcon in just a few weeks. There were only a few ways someone like Jack could make that amount of money in such a short amount of time. None of the options were a sure thing, and all involved risk, danger, or both.

In her travels as a transporter, Jack had learned if you held the bones at a certain angle in Wagers, it increased the probability they would hit flat on the first bounce. She knew if the first bounce was flat, the odds of her winning at Wagers would increase. Her last ten throws seemed to vouch for her technique as she was up as high as she had ever been.

"Well, are you going to throw?" grunted the dealer.

The High Hideaway was a space station orbiting Earth. It was no one's permanent home—a pit stop for those on the run, people looking to gamble or partake in things not available on the moon. Jack paused. She was in pain and needed a break.

"I'm going to have a drink first," said Jack.

With her left hand, which now looked like a paw, Jack signaled to the bot. She had a feeling today was her lucky day.

"Venus Thirst," she said as she winced in pain.

Jack's appearance was now more animallike, but she was still very human-looking. Those in transition chose a life of ridicule. They weren't yet true misfits but had completed half of the genome-editing procedures. If they had remained predominantly human, they could have concealed themselves, and yet many spent months if not years in the semitransitioned state, which was a testament to their journey. In a middle state, the being's body would try to reject the changes until the final transformation.

With her fanged teeth she bit the top of the Venus Thirst and popped the cap off. The drink gave her an energy boost and took the edge off the pain. It also took her confidence from a feeling that it could happen to a feeling it would.

Jack did the math. She was still short by half. She had taken out a one-thousand zurcon short-term loan from some Terrans as a stake to gamble at the High Hideaway. If she wasn't able to pay it back, the Terrans would beat it out of her and have her pay number locked and tarnished till it was buried in interest.

She was up to almost five thousand zurcon. It would be wise to quit while she was up, but it would have been wise not to take the payday loan in the first place. This was her only shot at getting the zurcon.

"Gambling for Helix Cells?" asked a misfit who looked like a zebra standing next to Jack.

"How can you tell?" asked Jack.

"Half the people in here are looking for a big payday for something that's quite out of their reach," said the striped misfit. "And those aren't exactly discreet."

He pointed to Jack's fangs.

"Where are you from?"

"I'm from nowhere," answered Jack.

"How long will you be at High Hideaway?" asked the misfit.

Jack replied, "I've learned it's never good to stay in one place too long. If you move on to the next thing, you won't be disappointed."

She tucked one hundred zurcon in her pocket. She decided that she was going to bet everything on her next roll.

Jack went back to the table and placed a 4,900 zurcon bet. If she won, she would be set. If she lost, she would be set back further than she had ever been. She wanted this so badly. She could endure the pain but not the waiting. She clutched the bones and threw her future down the table.

The first bone landed flat, bounced, and landed on a one. She would need two ones to win. The second bone's first bounce was flat. Jack fist pumped her left claw, certain it would land on a one, sealing her fortune. The next bounce hit a corner, spinning the bone for what seemed an eternity. She strained to see the bone's final position through the low lighting and smoke.

The bone landed on a zero.

36 · SKIRF

Three soft chimes nudged Emi from a restful sleep to wakefulness. The night before she had set Sadee to deliver her favorite ocean melody an hour before the IGIST summons, the morning wake-up call for the whole school. Sadee glowed brightly as Emi opened up her sleep pod and sat up, shaking off the grogginess from sleep.

She set the timer early with the intent of doing some prep work for Volta's class, but she couldn't resist grabbing the mask. Emi was infatuated with the creation. The waves in the morning sequence reminded her of Earth, and for a moment she felt a pang of homesickness and longed to go home. If only there had been something like her mask that day at the space compound.

The prototype of the mask was rather crude, but holding it, she saw its potential. The plague was an unstoppable force. Its power struck indiscriminately, causing catastrophic carnage wherever it appeared. The randomness and lethality of the plague's destructive energy created a blanket of fear that everyone on Earth wore as a heavy burden. In space Emi almost shed the burden, but it was still there lingering in the back of her mind. This mask could be the answer to that fear. All the components were there.

Emi saw it clearly in her mind. She was holding something that could make a huge impact. She would not stop until she brought this idea to life. She thought through how to make the mask better. Emi placed it on her desk and started jotting down notes.

She'd need to figure out how to shrink the filter but would also have to work through several other design elements. The mask must be comfortable. It would need to be stored so it could be easily deployed when necessary. Moreover, the design should be something great, a visual symbol that signaled a champion against the plague. Pretty soon she filled up five pages.

She glanced at the blank Agon application. She still had a month to fill it out. Before completing the form, she figured it would be good to know if she could get the air ionizer from Celeste Tusk. Volta seemed excited to explain the basics of air ionization to her, but she wasn't sure if he'd endorse her idea to Celeste.

Originally, Emi intended to explain how transformative the mask would be for the people on Earth. After her talk with Volta, she changed her strategy. To obtain his endorsement, she needed to emphasize the scientific importance of her invention.

Emi tucked the mask in her backpack. The success of her pitch depended on having a killer prototype. The morning summons chimed. She looked at the clock. Somehow the entire hour had passed. She had lost the entire hour thinking about the mask. She imagined Florin scolding her. *"Curiosity isn't enough . . ."*

***

As she walked to class with Sadee, Emi weighed her options. She needed to convince Volta that her Agon idea could be a scientific advancement. She could skip her morning session and prepare for Volta's assignment, but that would mean ducking out of Florin's session. She couldn't afford any more demerits. She needed to figure out a way to get the prep work done either on her breaks or during class.

As she approached Florin's class in the chemistry lab, she saw Hans floating in with another scout. He hadn't talked to her since the library incident.

"Hey, Hans," she called out.

He continued into the room without acknowledging her. Hans and Emi were lab partners in Volta's class and would have to talk soon enough. She was uneasy about talking with him, especially since she was behind on doing the prep work.

Florin called the class to order. Sadee hovered in the back of the room. Emi stayed linked to her, but whenever she tried to focus on the prep work for Volta's class, Florin seemed to look her way. Despite her best efforts, she made no progress on the prep work by the time class finished.

***

"Today is a working session," said Volta presiding over the class. "The preparation assignment was to calculate the right resistance in order to combine two devices together in a single circuit. In order for the circuit to work, both partners should have come with their preparation done. Today we'll actually build the circuit."

Volta walked around the room. Emi was seated next to her lab partner, Hans.

"Some P-lumins have already completed their projects."

Volta stood next to Ankor and Achimi and held up their completed assignment. Ankor's and Achimi's names appeared on the board as line leaders.

Volta walked over to Hans and Emi. She winced in anticipation of his inevitable discovery that she hadn't done the work. She felt devastated since she needed to stay in Volta's good graces to win his endorsement. Hans's avatar projected a fully completed simulation of the project. His simulation included his work and the work Emi was supposed to have done. Volta studied the simulation.

"Excellent job, Emi and Hans!" said Volta. "The simulation is perfect. Now you just have to assemble the actual circuit. Nothing like being paired with a scout, right? They make the present P-lumins do all the grunt work."

Volta went on to the next pair. Emi said in a low voice, "I didn't mean to skirf you, Hans, but I got caught up on my mask project. How did you get my section of the prep work?"

"Sadee sent it to me."

In the back of the room, Sadee displayed the Orion constellation and stars, creating an arrow shooting out of the archer's bow.

"Hans, you didn't have to do my section," said Emi. "I really do appreciate it, though."

Emi put together the breadboard, a base for prototyping electronics, applying the right resistance and completing the circuit. Because Hans had done all the calculations, she just traced along the simulation and had it done in minutes.

"Hans, I'm sorry for skirfing you, and I'm sorry about the Agon. It just means a lot to me to do this on my own. I kind of think I owe it to my parents . . ."

Hans interrupted. "Emi, Sadee explained to me why this is so important to you. I'm not a bully like Ankor or Achimi. I'm your friend. Don't worry about the skirf. I know it wasn't intentional. I'll support you however I can."

Emi wished she could hug the avatar. Instead, she bowed to Hans with her hands pressed together in the galactic symbol of thanks. The other teams were busy at work, building and testing their circuits.

Having checked on all the P-lumins, Volta stepped out of the room. Emi didn't want to miss her shot.

"Hans, I'm going to step out."

Emi grabbed her bag and charged out of the lab.

37 · ENDORSE

Emi closed the door behind her as she exited the lab. Volta was walking back toward her, so Emi pulled out her mask.

"What's this?" asked Volta.

"The plague killed my father and took my mother," said Emi. "I've created a prototype that I think can prevent this. The elongated beak houses a micro-air ionizer filter. This could save hundreds of thousands of lives and would be a key scientific breakthrough."

"Stunning. How did you shrink the filter?"

"I haven't yet," said Emi, "but I know this is the problem that needs to be solved. I know from you that if you can increase the concentration of ions, smaller amounts of palcerium are needed, and therefore, theoretically this should be possible. I just need to do the work."

"Oh, the joy of discovery!" said Volta, clapping his hands. "Yes. Yes! This is the right process. Keep asking questions, keep making assumptions, keep testing, and by space whatever you do, don't stop. Intuition is the fire that fuels these breakthroughs."

"I'd like to join the Agon, but in order to make this discovery, I need to get a full air ionizer."

"Ah yes, that will be a problem. Very expensive. Look, don't let constraints stop you. Plenty can be done through simulations. Just look at your assignment today. I entered the Agon as a P-lumin and failed, but I never quit. I kept going. My second attempt, I failed again. My third attempt, I failed. On my fourth attempt I finally succeeded. The facts are only relevant for today. Those who create the future find a way by doing the unthinkable work in the face of a million calls to quit."

"Volta, would you endorse this idea?"

"Emi, you don't need a professor's endorsement to enter the Agon."

"Yes, but do you know Celeste Tusk?"

"Yes, of course. She was very intrigued by my work for a time, but she lost interest when I wouldn't sign away my intellectual inventions to Tusk Enterprise."

"She said she would send me an air ionizer if you endorsed my work."

"Emi, if that's what you want me to do, I will endorse you. However, consider what Celeste Tusk would get out of this in regard to protecting your inventions. You don't become CEO of a space tech company in your twenties without protecting your own interests. Before I send over an endorsement, let's make sure you understand what you're getting into."

"She won the Agon!" exclaimed Emi. "And she said she believes in me."

"Yes, Celeste is a brilliant scientist, unequivocally so. I'm sure you'd learn a great deal from her. Also, I think I can help with some of the simulations. I'm not even sure you'd need an air ionizer."

"Really?"

Volta nodded. "You can do this."

The professor guided Emi back into the electronics lab. When they entered, Volta took the mask from her hands and gestured for her to sit back down. All across the room, lights were flashing on as the pairs completed and tested their circuits. Normally the class ended with a callout to the line leader and the instructions for the following day.

"P-lumins, please listen up. It is with great pride that I want to let you know one of your comrades is signing up for the Agon."

The students turned their attention from the circuits to Volta.

"Emi has created a prototype of a mask that could potentially prevent the plague from claiming any more victims on Earth. Let Emi be a symbol for this P-lumin class, embodying the ethos of IGIST. My challenge to you all is to give her something that will push her to rise to this great goal: encouragement."

He held up Emi's mask. A hush fell over the room, and all the P-lumins sat still. A few whispers of wonder floated in the air. Ankor and Achimi sat dumbfounded, and Sadee glowed green.

38 · FUTURES

Sooner or later they would find her. Jack had evaded the Terrans for weeks. If they caught her, they'd give her a thorough beating to ensure her next trips' earnings would be handed over to them. She was on the moon for now but needed to move on soon.

She ducked into a café and called Emi to update her on her current situation. Two weeks had passed since they last spoke.

"I'm doomed," said Jack exhaustedly.

"Jack, you must never abandon hope," said Emi. "There has to be a way. Why don't you settle into a transporting route and save up like you did last time?"

Jack cringed in pain and took a sip of her Venus Thirst.

"I can't wait any longer, Emi," said Jack. "And I certainly can't stay in the same place. I'm a runaway, a nomad, a wanderer. I've learned it's never good to stay in one place too long. If you move to the next thing, you won't be disappointed."

She looked over her shoulder to make sure she was still safe.

"There's no shame in running," she continued. "Emi, I called because you're the smartest person I know. I thought you could help me come up with a solution."

"Help me understand what I'm working with, Jack," said Emi. "How many zurcon do you have? How much do you need? And what is something you know that no one else knows?"

Jack clutched her pocket, feeling her zurcon case.

"I've got one hundred zurcon. I need ten thousand." She thought for a moment. "I don't know anything, Emi. I'm just a lowly space transporter. The bot knows more than I do."

She tilted her head toward the server bot.

"That's not true, Jack," said Emi. "You're brilliant. I know it. You've got to use what you have to your advantage. What do you know about the cargo you've hauled or some of the other jobs you've worked?"

Jack thought for a moment more. Everyone knew when goods got delivered, the value on that settlement, planet, or station would drop. Oftentimes space transporters would smuggle items or peel off a bit of the cargo and sell it. Anything meaningful enough to make ten thousand zurcon would get a person caught, and any profit she tried to make off an unusual bump in the flow of incoming goods could land her in jail.

"I'm desperate to get the zurcon," said Jack, "but I don't want to end up dead or in jail."

She looked toward the door again. She got the feeling she needed to move.

"We're exploring your options here," said Emi. "The key is to look at the problem from a different vantage point. You've got to know something that could be valuable."

Jack winced again then gulped down the rest of the Venus Thirst and set the empty bottle on the table.

"There's a routine job," she said. "It delivers the housing filters for palcerium. I worked the route several times. It's always the same. It's coming in next week. I don't see how this is valuable. If I knew when palcerium was coming, that would be helpful. Look, Emi, I've got to . . ."

Before Jack could finish her sentence, Emi interjected.

"Oh my God, Jack! There's a palcerium shipment inbound that's been delayed, but everyone is expecting that it's on track. They assume when the filters get delivered they'll be prepared and sent to Earth."

Emi stopped talking and crunched some numbers in her head while she searched the price of filters on Earth over the last six months.

"I don't understand," said Jack.

"Listen, you need to go to a trader today, and with your hundred zurcon buy a futures contract on the air filters. Once the news comes that the final shipment is delayed, that contract will be worth a lot."

Jack looked nervously at the door again. The Terrans could check the café any minute.

"Emi, this is the last of my zurcon."

"Trust me, Jack," said Emi. "This will work."

"OK, I've got to get moving," said Jack.

She closed out the session and pulled open a trading screen. She could buy the futures contract today. She entered in her info but paused before hitting "Submit." She checked the six-month forecast.

Everyone had the price dropping, and she was betting it would increase one hundred times over. She looked at the empty Venus Thirst bottle and hoped that Emi knew what she was talking about. She hit "Submit" and placed the order.

39 · VOLARiNG

"Is that her?"

Two girls floated above the sport court, looking down on the group huddled together, watching them.

"It's definitely her," said the taller of the two.

Emi's pod was lined up on the sport court to learn about volaring. She wanted to get back to working on her mask and wasn't looking forward to the mandated physical activity time. Looking up at the students floating, though, she became intrigued. The older IGIST students floated in lanes fifty feet in the air.

As IGIST rotated, it kept a minimum level of gravity on the main level. Off the main level, the gravity was near nonexistent. The lumins floating in the air lay facedown on a clear bag of water the size of a pillow. The bag was clipped with a small cable to a larger cable that created a lane. The lumins would push off with their legs and then move their arms in a breaststroke motion, pushing their arms till they extended forward and then thrusting them back to their sides.

The older students started pairing off with the first-years. The two girls docked their water bags at the ladder lanes and climbed down. They walked over to Emi.

"Remember us?" asked the shorter girl.

"Ripley and Gal."

"Yes, good memory," replied Ripley. "It's Emi, right?"

"Yes."

"All of IGIST is abuzz over your mask," said Gal.

Emi blushed.

"Well, let's get up there," said Ripley. "Gal, you stay with the scout."

Gal introduced herself to Hans, while Emi followed Ripley up the ladder. On top of the ladder, they had a perfect view of the whole campus. The sport court sat in between the Coliseum and the Bio Center. Behind them, Snow Tower loomed over the fountains on the catwalk. The lane pointed directly at the moon. Ripley reclined on the water bag and signaled for Emi to do the same.

"I'm going to clip you in till you get the hang of it."

Emi wobbled as she tried to get her balance.

"The key," said Ripley, "is to pick a focal point. When I go out, I look at the biggest crater on the moon in Lunar Park, and on the way back I look at Snow Tower."

Emi looked toward the moon and locked in on a crater. The move helped her find her balance.

"OK, now with your legs, push off and then push your arms forward and thrust them back."

Ripley kicked off from the ladder platform and floated out onto the cable. Emi pushed off with her legs and floated out too.

"Don't try too hard to balance," said Ripley. "Just keep your eye on that focal point, and the balance will come. Once you've got that figured out and get some motion, you'll want to try taking your gaze off the spot just for a moment to check out the views. That's the best part."

The older girl pointed down. Emi looked away from the moon and down to Earth. She remembered staring up at IGIST and dreaming of attending. Now she was here, and it was incredible. From space, Earth looked so fragile. A sense of purpose swelled in her. She would not forget about Earth or the people still there.

"If you think this is cool, wait till you get on a solar sail," said Ripley.

She gave Emi a tug and pointed her head forward while she continued to stroke to the other end of the lane. Emi struggled to keep up, but a few strokes in she got the hang of it and docked at the other side.

"Now for the return. Go on your back," said Ripley. "This is trickier."

Emi turned over and looked up at the countless stars. Being clipped in kept her from floating off into space. The backstroke wasn't coming to her. She kept straying away from the lane, nearly bumping into a P-lumin on her left.

"Easy, asteroid smasher," said Ripley.

The older girl pulled Emi back onto the track and gave her a push, sending her back toward the starting ladder. Emi flipped back over and looked at the Bio Center grasslands. Under an acacia tree she spotted the wonder that she had planted the night before the first day of school. Twenty-one days later the rose sprout glowed green. Mesmerized, she lost control again and floated into the lane on her right, bumping into someone.

"Get out of my lane," yelped the P-lumin.

"Sorry," said Emi, "Still getting the hang of it."

Floating on her back, Emi could not see the person she bumped into.

"Watch it, bygone," snapped Ankor as he pulled himself onto the ladder platform.

Ankor's response startled Emi.

"Wow, little green man," said Ripley. "Scared this Earthling will eclipse your first year?"

Ankor scowled.

Ripley laughed. "You went to Agoge, right?" she said, referring to the best primary school on Mars. "Your parents practically placed you into IGIST. You did no real work on your own. Let me offer you some insight. You're not special."

Ankor pulled his suit straight and climbed down the ladder. When he got to the bottom, he lifted his fist in a sign of defiance toward the older Martian. Ripley looked at Emi.

"Forget about him, Emi. He's just worried about being shown up by an Earthling with original ideas."

They climbed down the ladder and met up with Gal and Hans.

"Once TPFS kicks in and you guys get bored of IGIST, if you're looking for something interesting, we could use your help on our moon project," said Gal.

It was hard to tell what they were talking about, but Emi figured it involved a solar sail and really appreciated that they would even ask her. Hans and Emi said goodbye to Gal and Ripley and headed toward the dining hall. Sadee flashed images of Emi volaring, showing her floating with the stars in the background.

"Hans, volaring is amazing," said Emi.

"Looked great," said Hans in a semisad tone. "Someday I'd love to try it."

As they walked, something occurred to Emi.

"I know it must be rough being a scout, Hans. We're both outsiders trying to make it. But we will."

Ankor walked up behind Emi and Hans, cutting them off as he shoved between them. He looked back and said, "Enjoy the spotlight. It will fade, and everyone will find out what you really are."

40 · STOPGAP

Emi and Hans continued on to the dining hall, trying to ignore Ankor. Emi smiled at Hans's glowing hologram, and he smiled back. Despite his rigorous preparations for IGIST, Hans and the other scouts missed out on some of the wonderful in-person experiences that the school offered. The tones, cues, and first-person interactions were hard to grok via hologram. The scouts were well aware of this, and instead of stepping back from activities they couldn't participate in, they leaned in and observed so they could at least enjoy the context of the experience. The scouts came to lunch just to talk.

When they entered the dining hall, a hush fell over the entire crowd, and all eyes gazed at Emi. They walked to the first-year section in the back of the room. When they sat down at one of their tube's tables, the chatter resumed. Ankor and Achimi rolled their eyes at Emi as two second-year girls came over to the table. One was a scout.

As was custom when two scouts met, the girl and Hans's holograms faced each other and did the Scout Exchange greeting. It was the first time Emi had seen Hans do the Scout Exchange, and she couldn't help but smile.

"Good day. Are you Emi?" asked the other girl. She stood three and a half feet tall, and her skin glowed a honey yellow hue. This girl was in the minority at IGIST, even more so than her scout friend. Ganymedeans developed their midget builds in order to survive the Jovian moon's strong magnetosphere.

"Yes, nice to meet you. This is Hans and Sadee."

"I'm Olivia, and this is Janel. We're both in Volta's second-year class. He mentioned your mask. Do you mind if we see it?"

"No problem."

Emi pulled out her mask. Olivia held it up and examined it. She smiled and handed it back to Emi.

"I think it's really cool that you're doing this. I'm from Ganymede as you can probably tell. I love seeing someone other than a Martian getting some credit for once. If there is anything I can do to help you, let me know."

"I think you've got a shot at winning," said Janel. "Hans, let me know if you ever want to talk about being a scout at IGIST."

"Thanks," said Emi and Hans at the same time.

The two girls walked off.

"That was cool," said Hans. "Maybe we're not outsiders."

"You don't belong," said Ankor, interrupting them in a low voice.

"Excuse me?" asked Hans.

"Not you, scout. The bygone. She's exaggerating her skills. The mask is an incremental improvement at best."

"Ankor, just leave us alone," said Emi.

"It's an OK idea," said Ankor, raising his voice a little. "It's not great. I don't think it would even get an article in the *Factor,* let alone be a viable candidate for the Agon."

A small crowd of P-lumins huddled around the table, giving Ankor an audience.

"It might seem ambitious," continued Ankor, "but it's not. It's a stopgap solution. How many people would it really save? Is it really a scientific breakthrough? Will you even be able to create something that can work?"

"I will," said Emi.

"You may make something, but it won't help anyone."

"I'm an inventor," said Emi. "Who are you to judge my work? Are you going to scrutinize every idea I ever propose?"

"By space I will!" said Ankor in a loud, authoritative tone. "IGIST is for real science, not pet projects or pseudoscience. Volta is patronizing you. Giving you pride so that he might inspire something, but you can't make gold from dirt. IGIST can't risk having a girl like you tarnish our image. What happens if you actually make this thing, and people are dumb enough to believe it works?"

Ankor grabbed the mask and held it up high. The crowd had grown. Ankor crushed the mask in his hand and threw it on the table.

Emi was humiliated. She couldn't believe that Ankor would dare attack all her hard work.

"The plague is coming. The plague is coming. Now I put the mask on?" He fumbled with the straps. "What if I'm eating? What if I'm not close to it? What if we don't have enough? How is it powered? If the goal is to stop the plague, this won't do it.

"Distributing a solution that has to be put on in a single event isn't solving for an optimal outcome. A true scientist wouldn't shy away from tackling the problem, solving for the entire outcome. Preventing a single event is trivial. Let me break this down for you. This is a dumb idea—a damp cloth on the forehead of someone with a deadly fever. It will never prevent anything and certainly won't win any contest."

Emi tried to hold back her tears but couldn't. She grabbed the crumpled mask and stormed out of the dining hall.

41 · PERSIST

Although every fiber in her body loathed the plague, Emi had never actually hated a person before. It had been two days since Ankor lashed out at her, and she was still teeming with fury. In the library the glass walls were filled with equations; in one area someone had scrolled an equation that was clearly aimed at her.

Staring at it, she wanted something very bad to happen to Ankor. She felt a pang of guilt for wishing harm on someone else. Perhaps what she really wanted was to crawl into the deepest, darkest crater on the moon and bury herself in moon dust.

The equation represented two unknown variables, but instead of a *y*, someone had drawn a rudimentary picture of Emi's mask. The not-so-subtle sting in this school graffiti highlighted a flaw in Emi's approach: she wasn't solving the whole problem.

Since the conflict in the dining hall, Ankor managed to do three things. First, he became the line leader in every first-year class; second, he soured nearly the entire school on the notion that Emi's mask could ever be more than a point solution; and third, he consumed Emi's every waking thought like an unwanted virus.

The previous whispers of respect and awe had shifted to murmurs of pity. She overheard the word *bygone* too many times to count. In the wake of this ruination, Emi tried to channel the vitriol she felt for Ankor into motivation to finish her project.

Others might have given up at this point, but not Emi. Her motley crew of supporters stood by her. Hans and Sadee rooted her on. She received a positive note from Celeste, encouraging her to continue her research and claiming that she was excited for an update.

Her biggest cheerleader turned out to be Volta. The professor could hardly tell her what day of the week it was but could casually make the inner workings of nested infinite square roots sound exciting. He was oblivious to the P-lumin drama. Emi couldn't resist his invitation to provide her with a simulation of the air ionizer. She intended to take a stab at her homework for Florin's class, but after Volta's demonstration she couldn't take her mind off the model.

***

On the walk to class with Sadee the following morning, Emi knew she would have to face the music with Florin. She made it through the morning session with no drama. As the class broke for lunch, Florin approached her.

"Emi, can you stay behind for a moment?"

"Yes, Florin."

"Sadee, please wait outside."

She heard a few snickers from the Martian posse as they exited the room. Emi pulled up a chair to Florin's desk.

"Emi, do you want to be successful here at IGIST?"

"Yes."

"Missing your meeting and now missing your homework are not the actions of someone who wants to succeed at IGIST. To be successful, you have to do the work. I'm going to have to give you your second demerit for missing your homework. If you get five demerits as a P-lumin, you'll be dropped from the school. Do you understand?"

Abashed, Emi looked down at the floor. "Yes, Florin, I understand."

Florin remained unsympathetic and continued in her monotone pitch. "I suggest you make your studies your number-one priority. Focus on those first."

***

"I don't care for Florin," Emi messaged Sadee as she walked out of the class. "But I need to focus on my studies or I might get kicked out of IGIST."

"No Agon?" replied Sadee.

If Emi dropped out of the Agon, she could focus on her studies one hundred percent, but it would be admitting to Ankor and everyone else that they were right. If she didn't get her studies in order, the risk of her getting kicked out would become all too real. What would happen to her if she got kicked out of IGIST? Where would she go? She clutched her bag. Her precious mask was more than a project. This was her identity. It was being challenged, and she knew she must protect it. She still believed it would work and save lives. She could solve this problem.

"I can do both," Emi messaged back. As she walked to class, she directed Sadee to pull open a detailed calendar for the next two weeks. Emi blocked off time for homework right after class. She intended to prioritize her homework after school, knock it out, work on the mask for an hour or two at night, and then get up and do an hour of schoolwork before class.

***

Throughout the rest of the day, Emi felt good about her plan. After her final class, she hurried back toward her room. On the way back she saw a virtual bulletin board listing everyone who had signed up for the Agon. In the last sign-up slot, someone had spray painted *Stopgap* over her name. Emi clutched her bag and ran to the electronics lab.

***

As Florin walked across campus, she saw Emi look at the board and then run toward Volta's lab. Florin walked up to the Agon sign-up list and shook her head. She walked over to the electronics lab, expecting to find Emi in tears. Instead, she found Emi and Volta studying the model. They were so consumed by their work that they didn't notice Florin walk in.

"You're very close," said Volta excitedly. "If you exchange these two components, I think it will get you close to the size you're aiming for."

Florin cleared her throat loudly, trying to get their attention, but they were too focused on the work. Sadee messaged Emi, "Look up."

"Hello, Florin," said Emi, startled.

"What are you working on?" asked Florin.

"Emi's made some amazing progress here," said Volta. "She's really quite gifted. Using the simulated air ionizer, she's mapped out a way to make it an order of magnitude smaller. I think she's a few tweaks away from getting to her size goal, which would be a major breakthrough."

"Volta, can I talk to you for a second?"

He nodded, and the professors walked out of the lab. Emi gave Sadee a look, and the drone floated to the front of the room, aiming her directional microphone at the door.

42 · FLUX DISTRIBUTOR

Sadee and Emi listened from inside the electronics lab as Volta and Florin spoke outside the door.

"You're being small minded," said Volta. "Our job is to light the fire of innovation, not snuff it out."

"She's not ready," said Florin. "P-lumins are supposed to be building a foundation and developing the skills and habits for a lifetime. You're encouraging bad habits."

Silence. Emi imagined Volta staring back at Florin with his intense gaze. Finally, he spoke.

"You're wrong, Florin. She's chasing the light. I've been there. If you see an idea clearly, you must go after it with all your might and never slow down. Stopping to explain it to others along the way who don't get it is the surest way to kill the spark that can change the future."

"Have you seen her weight?" asked Florin. "She's withering away. I don't think she's eating, and she's missing all her schoolwork. This is not us helping. A young brilliant mind needs to be given some guardrails to protect her from herself. You're showing her a spaceship's warp drive before she knows how to read a star map."

Again, there was silence.

"We're at an impasse," said Volta. "I'm going to speak with Archimedes."

"So be it."

Volta turned and headed toward Archimedes's office. Florin returned to Volta's lab and found Sadee hovering by the door. She gave the drone a stern look.

"Emi, come with me."

***

Ambling along the catwalk, Emi observed the Big Dipper while Florin spoke, strolling beside her.

"Looking up at the stars clears my thoughts and calms my mind. Realizing I'm just a small speck in the vastness of space sharpens my thinking and gives me an appreciation for what I can actually affect."

Emi nodded along, and Florin continued.

"Emi, when I first started at IGIST, I felt like an outsider. I admire your determination to stop the plague. However, I think your behavior has become self-destructive. You've got an amazing opportunity to learn here at IGIST. As a P-lumin, you don't need to prove anything to anyone, especially to the Martians."

Emi nodded as they passed by the fountains of IGIST. Something changed in Florin's tone. Instead of flat and monotone, her voice sounded empathetic. It was the first time in what seemed like an eternity that Emi felt like she was talking to another Earthling. As they bonded, the campus struck Emi as wondrous yet far less strange. When they arrived at the bottom of Snow Tower, Florin pointed to the top.

"Do you know what Snow Tower does?"

"No." Emi knew Snow Tower was important, but she didn't really know why.

"During the early phases of space exploration, the first astronauts who stayed in space longer than two to three years were at high risk of sudden death. They called this the fatal space cliff. The best scientists in the universe assumed this was from prolonged exposure to increased radiation caused by cosmic rays. To protect against this, thousands of radiation protection suits were created.

"None of them worked, except one. The Crew 3006 was a cutting-edge space design with integrated electronics. To check that the electronics were working every day, the astronaut would push a button that sent a frequency test throughout the suit. If everything was good, it would show green. Suddenly, astronauts could live past the fatal space cliff and venture farther into the galaxy. It was a major breakthrough."

Emi nodded, following along.

"Berlin Snow was an engineer for the company, O, which designed the suits. What he knew was that the Crew 3005 was identical to the Crew 3006, except it had only an oxygen tank and no electronics. The same exact material that was meant to stop the radiation worked in one suit, but not the other. Berlin Snow deduced that material preventing radiation might not be the issue. He reframed the problem. Instead of asking, 'Will preventing radiation through a material overcome the fatal space cliff?' he asked, 'What changed to overcome the fatal space cliff?'

"The problem was not blocking the radiation through the material, otherwise the Crew 3005 would have theoretically stopped it. By reframing the problem, Berlin Snow came to realize that Crew 3006 success was really a happy accident. The true lift to overcome the fatal space cliff was the push-button frequency test. What Berlin Snow discovered was that the challenge in overcoming the fatal space cliff wasn't about protecting humans from radiation, it was about protecting their microbiome.

"All humans have microorganisms that reside in the body. There are actually one hundred trillion bacterial cells in the microbiome. This microbiota is infused within the human cells and has a symbiotic relationship with the human host. In space the microbiome reacts to several different variables, such as lack of gravity and prolonged exposure to radiation. What Snow discovered was that the daily frequency test stimulated the microbiome, keeping it alive and functioning properly for a time.

"With his newfound insight Snow proposed a vast 'flux air distributor' that would send a frequency to everyone in space. This frequency carried the formula for a healthy microbiome that could survive in space. All space colonies, spaceships, and space stations could overcome the fatal space cliff by simply receiving that message and synthesizing the microorganisms that would join the microbiome and keep it healthy. Berlin Snow was also one of the founders of IGIST, and his proposal was to create the Bio Center to foster microorganisms that could survive in space, and then place the flux air distributor beacon at the top of the Institute's obelisk tower to analyze those microorganisms and distribute the formula to recreate them throughout space."

"Amazing!" said Emi, looking up at Snow Tower.

They walked around the polished base of the tower, and Florin went on.

"I know how hard it was for you to get to this moment. Just being here is a galactic accomplishment, and I'm in awe that you don't think that's enough. That drive can be a powerful force, but make sure to apply it correctly. I've seen lots of P-lumins flame out trying to be the best or the smartest. Your first year should be about finding out who you are and what you're passionate about.

"I'm not asking you to drop out of the Agon or to stop working on your mask. But you need to make sure your studies are your number-one effort. Also, I think you'd be surprised by how much more you can do if you take the time to really understand the problem through a reframing exercise, not to mention the value you would get out of learning some first principles. Do the work first, and if you have time, pick up working on your project."

Emi nodded in appreciation.

43 · ZURCON

The Terrans looked at the picture, studying the woman they were supposed to find.

"If she can't pay, it says to rough her up," said the Terran lady.

The mohawked leader studied the photo and touched the scar on his face.

"If she doesn't have the zurcons . . ."

He paused and put his hand on his chin.

"We're going to kill her."

***

Jack sat next to ten empty bottles of Venus Thirst. She had been holed up on the moon for the past eight days. Her pain was excruciating. She needed to finish her transition but had spent her last zurcon on air filter futures contracts. She had no money and was almost out of hope.

A news message alerted her—something about Tusk air filters. People were rioting on Earth. Her ears perked up. The next available filters would be delayed for nine months. Could it be Emi was right?

Jack ran to the nearest bank. She hadn't been in public in more than a week to avoid the Terrans. She'd been shamelessly running and hiding for so long. It was her nature. She didn't care now. She needed to know.

***

"What's the price of an air filter on Earth?"

"Well, yesterday it was . . ." The teller paused with a bemused look on her face.

"That's odd, it's not giving me a price," she continued. "Wait a minute. By the moons of Jupiter, it just multiplied by one hundred."

Jack grinned, her fanged teeth showing. She pumped her fists over her head in triumph and howled in celebration. She left the bank and called Emi as she ran back to her hideout.

"Emi, those futures are worth more than ten thousand zurcon," said Jack, smiling. "I can't thank you enough. I'll be able to make Esteem!"

44 · ALTER

Florin looked at the time. She had offered to help Emi with her classwork but wondered if her student would show up. When Emi and Sadee entered Florin's lab, Emi looked like she hadn't eaten or slept in a few days.

"This is a great start, Emi. You've shown up. That's usually the hardest thing to do," said Florin in a comforting voice. "Let's start by reviewing today's lessons."

"Solid, liquid, gas," said Emi, listing off the phases of matter.

"Right, and what are the two ways we change the properties of matter?"

"Chemical and physical."

"Yes. Excellent. How's your homework coming?"

Sadee glowed yellow and displayed a straight black line.

"Shut up, Sadee," responded Emi.

"Ah, I see," said Florin. "Learning the principles of chemistry can be done two ways. The first is to go through an exercise of enduring thousands of hours of simple but tedious memorization. This is akin to digging a trench in Lunar Park with a spoon."

Emi laughed. Florin placed two bowls on the table. One contained a white liquid, and the other held a black liquid.

"The other way is to show it."

Above the first bowl she held the dropper and squeezed one drop. The white liquid quickly expanded up and turned into a hard substance that looked like a mushroom.

In the second bowl she added another drop, and the black liquid suddenly exploded with different colors and then, after a few seconds, hardened into a waxlike substance.

"Turn them over."

Emi dumped out both bowls, confirming that their contents had turned from liquids into solids.

"With matter it's pretty simple to see that something can change its physical property from a solid, like ice, to a liquid, like water, and then back to a solid. I struggled with the same concept until I saw it demonstrated."

Florin placed the two solid objects into two larger bowls and started to hum softly.

Nothing stays the same, don't pass
No static, don't falter
Phases of matter. Solid, liquid, gas.
Look at yourself and alter
States are fluid and reversible.

As Florin hummed the song, Sadee glowed tiger stripes, reminding Emi of Jack singing the Polar song. Florin sprayed a mist onto the objects, and they transformed back into a liquid state.

"Chemistry is like magic," continued Florin, humming the last line again. *"States are fluid and reversible."*

Sadee played the melody from the song.

"I've got it!" said Emi. "This is so simple."

Florin's demonstration unlocked Emi's mental block, and she quickly jotted down the answers for ten problems on her sheet.

"Emi, are you eating all of your meals?" asked Florin.

Emi looked up. "Sometimes I get so consumed with my mask project that I forget to eat."

"Consumed?"

"Oh yes. Volta calls it chasing the light. When I get in the zone, I sometimes can't stop working on the mask for hours and hours."

"So, how is your mask project coming?"

Emi sighed, her lips trembling. "I can't stop."

Emi dropped her head in her hands. Florin placed her hand on her shoulder. "I've gone through it in my head a million times. Ankor was right. They're all right. The mask only is a stopgap. But, but . . ."

"Emi, it's OK. It's OK to stop."

"I can't," said Emi. "I know there's something that can stop the whole plague. I can't just stop."

"OK, that's enough for today," said Florin.

They walked out of the lab and toward Emi's room. Off in the distance some lumins volared above the school.

"I'm worried about you, Emi," said Florin. "You need to ensure you're taking care of yourself. Be wary of 'chasing the light' before you've got a good base underneath you. Learning the foundations of science will help you grasp new concepts. If you remain so focused on a single approach, you may miss an even bigger opportunity."

Florin pointed to the lumins floating on their water bags. "You need to find an outlet to relax and you absolutely must eat. Can you do that for me?" Emi nodded, and Florin continued.

"We've got a few big events coming up, so we'll have no homework, but that's meant to free P-lumins up to focus on projects geared toward first-year interests, not the Agon. Tomorrow's a big day. The entire universe will be tuning in to see the discovery from Fortna. Why don't you take a few days off from working on your mask and try to relax?"

Emi walked back to her room with Sadee, while Florin approached Archimedes's office.

***

"I'm worried about her, Archimedes. She's very similar to Leo Conca. I'm certain she has inventor's weakness."

45 · FORTNA

"What's all the excitement about," messaged Sadee. They rode in the gondola to get across campus to the auditorium.

"There's been a discovery," said Emi. "Everyone in space is tuning in to see what the explorers found."

"It's going to be announced by a scout," said Hans, grinning ear to ear.

The gondola touched down, and the P-lumins rushed into the auditorium. Their first-year section filed in together. Ankor slipped in between Emi and Hans.

"They're going to do something special with IGIST, I heard," Ankor said as they took their seats. The professors called for everyone to settle down. Archimedes stepped on stage, and a hush fell over the crowd.

"Luminaries, today we have some astonishing news," said Archimedes. "Live from the Kelorean solar system, we will be watching Nico Fortna, one of our very own IGIST grads, make a big announcement."

Fortna's image from his spaceship appeared above the audience. The crowd broke out in wild applause and cheering. Fortna wore a black T-shirt with the word *IGIST* across the front in teal letters, showing his athletic build. In the top right-hand corner of the image, a picture of a planet was rotating.

In a deep, confident voice, Fortna said, "Tomorrow we'll be touching down on a new planet in a new solar system."

The luminaries leaned in as he went on. "I'd like to dedicate this to the other scouts who risk their lives pushing the boundaries of exploration."

Several luminaries nodded and acknowledged the scouts at IGIST. The cheers continued, and the staff signaled for the crowd to calm down.

"I've always believed that out in space an unbelievable presence is waiting to be found," said Fortna. "Today is that day. We're orbiting Linus77. I've waited my whole life for this, and we've finally found it. We believe Linus77 is a habitable planet."

He pointed to the image on his screen. "It's beautiful, isn't it? The planet has two rings, and below this white atmosphere is a cold ocean with a network of channels with flowing water under a thin cloud cover. This is particularly important because it's the first habitable planet we've found in one hundred years. We also believe Linus77's three moons are habitable." The screen switched to an image of a whitish-gray moon with thin, gray-blue veins of flowing water. "If we can set up a base here, it will open new vistas in the adjacent galaxies for millennia to come."

The energy in the audience was high as they hung on Fortna's every word. Clicks went off as P-lumins and others snapped shots of Fortna.

"Looking at Linus77, if you had any reaction like I did, your mouth is watering. We have some challenges, though. The force of gravity down there is much stronger than we anticipated. It's so strong that none of our current equipment, specifically low-altitude flight gear, will work. There's nothing like traveling through space and time only to find the right-size lock but to have brought the wrong-size key. Some might call our situation dire, but I've got a secret weapon. I'm going to pop into my alma mater to discuss it."

Fortna paused, and suddenly the image went dark. He emerged in the auditorium as an avatar hologram, and the crowd started to cheer again. The IGIST alum walked toward the stage, passing Emi and Ankor. When he spotted Hans, he stopped and raised his fists to his chests with his elbows out. Hans instinctively stood up, and the two performed the Scout Exchange. As they did the gesture to release their arrow from Orion's bow, the crowd cheered. Fortna continued toward the stage. Emi leaned over to a beaming Hans and remarked, "That was so cool!"

Fortna stopped in the middle of the stage and held his hands up.

"We'll have to engineer our way through this. There's nothing we can't overcome together."

A video showed large canyons with white water crashing through ice and rock. Fortna's hologram avatar pointed to the scene. A rough sketch of a robot vehicle appeared.

"Instead of planes, we'll need to design rideable rover mechbots that can handle the gravity and the rugged terrain."

Fortna continued on, describing how they would be accepting design suggestions from across the galaxy through crowdsourcing. He believed that IGIST luminaries would lead the way, proposing creative solutions to overcome the challenges they would face on Linus77.

Fortna faced the IGIST crowd and said, "As old stars die . . ."

The crowd boomed back, "New stars are born!"

The scout's hologram disappeared from the auditorium and showed back on the screen. The video then displayed Fortna's ship deck, where several scouts were at work.

The assembly broke, and as the P-lumins filed out, Hans and Ankor discussed how they might assemble such a robot. Emi tagged along.

"We can help," said Ankor. "We could create a design for his robot."

Ankor and Hans spoke excitedly about the possibilities as the first-years crossed the catwalks.

"Fortna is leading," said Hans. "This will mark a key milestone in the exploration of deep space."

"It's all possible because of Snow," said Emi, pointing to Snow Tower. "Explorers can go past the space cliff because of his insight."

Ankor and Hans turned to Emi.

"That's a stretch, Emi," said Hans. "Scouts risk their lives to explore new areas."

"Yes, but Snow's ideas paved the way for them to even have that chance," said Emi.

Ankor chimed in. "Snow's insight would have materialized sooner or later. It takes courage to pioneer strange, new lands where your tools and instruments might not work."

"Did you know the scouts don't have a plan B?" asked Hans. "We're out searching for outposts to expand civilization. This is crucial for the Spacefaring era to continue. For every scout like Fortna, there are thousands of scouts who die a cold, lonely death when they run out of supplies in deep space."

"But Snow—"

"Emi, enough about Snow," said Hans. "Today millions of people were inspired by Fortna and the scouts. Don't ruin that."

46 · First Principles

Before class, Hans and Ankor sat next to each other. They discussed Fortna's challenge. Emi muttered, "This place flipping sucks," and wrote *TPFS* on her tablet. Florin walked by and called the class to order.

"First principles are a way of looking at a problem and breaking a situation down into its fundamental pieces and then putting them back together," said Florin. "Most people reason by analogy because it's the fastest way for us to synthesize information. For example, how could we inhabit one of Linus77's moons?"

Florin repeated back the ideas coming in from the students.

"Printing homes, applying Sappho's formula . . ."

She turned to the board and sketched a cursory map of Linus77 and its three moons, depicting their water supplies with blue lines. On the upper corner of board, she drew a sunlike star and labeled it *Renewable Energy*.

Emi had learned more about the Kelorean solar system from reading Fortna's paper "A New World."

Florin turned back to the class and continued. "Most of these ideas are reasoning by analogy—that is, taking what you know works and applying it to the problem. Despite the benefit of speed, this method has some drawbacks. If we only reason like this, we often end up justifying why we do things based on thinking 'that's how it's always been done.' To make big breakthroughs and solve big problems, we must reason from first principles. We must challenge the status quo. We start by challenging why this is done a certain way and asking whether it can be done differently. Reasoning by first principles would entail distilling a problem down to its basic parts and asking how can we accomplish our goal in a new way."

Emi jotted down notes as Florin continued to speak.

"So, how might we use first-principles thinking to analyze our goal? Let's start by breaking down the problem and focusing on the fundamental truths. What do we need to live?"

Florin wrote the students' suggestions on the board and repeated them back.

"Dwellings, sustenance, oxygen . . . Good. Good. Already have oxygen." Florin drew a line connecting the word *oxygen* to the blue water on the moon diagram, which she then labeled H_2O. She pointed to one of the moons and asked, "What else do we know about this habitat?"

Emi blurted out, "The force of gravity on Linus77's three moons, in contrast to the planet, is slightly weaker than that of Earth as Fortna mentioned in his paper."

"That's right," Florin replied, smiling. She turned to the diagram of Linus77 and wrote: $F_g > 9.8\ m/s^2$. Beside each moon she put: $F_g < 9.8\ m/s^2$. She resumed her lecture. "Using first-principles thinking, we're able to see that all we really need are the raw materials for homes, offices, gardens, et cetera. Had we only reasoned by analogy, most if not every step of our plan would have amounted to a complete waste of resources."

The P-lumins nodded, enthralled by Florin's lecture.

"Now that we understand first-principles thinking, let's apply it to our big idea for the day. Examining substances at the molecular level helps us understand the building blocks of life," said Florin. "We can break down this approach into different levels to make it easier to understand. Starting from the universe, we go down to the galaxy to the solar system to the planet to the biosphere to the ecosystem to the community to the population to the organism to the body system to the organ to the tissue to the cell to the molecule to the atom."

The screen scanned from an image of the universe through those phases, ending with the atom.

"The smallest building block of matter is an atom. These atoms come together to create molecules. When you mash this stuff up in different arrangements, you get everything from organisms to planets to galaxies. We describe arrangements of atoms with chemical formulas like H_2O. It represents two hydrogen atoms bonded to a single oxygen atom. We can arrange the different elements in infinite ways, creating everything in the universe."

Florin continued. "By rearranging elements, you get different outcomes. Anything can be changed at the molecular level."

Emi messaged Sadee, "What if?!"

Florin was showing the elements and their properties on the board. Emi stopped paying attention shortly after Florin showed the formula for water. On her tablet Emi listed out:

- TPFS
- First Principles
- Reframing the Problem
- Eureka!

What if they could get the chemical formula for the plague and run simulations to see what would change by adding different elements? They just needed to get the formula and build the simulation.

For the rest of class, Emi sketched out how she would build her model to test the different arrangements. She also listed out the dates. Eleven days remained until the deadline for the Agon submission. Then she would only have twenty-five days before the actual competition.

Emi's excitement beamed on her face. She looked down at the bulge of the mask in her bag and felt a twinge of regret. At that moment she decided to abandon the mask. She imagined that Volta would be disappointed in her. The mask project had been demanding yet fun, and she had essentially solved it. She just needed the filter to prove it out.

However, the mask was just solving for a portion of the overall problem. It wouldn't be a viable contender for the Agon. By breaking down the problem to the molecular level, she was certain she could come up with a formula that would eradicate the plague, rather than just block it through a mask.

At the end of class, Emi approached Florin and showed her how she reframed the plague problem. She would use first-principles thinking to create an antidote. Florin clapped her hands and showed Emi initial signs of encouragement, but Florin's excitement drained out of her face as she spoke.

"Emi, I know you may be thinking that you could enter the Agon with this. I want to encourage you to follow your passion. 'Chasing the light,' as Volta would say. However, I want to temper your enthusiasm with some hard truths. In biochemistry and in all science, theoretical probability is what we expect to happen. With all the formulas you can map everything out. However, there is another step: the application of theory. When we try to apply our theory in the real world, oftentimes there are unforeseen changes."

Florin explained that the Agon rewarded applied science. Emi started to whimper. What Florin was telling her was that she might be close, but she was still an impossible distance away.

To create a cure, she needed more than a model. To win the Agon, she needed more than a model. Standing in between Emi and her dreams was a gigantic impossibility that she couldn't overcome.

Florin articulated the impossibility with her final sentence: "Emi, in order to really solve this, you would need a live sample of the plague to show that your antidote works."

Emi sighed. Under her breath she muttered, "TPFS."

47 · JiLLi

As Emi walked back to her room, she gazed at Earth and longed to go home. Now more than ever she wanted to be back in her old room. Sadee pinged her. Emi had a message from Celeste. She indicated to play it, and an image of Celeste appeared.

"I've sent you an air filter."

Emi sighed. "What's the use?" she messaged back to Sadee.

On Earth, Emi had always been the smartest. She wasn't a showboat, but deep down she took great pride in knowing that ninety-nine percent of the time she was operating at a higher level than everyone else. On Earth she felt most comfortable talking with grown-ups and smart older students.

At IGIST she felt the opposite. Her most meaningful conversations had been with the wardens, who weren't exactly known for their intelligence. She was never going to be the line leader in her first year at IGIST. That was never her goal, but her realization that everyone in space turned a blind eye to the bygones sickened her. How could they all ignore their ancestry as if they had no connection to Earth? Emi felt responsible for the bygones. If Emi could achieve something great, maybe she could redeem the people of Earth from the plague so that they all could have a chance to make an impact.

Emi looked across the campus at the Coliseum. It used to elicit joy for her to see the grand pillars and imagine herself revealing her amazing scientific discovery. Looking at it now, she felt a sense of suffering that only weighed her down deeper into depression. If she quit, she would be the laughingstock of the whole school. If she barreled ahead with the mask, she would not be a contender and would have to relive the hard truth that Ankor had delivered in the dining hall, this time on an amplified stage. She messaged Sadee, "TPFS."

As she approached her pod, she saw Balin with someone she had never seen before. She smiled and ran up to give the yak-man a hug.

"Emi, this space transporter has a delivery for you," said Balin. "They said that they know you from Earth."

Emi couldn't believe it. Standing in front of her was a magnificent creature. A blue tigress misfit with black stripes and glorious copper-bronze hair stood tall, exuding grace, beauty, and strength.

Emi recognized the misfit's kind, gentle eyes and reached out to embrace her dear friend. Her lithe tail swayed from side to side. Sadee glowed blue with tiger stripes.

"Jack!"

"You do know each other," said Balin, smiling. "I'll leave you to catch up."

"Emi, it's so good to see you," said the misfit, picking her up and swinging her around. "I brought you this package from Tusk Enterprise."

Jack handed Emi the small package, and she slipped it in her pocket.

"Jack, you look incredible," said Emi. "I'm in awe. You did it. You really did it, and you look amazing! How do you feel?"

The misfit hummed the Polar song and spun around.

"I go by Jillican," she said, smiling, "but you can call me Jilli."

"So, where do you live now?" asked Emi as they walked back to her room.

"I'm a nomad, remember?" responded Jilli. "I'm always looking for new experiences."

Emi nodded as Jilli went on. "And if you keep moving, you can't get hurt."

The misfit paused as they sat down on Emi's sleep pod. "So, how is IGIST?"

Emi shook her head.

"I hate it here. This place flipping sucks, Jack—I mean, Jilli," said Emi. "I miss my home. I just want to go back to Earth. I miss my dad. I just don't belong here."

"Emi, I'm so sorry to hear that," said Jilli. "I hate to see you losing yourself."

Emi described to Jilli her journey at IGIST thus far. Emi showed Jilli the mask and explained how it would work. She had gone so far as to mock up two prototypes, gesturing to where they sat in a corner of her room. Her design was good. She opened the filters and showed Jilli how they would work inside the mask. She ran the function check, and it showed green. With the filter that Jilli had delivered, Emi would have enough palcerium to put in each mask.

While Emi talked, Sadee delivered them some Venus Thirsts and comet cake.

Emi then described how Ankor and the other Martians had tormented her and recounted the blowup in the dining hall. She explained that at first, she stayed persistent, thinking that they were fools, but after learning first principles and reframing the problem in Florin's class, she had concluded that the mask was, in fact, a point-solution approach to just a portion of the larger problem.

Emi added how she had even built a model that could identify the molecular structure of the plague and had started to run simulations but had stopped when she realized she needed a live sample of the plague for it to actually work.

During the whole conversation Jilli just listened, nodding along as Emi explained her predicament.

"You've been here for me through everything," said Emi, giving her misfit friend a hug. "I think of you as"—she paused—"family. What do you think I should do?"

Jilli got up and paced around the room. "What if?" She paused and finally sat back down, looking uneasy.

"Emi, what if we went to Earth to get a live sample of the plague?"

48 · ALVIN

Emi walked to class and took a seat outside the room. Volta was running late, and everyone milled about, discussing the first-year project. During their first year in electronics, the P-lumins were tackling something that very few people their age could accomplish. Despite her classmates' excitement about the upcoming project, Emi was completely distracted by Jilli's idea.

Having finally arrived, Volta swaggered into the lab, holding several mechanical parts. The students filed in behind him. Without any acknowledgement that he was fifteen minutes late, Volta brushed back his flowing hair and called the class to attention.

"Today is a very exciting day," said Volta. "We've spent the first few weeks building a base understanding of circuits and the different components that can be controlled by a microcontroller."

Volta pointed to the board, which then turned from a black screen to reveal several images of robots.

"Now it's time to put it all together."

Volta's excitement overflowed as he picked up some of the parts.

"Every year each P-lumin tube builds a robot that aims to accomplish a particular task. Whichever team succeeds will get the rest of the course off."

All the P-lumins leaned in, excited about the robot assignment. Volta held up a robotic chassis with two arms attached and then set it on the table next to a valve.

"Last year's task was to build a robotic arm that could close a valve near a leaking pipe. I've got the winner here. The tube called him Alvin. We try to pick real tests that explorers are coming up against."

One of the robotic arms waved to the class, and everyone giggled.

"I've learned, from tackling these experiments, that persistence pays off. If you can see the light at the end of the tunnel, you're close to a breakthrough. You must remember, though, the robot just needs to execute the task. It doesn't need to be perfect, but if you can break it down into steps that, say, a one-year-old could follow, then you're closer than you think."

Volta pressed a button, and the robot came alive again. Its arms tapped around, reaching for the valve, its motions choppy. One hand finally grabbed the valve. Once it had a grip, it waited for the other hand to find the valve before both hands reached the valve's circular handle. In a jerky motion it thrust to one side, turning the valve handle. The robotic arms released their grip and repeated the motion three times, finally opening the valve. The class cheered.

"Bravo," said Volta. "Nice job, Alvin."

He gave the robot arm a high-five. The class laughed.

"For this year's trial each team needs to design a robot that can travel a distance of fifty meters carrying twenty-three kilograms."

On the board Volta drew a line representing the distance. The P-lumins were not impressed. All of them had already built a robot that could do something this simple. Adding the weight was a trivial issue to solve.

"Now for the daring part," said Volta, smiling. He wiped out the middle of the line that he had sketched on the board, making a gap.

"At the twenty-five-meter mark, your robot needs to detect a one-meter gap and jump over it."

The P-lumins gasped.

"With the payload!"

Alvin's arms clapped. The class cheered, affirming a difficult task was exactly what they wanted. Volta clasped one of Alvin's hands and raised it in the air.

"If you can create a jumping mechanism, it will help Fortna and the scouts on Linus77. Now get to engineering!"

As the line leader, Ankor wasted no time organizing the three pods to begin the robot assignment. Up until this point the twelve first-year students in their tube hadn't really worked together. They spent time together during meals and volaring. Their rooms were all close together. Several of them studied together, but Emi had always gone off on her own. Now they would have to work as a team. Emi wasn't thrilled about having to work with the Martians, but while they talked through their robot plan, Emi thought through her own plan to procure a live sample of the plague.

"We must focus on the most difficult part of the challenge," said Ankor.

He broke the problem into three pieces, pushing the team to solve the hardest parts first. Each pod would tackle one of the parts: identifying the gap, the lift mechanism to jump above it, and the ability to land again without crashing.

Emi and Hans's pod focused on the jump mechanism. Emi reviewed her own notes and tried hard to find reasons to pick apart Ankor's plan, but he was proving to be an inspiring leader. Ankor's meticulous leadership made her even more focused on what she was sketching on her pad.

"If we master the robotics task, we can submit some of our ideas to help Fortna," said Ankor. He pushed the team with a fierce sense of urgency. His confidence was contagious. Each group worked hard to get its piece right.

As her peers got up after class, Emi examined the sketch on her tablet. It was a map of IGIST, the moon, and Earth. In between the moon and IGIST, Emi highlighted the solar-sailing lane. She also checked the reports of the most recent plague outbreaks on Earth. In order for her plan to work, she would need to convince Gal and Ripley to give her a ride to the moon.

49 · SOLAR SAIL

Emi's heart raced as she reviewed the scheme with Sadee. Starting tomorrow, the first-years would have a week off from class to study for midterms. During this time many P-lumins would visit the moon for a day or two to meet their friends and families. It was the first window when they could leave IGIST. In order for the plan to work, Emi would need to go for six days.

The plan hinged on two things. First, during lunch she needed to track down Gal and Ripley and convince them to take her to the moon. Second, she needed to explain why she was going to the moon for review period. Emi needed a good explanation for the two people who would notice her extended absence: Florin and Hans.

***

In Volta's class Emi explained to Hans, "So, I'll be going to the moon for the review period. My friend Jilli is going to meet me there. I'll stay up to date on my sections of the robot task and send them to you so you can submit them into the larger project."

Hans's glowing avatar just nodded. For him, the idea of a review period was less interesting since he was never physically at IGIST in the first place. If he had any suspicions, they didn't come across to Emi.

***

When lunchtime came, she spotted her other friends.

"Ripley," called out Emi.

Gal and Ripley looked up from their lunch.

"Hey, Emi, what's going on?"

"I was wondering how your moon project is going."

They looked at each other. Gal signaled for Emi to lower her voice.

"Emi, that's a secret project, if you know what I mean," said Ripley.

"Ah, I gotcha," said Emi. "I was wondering if I could catch a ride with you on your next solar-sailing trip. I'm going to the moon for break and thought it would be cool to go back and forth via solar sailing."

As a P-lumin, Emi would need an older sponsor to take her solar sailing. Ripley and Gal were her only shot.

"We're pretty loaded," said Gal.

Ripley looked at Gal and turned back to Emi. "Give us a sec, Emi."

The two older girls turned to each other and appeared to be B2B messaging.

"See, our project is all ready to go," said Ripley a moment later. "We've just got one last hurdle to figure out."

"Of course!" exclaimed Emi. "What's the problem?"

"Well," said Gal. "We've got some precious cargo we need to get from IGIST to the moon—discreetly, if you know what I mean. Could you meet us tomorrow morning?"

Emi thought for a second.

"I know a space transporter who knows every trick in the flight book," said Emi. "I'll be there tomorrow and see if she can come."

***

Emi ran back to her room. She had scheduled a one-on-one with Florin to explain why she was going to the moon. Before meeting with Florin, though, she had one last thing to do.

She scanned the application for the Agon. It wasn't due for a couple of days, but she'd be traveling to Earth on the due date. She checked the box for individual.

She deleted her previous write-up on the mask and rewrote the "Question/Proposal" section, outlining how many people the plague had killed on Earth and how it was possible to detect the molecular structure of the plague. Her breakthrough would be using a chemical reaction to change the elements of the plague and counteract its devastating effects.

Prior to the Agon, she would need to fill out the rest of the report, highlighting her research, her method and testing, the results of her test, and finally, an application presentation and conclusion. Sadee reviewed her work, glowing green. When the drone finished, Emi hit "Submit."

She rehearsed with Sadee what she would tell Florin. "I'm really burned out and you had suggested I take some time for myself. I'm going to really dive into my review work for a few days, then meet a friend and be rested and refreshed for midterms."

It wasn't perfect, but even if Florin objected, Emi would be fine as long as she passed the midterms. Emi was pleased everything was coming together.

Emi received a message from Florin, saying she couldn't meet for a few days. Emi weighed her options. She could delay her trip, or she could press on. She messaged Sadee to wake her at 3:00 a.m. so she could meet Gal and Ripley at 4:00 a.m.

50 · ROVER

"Here it is," said Gal to Emi and Jilli early Monday morning.

Beside Gal, Ripley inspected the solar-sail craft. It consisted of a solar cell that contained the actual solar sails. The solar cell would be released from the cabin. Once extended, the solar cell unfolded into a square-shaped sail composed of four separate sails made of mirror fabric.

The sails used radiation pressure exerted by sunlight on the large mirror sails to create propulsion. Using a drag jib off the back of the cabin, the solar sailors could either steer the craft gracefully from point A to point B or navigate it through obstacles to demonstrate their skills.

"Here's our problem," said Ripley. "We need to get Rover here into the cabin but not get caught on incoming inspections."

Emi looked at the rover, a robot the size of an autonomous lawn mower. The tires were oversize and ruggedized with tread. The tires and the body of the robot were painted a moon-rock gray.

"What are you thinking?" asked Jilli.

"Well, we were thinking we'd put it in a crate and drag it behind by the jib," said Gal.

Jilli laughed out loud. "That will work to get it there, but you'll certainly get checked," she responded.

Jilli walked around the cabin of the ship.

"Amazing solarcraft," said Jilli. "This is the same model used in the Star League Solar Cup. Are you racing it?"

"We are," said Gal. "Aside from Rover, the Solar Cup is our main focus this year."

The Star League Solar Cup was a match between two solar-sail crafts racing from Venus to Earth. The teams would have to circumvent a series of obstacles in their path. One solar-sail craft was the defender, and the other was the challenger.

"We're the IGIST team," said Ripley. "We've got some awesome new techniques that'll help us wrest the cup from Apollo."

The two older girls pointed to the lane between the moon and IGIST and explained how they navigate the simulated obstacles. Meanwhile, Jilli examined the back of the sail craft.

"Are we talking about the Star League Solar Cup or how to smuggle this thing?" asked Jilli.

Ripley and Gal turned back to Jilli.

"This is it," said Jilli, pointing to the escape pod that would be used in case of an emergency. It also housed extra oxygen masks.

"Are you suggesting we lose the escape pod and put the rover there?" asked Gal. "What will happen if we wreck?"

"Well, that won't happen," said Ripley.

"We can't," said Gal.

"We don't have much time," said Ripley. "She who dares, wins!"

Ripley unlatched the escape pod and started to remove the contents.

"Bring over the rover," said Ripley.

Gal and Emi pushed the rover up to the escape pod.

***

For a moment Emi had a twinge of regret. Florin would be so disappointed in her.

"Want to sit shotgun?" asked Gal as they climbed inside the cabin.

As Emi climbed in the cabin, her guilt faded away a little. She'd be fine, she told herself. Nothing great ever happened by playing it safe. She was worried about what Florin would say. Maybe she should have delayed the trip. She justified her choice by reminding herself Volta was a proponent of "chasing the light." Archimedes also told her nothing great happens by following the rules.

"Let's have her sit in back and I'll explain Rover," said Ripley. "You're all clear for travel?"

Emi nodded yes.

"Let's start the show," said Gal. She pulled down a lever, and the solar cell shot out into space. Suddenly, the sails expanded. As soon as they were out, the cabin shot off the IGIST deck and thrust into the lane.

Emi looked down on IGIST. Snow Tower glowed against space, and the torus looked magnificent.

In the main cabin Ripley pointed through the module where the escape pod had been and that now held the rover. She handed Emi a thin wire mask. The wires were so thin the mask was practically invisible.

"Put this on," said Ripley. "The mask will stop facial recognition."

As Emi put on the mask, Ripley explained their project. She pointed to the center of the rover. A magnifying-glass lens sat in the middle of the machine. "We've been working on this rover for over a year. The rover is the biggest Sputnik prank ever. We've built the rover with this special magnifying lens."

The older girl pointed to the bottom of the rover.

"On the bottom we sprinkle this material. When the sun shines through the magnifying lens at an intensified rate, it changes the composition . . ."

As Ripley explained the technical process that occurred, Gal interrupted her. "The result is that forty-eight hours later, the moon rock that has been exposed turns from gray to black."

Emi traced the magnifying lens.

"You know Lunar Park?" asked Gal. "Where we first met?"

"Yes, right by Apollo."

Gal put on a wire mask.

"Exactly. We're going to set this puppy loose. We've got it programmed to run for a day and half. By the time they realize it's happening, it'll be too late. From the moon it will just look like black streaks. From IGIST you'll be able to make it out. And from Earth . . ."

Emi's face froze when Gal said Earth.

"Who's going to be able to see it from Earth?" asked Emi nervously.

"Well, everyone on Earth," said Ripley. "It's going to be epic. We've got several satellites from space and telescope cameras from Earth all teed up for the big reveal. You see, right now we're at a waning gibbous. Over the next three days as it turns to a full moon, it will show our work: the most epic Sputnik prank in history scrolled across Lunar Park miles wide."

Emi tried to act impressed and focused but was preoccupied with her plan. Emi couldn't tell them. She would afterward, but it was too risky now. She messaged Sadee to be sure.

"Are you sure you don't want to help?" asked Ripley.

"Ripley and Gal, thanks so much for letting me ride along. Your Sputnik prank sounds awesome, and I'd love to help, but Jilli and I have things to do."

"OK, cool. Remember to keep your mask on as you get off the shuttle. We'll see you Sunday, around noon," said Gal.

***

When the sail craft landed, Emi hurried to follow Jilli to the Earth shuttle takeoff point.

51 · FRiSCO DiSCO

"Set the timer," Emi messaged Sadee. They only had a six-hour window to get the job done and get back to the shuttle. Emi and Jilli both wore cloaks. Emi pulled the hood over her head. She kept the wire mask on to hide her face.

Over the last two days, they had traveled from the moon to Earth, during which Emi and Jilli had plotted how they would retrieve a live sample of the plague. On the news they saw that an outbreak had occurred at the Rockland School the day before. Watching the event, Jilli and Emi determined their familiarity with the school layout would be a major benefit.

A stroke of serendipity had provided a landing and launch in the same day. The next spaceship going from Alexandria Compound to the moon was scheduled to take off at midnight. Emi and her crew needed to race against the clock to get the sample and make it back to Alexandria by ten in the evening for the last check-in call.

In the Hyperloop ride from Alexandria to Rockland, Emi and Jilli reviewed the plan. There would certainly be armed robot guards to protect against looters. The sanitization period lasted four days. The first three days, a person would be at great risk of a plague flare-up. On the fourth day it was very low probability. Standard protocol was to wait four days, then on the fifth day wash everything down with a special chemical that wouldn't stop an active plague breakout but would restrict any dormant plague cells from flaring up. During the sanitization period it was common for bandits to break in. The risk of being exposed to a plague flare-up didn't faze them, apparently.

Tusk air filters had built-in canisters that kept the plague residue contained. The canisters would be removed, cleaned, and restored during the sanitization period. If Emi and Jilli could get to a filter before they were removed, they could obtain a live sample. They also needed some kind of diversion to draw the majority of the guards away from the filter point so they could grab it and get it back to the shuttle.

Sadee beamed a layout of Rockland's campus. Five filters ran all the air through the school. The majority of them were at the front side of the building and were all lit up, viewable from the main entryway. It would be too risky to go after one of those.

Emi circled the math building. It was behind the gym in the back of the school. They would need to bypass an eight-foot wall to get to it, but if they could, the filter on the back corner of the school would be the easiest to get to and retrieve without being noticed.

***

Emi and Jilli lay in the field about one hundred yards from the school. It was close to dusk. They had decided it would be safest to do the operation after sunset. Red glowing guard robots cruised around the perimeter of the school.

"Something's not right," said Emi to Jilli.

"What's going on?"

Emi's eyes were closed, and Sadee was live streaming an image of the school's perimeter. On Sadee's live stream Emi saw numerous teachers at the school. They were packing up equipment so that it wouldn't get ruined during sanitization or pillaged by scavengers.

"There are teachers inside," said Emi. "Not just one or two, but maybe fifty. There are four in the math building alone."

Their diversion would be focused on the front of the school. Once it turned dark and they were in position, Emi was to message Sadee "Frisco Disco," the code words to start the diversion. Sadee had hacked three of the school's coaches in the parking lot to drive into the front wall. It would surely trigger the guards for twenty minutes as they tried to contain the breach, but there was no way it would draw all the teachers out. If anything, they would probably hunker down to protect the equipment they were trying to get out of there.

"We'll have to plan another diversion," said Jilli.

"We don't have time," replied Emi. "We'll be caught for sure. There is no way we can get in and out with them there. We need to think about a plan B. We'll have to regroup and catch the next flight."

"Emi, the next flight isn't for a week," said Jilli. "And the closest plague outbreak outside of Rockland is two hundred miles away."

Jilli stood up and took a step toward the school.

"Wait, Jilli. Please wait."

Emi grabbed Jilli's cloak and pulled her to the ground.

"Let me size up the situation," said Emi. "There are just too many teachers to get out of the building. Let me think for a second. What if . . ."

She sat silently and thought through her options. Nothing. Every idea she had was worthless. They had come too far to fail, but she didn't see a way out of this. As she thought for ten minutes, dusk turned to darkness. Suddenly, all the teachers bolted out of the buildings and headed to the front courtyard.

"What's happening?" asked Jilli.

"They're all going to the front courtyard," said Emi. "But why?"

It was a full moon, and its illumination shone down on Emi and Jilli. Sadee live streamed an image of the teachers pointing at the full moon. Emi looked up. The full moon glowed spectacularly. Lunar Park looked particularly magnificent. Scrolled across the perfectly glowing park, black bold letters spelled out *IGIST*. In the *T*, a small circle with antennas represented Sputnik.

"Oh my gosh," said Emi, "I can't believe they—"

"Frisco Disco!" Jilli grabbed her. "There's no time. It's now or never. Frisco Disco, Emi. Frisco Disco!"

Jilli ran for the fence. Emi got up, quickly followed behind her, and messaged Sadee, "Frisco Disco." Within seconds they heard a loud bang. All the perimeter robots' glowing images surged toward the front of the school.

Emi and Jilli quickly climbed the fence and sprinted toward the math building. They navigated an outside hallway that led to the filter station. Once they got there, they stopped running and leaned up against the edge of the building. They would have to pass two doors to get to the filter. Emi looked up and saw an alarm. If a teacher were still in the room and were to pull the alarm, it would draw the guard robots immediately.

Emi and Jilli silently leaned against the wall and then headed toward the filter.

"Freeze," yelled someone.

Emi and Jilli turned around. Mr. Lemore stood with his hand on the alarm.

"Drop the hoods," said Mr. Lemore.

His eyes widened. "Emi?"

52 · COLLECT

Jilli pulled down her hood.

"Dad."

Mr. Lemore stood speechless.

"Dad, it's me, Jack."

"No," said Mr. Lemore.

"Dad, you must help us. We need to—"

"Stop."

"But Dad."

Jilli walked toward her father.

"Stop!" yelled Mr. Lemore.

"Let me explain," said Emi.

"I will not let you explain, and I will not help you with whatever you're doing," replied Mr. Lemore.

"Dad, please."

Jilli reached out her hand, and Mr. Lemore slapped it away.

"What are you doing, Jack?" said Mr. Lemore. "Stop pretending to be whatever you are trying to be."

"I was pretending to be Jack," said Jilli.

"You are not my daughter," said Mr. Lemore.

Jilli stomped her left foot and hissed, "Forget you."

Jilli grabbed the case and ran back to the filter.

"There's been an outbreak," said Mr. Lemore in a high-pitched, hysterical tone. "Stay away from the filter or you'll kill us all. Emi, what are you doing?"

Jilli opened the latch to the filter door. "Mr. Lemore, we need the filter," said Emi. "I'm now at IGIST . . ."

He yelled down the hallway. "Leave the filter alone!"

Jilli reached in, pulled the filter out, and put it in the case. Mr. Lemore immediately pulled the alarm. Red lights flashed. Jilli moved back down the hallway toward them. Emi could see the robot guards' lights moving in their direction.

"Mr. Lemore, please listen," said Emi. "I'm at IGIST. I've created a model that will stop the plague, but I need a live sample to prove it. Jilli is helping. Please, if we get caught, we'll never be able to prove that it will work."

The red guard bots were seconds away. Mr. Lemore stood in front of the classroom door. He stepped aside and opened it. They were sure to be caught. Mr. Lemore stared at them. His face softened from a sort of fearful astonishment to the compassionate eyes Emi recognized.

"Quick, get inside," he said.

Emi and Jilli ran to the back of the classroom. Mr. Lemore stayed in the hallway and shut the door behind them. Five guard bots descended on Mr. Lemore and scanned the hallway. He showed them his credential badge.

"I saw them running down the hallway from the filter," said Mr. Lemore to the guard bots. "I pulled the alarm as they were running that way."

He pointed to the front of the school near the courtyard. Four of the bots headed in that direction. One remained behind and scanned the hallway one more time. The guard bot opened the door to the classroom that Jilli and Emi had entered. The classroom was empty, and the window was open.

53 · INVENTOR'S WEAKNESS

Emi and Jilli raced from the Hyperloop station to Alexandria Compound. In her backpack Emi had the plague in a transparent canister. She pulled the double-sealed container out. Jilli handed her a blue hair-gel dispenser. It looked as if this wasn't the first time Jilli had smuggled something up to space.

"This will get us through the customs exit," said Jilli.

Emi breathed a sigh of relief as they waited in the station. The shuttle would launch in one hour. Sadee pinged her with a notification of an incoming call. It was Florin. Emi signaled to Sadee to keep her video off but to accept the call from Florin. Emi stepped into a private space to take the call. Her professor's image projected onto a wall.

"Hello, Emi, how's the moon?" asked Florin. "I'm sorry I had to reschedule our meeting but wanted to touch base with you on your leave."

"Thanks for checking in," said Emi. "Something's wrong with Sadee's imager. My trip has been good. I've been diving into my review work for a few days now and also got to see my friend from Earth."

"That's great, Emi," responded Florin. "When will you come back to IGIST?"

"In a few days," said Emi. "I plan to come back Sunday before midterms."

"Before we sign off, I want to show you something," said Florin.

Emi gulped. Florin pulled out Emi's IGIST model and pressed the red button. A hologram image of Emi appeared. *"My name is Emi, and I was born to go to IGIST . . ."*

Emi listened to herself explaining that, shortly after her mother discovered the steps to create a glowing plant, she was infected by the plague and moved to quarantine, never to be seen again. That was Emi's motivation to get into IGIST. If she gained acceptance, she'd stop at nothing to create a cure for the plague. The hologram video closed with Sputnik flying across before the image flickered out.

Florin looked into the camera. "Emi, I wanted to show you this because I'm worried about you. Have you ever heard of inventor's weakness?" she asked.

"No."

"At IGIST we often see great inventors chasing the light with so much passion that they take an ends-justifies-the-means approach. This win-at-all-costs mentality drives them to do things that are bad with the justification that their breakthrough will cause enough good that it will be worth it.

"Emi, someone succumbs to inventor's weakness at the point when they become so obsessed with their goal that they will do anything to achieve it. You have all the potential to be a great scientist. Your drive and determination are more impressive than anyone's I've seen before. This is, no doubt, your greatest strength, but I'm sure it's your greatest weakness as well."

Florin paused and made a comforting gesture to Emi. "With what happened to your parents, I understand your desire to come up with a cure for the plague. Just make sure you don't cross the line. I care about you a lot, Emi, and sincerely want what's best for you. I'll see you when you get back."

Florin's image flickered and disappeared. Emi sighed. She felt agony over what she had done. It wasn't too late. She could leave the plague on Earth and go back to space with a clear conscience. She wondered if Florin knew what she had done. How could she? She really did believe Florin cared for her. When she spoke, Emi felt as if her mother was talking to her. But Florin didn't know. She couldn't know what Emi had done. Florin was the one who had told her she needed a live sample to win the Agon.

Emi remembered Celeste telling her about the moment she knew she had something with her insight into palcerium. Also, Archimedes had encouraged Emi to make something of her ideas. What did Florin know? She had never won the

Agon. Volta even said she had never chased the light. Emi was excited and relieved she had taken the risk to get the plague.

"Boarding in two minutes," voiced the loudspeaker.

Emi clutched her backpack with the container and headed toward the boarding line.

54 · THEY KNOW

Emi tossed and turned in her sleep pod. In her dream, Emi walked down a hallway with equations covering the walls. She smelled something, the distinct smell of a unique fragrance triggering her memory. It was the strong aroma of her mother's plant. At the end of the hall was a door. She opened it. In the center of the black room, a glowing plant shone brightly. She walked over to it, and the plant's light illuminated her as she leaned in and inhaled. The plant smelled like a heavy forest after a rain shower with a subtle note of cinnamon and cedar wood.

"Be alone, that is the secret of invention . . ."

She heard her mother's voice.

"Mom," Emi yelled. "Mom, are you here?"

Emi reached out to touch the plant, and it vanished. The room became black. She could feel her mom's presence.

"Mom?"

Her mother's voice carried softly through the black room, seeming to come from the other side of the door. "Max, come quickly."

Emi walked back through the black room and tried to open the door. It was locked. She knelt down and looked through the keyhole. She saw her parents in her mother's lab. Her father was bringing her mother an instrument. Suddenly, Emi's mother jumped up and gave her dad a hug. "We did it, Max! It worked. It actually worked."

The voice vanished, and Emi woke up in her sleep pod, confused for a moment where she was. She sat up, trying to shake away the exhaustion. As she got her bearings, she recognized her room at IGIST. A ray of light shone on her face.

"Hurry up, Emi, or you'll be late," messaged Sadee.

As Emi got her bearings, a wave of excitement came over her. She tapped Sadee. "Why didn't you wake me, Sadee?"

Sadee sent her the logs showing that the morning sequence had gone off five times before she sent the final message. Emi quickly threw on her jumpsuit and peeked under the bed. There it was. She had done it. She had the live sample. As she looked at the case, her eye flared in pain, and she could faintly hear the sound of the plague popping. "Do you hear that, Sadee?" The drone signaled no. Emi turned away and shook her head as the phantom sound disappeared.

Emi couldn't contain her enthusiasm. She was desperate to start diagnosing the sample, but first she had to make it through a long school day. Emi looked at the display in her room. Roll call would sound in a few minutes. Her calendar showed it was twenty days until the Agon. She debated skipping class but knew it would be too risky.

She stared at the canister. Inside, the plague morphed and remorphed, causing miniblasts. Looking at the plague, she felt equal parts excitement and fear. She had passed the point of no return. She had gone after the pursuit of her deepest desire, and now there was no going back. She desperately wanted to get to work on finding the molecular makeup of the plague sample that she had risked so much to obtain. Sadee dinged her with a reminder.

"OK, we've got to go." She grabbed her kit and ran out the door.

***

The entire tube was lined up for roll call.

"We know," said Ankor in a near yell. Emi's heart dropped. All her tubemates were staring at her. Sadee turned yellowish-green.

Ankor paced in front of the line of students with his left arm behind his back and his right arm raised in a questioning motion.

"How could you do it, Emi?"

Emi stood frozen. How did they find out? She heard a faint crackle. She turned around and looked at her pod, then at Sadee, then back at Ankor and her classmates. Her instincts told her to run, but no one moved. Could they not hear it? She stayed still, eyeing her classmates.

Ankor continued to pace in front of the group, but she couldn't make out what he was saying. Snap, snap. Like a whip, the noise got louder and louder. She turned around again. Nothing. Was the noise in her head? She scrambled for what to say but couldn't speak. She felt an asteroid in her stomach. She regretted bringing the plague up to the station. They'd confiscate the sample, and she'd certainly get kicked out of the Agon and most likely expelled from IGIST.

Volta walked up to the scene and barked at Ankor to get in line.

"Emi, how could you have done this?" asked Volta.

Emi cleared her throat. Sadee nodded at her. She had to come clean.

"Volta . . ."

As she started to speak, Ankor interrupted her. "It's not fair, Volta."

Emi's face looked puzzled. Sadee sent her a B2B message, "What's he talking about?"

Ankor continued. "We know, Emi. You submitted your plague simulation for the Agon. While you've been working on that useless simulation, we've made real progress on our robot. We've even sent design sketches to Fortna and the Kelorean team to get their feedback."

Emi breathed a sigh of relief.

"Ankor, calm down," said Volta.

Florin walked up to the group. "Volta, finish roll call. Emi, let's just you and I go for a star stroll."

Florin shooed Sadee back to the pod, put her arm around Emi, and headed toward the catwalks with her. The sun was shining on Snow Tower, and the fountains were in full effect with the star-lit sky as a backdrop. As they walked underneath the spray of the fountains, Florin wrapped her arm tighter around Emi.

"Emi, the first-year robotics team has done so well that Fortna encouraged them to sign up for the Agon. I assume you've been so busy studying for midterms on the moon that you haven't kept up with the robot project."

Emi replied, "I've been submitting my sections to Hans."

"Your team feels your contributions aren't that great," said Florin, "but you're still on their team."

Florin sat down on a bench facing the fountain.

"Emi, you can't sign up twice for the science contest. Since you're already on the robot team, your personal submission is keeping the rest of your tube from participating."

Florin spoke in a calm tone.

"We've only ever had a handful of first-years sign up, and they've never even come close to succeeding. This year there was certainly a buzz about you potentially submitting with the mask, and now your robot team's interested in joining with the robot they're creating. You guys can't do both."

Emi paused for a second and then responded, "I'm staying in the competition."

"But, Emi, you have no chance at winning with just a simulation."

"Florin, I'll find a way. Look, I started with the mask, and you told me to reframe the problem. I've done that, and now you're encouraging me to quit? That goes against everything we've been taught. I'll find a way to make it more than a theory."

"There is no way," said Florin, shaking her head. "Let's walk back."

"I'm not dropping out."

As they approached the dining hall, Volta was waiting for them outside. Florin shook her head no.

"No. What do you mean no?" asked Volta. "She can't possibly win with a simulation."

"Wait here, Emi," said Florin. The professors stepped a few feet away. Emi instructed Sadee to listen in on them, but when the drone activated her microphone, the black arrow on her orb froze and then blinked repeatedly, and they heard a loud buzz. Volta shot her a look and waved his index finger in a no sign. He had blocked Sadee. The professors walked back over, Volta scratching his beard.

"You have no chance," said Volta. "However, we can't keep you from signing up. Because you signed up first, you're blocking your tube. Here are your options. You can stay signed up and block your tube. You can revoke your submission and submit with your tube. Or the final option Florin and I have discussed is that you can remove yourself from the tube and the robot team. If you do this, you'll have to do another electronics project on your own to catch up, which will be very difficult with your current workload."

Volta paused. "Listen, Emi, make the right decision. Just revoke your submission and team up with your tube. You can do this project next year."

Florin nodded as Volta spoke. Emi shook her head no.

"I'm sticking with my submission," said Emi.

"I'll give you one more chance to rethink," said Volta.

"I'm committed to stopping the plague."

"So be it."

Volta pulled Emi's arm and marched her over to her tube. Ankor, Hans, and her other tubemates looked up at her.

"Listen up. As of today, Emi is no longer your comrade. She has made a very brumby decision to remove herself from your tube so that you can continue on as a team with your robot project and enter the Agon."

Her entire tube looked stunned.

Volta pulled Emi over to an empty table.

"Here you go," said Volta. "A lone table for a lone girl."

Volta gave her a look of exasperation and stormed off. Everyone in the dining hall stared at Emi. She didn't care. She wondered if her mother would be proud. Utterly alone, Emi couldn't wait to get back to the lab and start working. That was her place of solitude.

55 · ALiBi

Emi looked around the library and wondered if anyone suspected what was in her backpack. For weeks Emi's backpack had bulged with her treasured mask. Today it hid something different: the canister containing her newest prized possession, a live sample of the plague. She'd been on the edge of her seat all day waiting to look at the sample, but now she felt hesitant. It seemed so simple. She just needed to look at the plague under her electron microscope and determine its molecular makeup.

The library at IGIST was a strange place. In the main section there were several older luminaries studying, but it was deathly silent. It was weird to Emi that one could be surrounded by people and yet still feel so alone. She could hear the faint crackle. Her eye flared up, and the numbness gave way to a quick burst of pain. Emi's heart rate increased, and she looked at her trembling hand. All the students carried on studying, oblivious to what was going on in Emi's mind.

She checked out a private room in the microbiology wing and headed down the corridor. Once all white, the walls of the corridor were overflowing with equations illustrating the different phases of physical and chemical reactions. A sketch of a ball-and-stick model showed atoms and the bonds between them. Quotes were scattered between the equations and drawings. *TPFS* was written in almost every language, and there were several variations like: "IGIST is suffering TPFS," "IGIST is 1 percent inspiration and 99 percent TPFS," and "The wise luminary looks into space and knows TPFS."

Emi lost track of the wall graffiti as she walked down the corridor. Every step she took she could hear the sound of the plague grow a little louder. Sadee's presence did not help. Her metallic orb shape and glaring lights only highlighted that she wasn't a real person. Emi thought she wanted to be by herself, but now she found herself scared at the thought of being alone. The more obsessed she became, the louder the plague sounded, and the louder the sound, the more pain and trepidation she felt. What if she couldn't break down the plague? What if her whole approach was wrong? What if this was unsolvable?

She slammed the door to the room and took a deep breath. She pulled the canister out of her backpack. The plague had come alive inside the canister. She became captivated by its movement. The plague's cloudy substance was offset by tentacles that reached out of the cloud and thwacked the glass, then writhed back inward to the smoky substance. The plague never remained still. It constantly morphed and changed shape.

Emi sat down and pulled out her microscope. The electron microscope enabled her to view each individual atom in a molecule. She carefully placed the canister under the microscope. It was happening. She had the live sample. This first step should be the easiest part. In seconds she would be able to determine the makeup of the plague. After she had found that, she could start the second step, which would be modeling which parts of the molecule to change to diminish the plague's lethality. This second step could take a lot longer, and the Agon was less than three weeks away. She turned on the electron beam and tipped her lab glasses up. She looked at Sadee.

"Here we go."

Emi shut her left eye and leaned her right eye into the microscope's eyepiece. As the image came into focus, it looked like a whole new universe. Under the microscope breathtaking, vibrant colors displayed countless shapes and formations. They all moved in such harmony. For something so deadly the plague was dazzling. Emi zoomed in on a cluster of brilliant yellow spheres with tiny spikes poking out of them. They were consumed by larger, spiral-shaped cool blue structures. The blue spirals corkscrewed into each other, making a larger, ball-shaped object. Emi lost track of time, zooming in and out, studying the complexity and beauty of the plague. Finally, Sadee interrupted her. "Share an image."

Emi zoomed into the molecular level and pressed the capture button to take an image and then pulled away from the microscope.

"Sadee, the plague is something spectacular. I've never seen anything so amazing," said Emi.

"Floppy molecule," messaged back Sadee.

"Huh?" replied Emi.

She looked at the image she had shared with Sadee. The magnificence of the plague was not captured in the image. It was blurry, and the molecule was barely recognizable.

"Brumby," cursed Emi.

At the molecular level the plague was too active to get an image with her simple electron microscope. They would need to use a more powerful microscope that could cryogenically freeze the plague to capture its molecular makeup. Emi looked at the time. It was well past midnight. She couldn't wait until tomorrow. She knew exactly where to go.

Emi shoved the canister in her backpack.

"Sadee, follow me."

They raced through the corridor. There were still several luminaries studying, and they passed a tall older girl who furrowed her brow at Emi. The girl was wearing an Apollo backpack. Emi had gleaned that students from other Star League schools, such as Apollo, could take classes at IGIST and explore the Institute's facilities.

Outside the library Emi eyed the Bio Center.

She looked up at the gondolas. The campus was dead, and she didn't want to call attention to herself. Emi and Sadee headed across the catwalks toward the Bio Center.

Emi looked through the front door that faced the rainforest. She tried opening the door, but it was locked.

"Let's try the side door."

Emi and Sadee ran around to the side door that opened to an ocean region. Locked again. Emi looked across the way and saw the volaring ladders. She remembered seeing the grasslands from up above. It was the only section of the Bio Center that was not enclosed.

"Come on." She signaled to Sadee.

At the top of the ladder, Emi unclipped the volaring bag and hooked the five-foot safety cable to Sadee.

"Go," she messaged Sadee. The drone started to pull her, and she wobbled on the volaring bag. She looked to her left at Snow Tower and the fountains of IGIST then started to slip. *Pick a focal point,* she remembered Ripley saying. She turned forward and focused on the opening pointing down to the grasslands exhibit in the Bio Center. As they floated toward the Bio Center, she was certain no one was watching. She wondered if it would be recorded. What would she say if she got caught? The volaring bag wobbled again, and she thought of Ripley. *That's it,* she thought. *Sputnik.* She needed to think of a good alibi around a Sputnik prank.

Sadee pulled her down to the ground, and they landed in the center of the grassland. She surveyed the acre of the savanna. Golden waist-high grass covered the entire section. Ten acacia trees dotted the mini-Serengeti, fanning their branches and leaves over the grassland. Emi walked over to one and clipped her volaring bag to it.

Emi messaged Sadee, who then responded, "I'm not a lawn mower."

"Come on, Sadee. We need an alibi."

Emi took a few moments and plotted out the savanna and then sent Sadee the instructions.

"Fine. I'll do it."

Sadee dropped a compartment open, lowered one of her propeller blades, and started to cut the grass.

56 · COLD TRAP LAB

Emi ran to the back of the savanna where doors opened into the Bio Center laboratory. There were two adjacent rooms known as the Cold Trap Lab and the Capture Lab. One camera monitor covered both labs. Emi reached up and placed tape over the camera. The lab was an electronics-free zone. Guarded by an electromagnetic pulse shield to protect the equipment, the cold trap would zap any electronics in the lab.

The cold trap held a cryogenic molecular sieve that would freeze a sample of any item. Once a sample was frozen in the second room, the Capture Lab, a powerful electron microscope could take a molecular image of the sample.

Emi needed to get a frozen sample of the plague from the cold trap and then take the picture in the Capture Lab. Her heart was not racing at all anymore. A surge of pride grew in her heart as she removed the canister. She was so close. She felt calm and steady. She was alone but didn't feel lonely. Her inner scientist was blooming.

Chasing the light alone, she felt the beauty of the plague as she looked at the canister. Her thinking was clear, and she felt worthy of IGIST. She reveled in the solitude as she prepared the canister under the cold trap chamber.

Outside the cold trap, Emi triggered the freeze sequence. Liquid nitrogen shot into the chamber, freezing the top part of the plague. Inside the chamber, a small clamp cut a thin slice off the frozen block, creating an enclosed specimen slide.

A light on the door showed green, and Emi entered the Cold Trap Lab. She opened the chamber and grabbed the enclosed specimen slide. She left the chamber open and ran next door to the Capture Lab. As she placed the specimen slide under the superlative electron microscope, Sadee entered and hovered around the door.

"Sadee, you can't go in there," messaged Emi. "It's an EMP zone. You'll get fried. Come check out the specimen slide."

Emi peered through the microscope. A similarly mesmerizing scene appeared, although this time it was completely still. It also looked as if the universe had been crystallized and painted a whitish blue. She gazed at the sample specimen for a few minutes. Finally, Emi snapped the image from the microscope and sent it to Sadee. She signaled back that it had been able to capture the molecular analysis. Emi heard the crackling sound. At first, she thought it was the phantom sound in her head. Then she heard an awful sound. *Wuh-PSSSH,* crack! Through the glass she saw that she had left the chamber open. The plague had thawed and now was expanding—rapidly. An explosion of dark cloud emerged next to the cold trap chamber, and long fractal tentacles shot out, expanding the plague. Emi looked. She wouldn't make it to the door.

Sadee pressed the door button, sealing off the Cold Trap Lab. Emi pressed the freeze sequence, and the entire room was sprayed with liquid nitrogen. The plague froze in the air and fell to the ground, shattering into a million pieces.

"Open the door, Sadee."

Emi grabbed a pair of gloves and took the canister, which the cold trap had automatically resealed. She stuffed it in her bag and returned to the Capture Lab.

"Shut the door, Sadee, and initiate the clear-room sequence."

Large vents in the roof blew out highly pressured air, pushing all the contents of the room into the Tusk air filters that ensured all dangerous residues would be cleaned.

Once the sequence was over, Emi and Sadee walked back out to the savanna. Emi was mortified. How could she have been so careless to leave the chamber open? If it hadn't been for Sadee . . . well, she didn't want to think about that.

She unclipped the volaring bag and clipped it onto Sadee. The drone pulled her up through the opening, and she smiled as they cleared the gravity field. She'd done it. She had the molecular breakdown of the plague. Now all she had to do was run the simulation to see what additional elements could cause a chemical reaction and minimize the plague's lethal effects.

When she saw the savanna, she laughed. Across the grass Sadee had mowed *TPFS*.

57 · NIGHT TERROR

When Emi got back to her room, she was too worked up to go to sleep. Her excitement was hard to contain. She tried calling Jilli. Jilli sent back a message, "Talk tomorrow."

"OK, I've got some news," messaged Emi. "Big breakthrough. Figuring out plague makeup is done. Now on to step two to figure out what will cause a reaction."

To wind down, Emi scanned the news from Earth. There was an article about Terrans targeting misfits. The misfits' annual Esteem celebration would take place in Reykjavik, Iceland, a misfit-friendly city. In the past, several misfit-friendly cities had been attacked during the Esteem celebration.

The report included a picture of a former Legion member. He had been found dead five miles from the Hyperloop station. The man had no eyebrows, and his clothes contained traces of the plague. He was described as a smuggler. There was a concern that the Terrans were gearing up for an outbreak at this year's event.

"Stay away from Reykjavik," Emi messaged Jilli. No response. Emi would tell her tomorrow on their call. Emi finally became tired and climbed into her sleep pod.

In no time she was asleep, tossing and turning in her pod. In Emi's dream she stood in a corridor at IGIST. There were equations and quotes on the walls, leading to one door at the end of the hall. She tried to open the door. It was locked.

Through the door she heard Jack Lemore humming the Polar song. Emi pounded on the door.

"Jack. Jack!"

She tried to open it to no avail. Underneath the handle of the door was a keyhole. Emi peered through. Jack Lemore appeared in her tigress form.

"Jilli," yelled Emi.

The keyhole view opened onto a beautiful snow-filled countryside. Jilli walked along, unable to hear Emi. Up above Jilli, a crowd of misfits celebrated in the snow.

Emi heard the sound of the plague. She pounded on the door.

"Jilli, get out of there!"

The sound of the plague got louder and louder. Emi looked through the keyhole. The plague was coming at her. A tentacle reached out through the keyhole and touched her eye, causing a searing pain.

Emi woke up drenched in a cold sweat. She held her hand to her eye, which was numb. She needed to warn Jilli.

58 · BRUMBY

The next morning Emi remembered one thing from her restless night: she needed to warn Jilli. She immediately called her. After telling Jilli about her breakthrough finding the molecular makeup of the plague, Emi warned her about going to Iceland.

"I must go to Reykjavik," responded Jilli.

"But why? There is certain to be danger. You got lucky with the plague the first time."

"Emi, you've taught me that strength comes in many forms," said Jilli. "As misfits, we must show up in the face of these threats. If we disappear or hang low, that is exactly what these cowardly Terrans want."

"Jilli, there's got to—"

"Emi, I'm going," said Jilli, interrupting her. "I decided long ago to live life on my terms."

The hologram faded away. Emi sighed, frustrated. If she couldn't stop Jilli from going, maybe she could have a solution for her in time to take to the Esteem celebration. She couldn't wait to get through her class and spend some time analyzing her model results. After discovering the molecular makeup of the plague, Emi knew she was on the right track.

Before she could go to the library to review her simulations, she needed to turn in her electronics project. Emi walked over to the electronics lab, where her tube was working on their robot project. In the center of the room, a three-dimensional image of their design floated above a workstation. Volta stood with the tube.

"You see, by placing wheels on pneumatic hinged legs, we can enable the robot to jump," said Ankor. "The air compression helps with the landing."

Emi and Sadee sat off to the side of the group. Ankor continued to direct the team while Hans came over to Emi.

"How's your electronics project going, Emi?" asked Hans.

"I'm finished," responded Emi. "Volta said my mask could count as my project. I'm actually really impressed by the robot design. Who came up with the hinged wheel?"

"That was my idea," said Hans. "How have you been, Sadee?"

Sadee's orb turned into a savanna grassland, and the light golden grass appeared to blow in the wind.

"I had a feeling that was you two," said Hans. "Cool Sputnik!"

Sadee glowed green.

"You didn't have anything to do with the moon prank, did you?"

Sadee shared an image from Earth, showing the word *IGIST* scrolled across Lunar Park.

"Sadee, cut it out," said Emi. "No, Hans, the moon was some seniors. It did inspire us to do the Bio Center prank though. Shh! Here comes Volta."

Volta approached, and Emi turned in her report for the electronics project. He asked her a few questions and then turned his attention back to the robot designs.

"Hans, I'm going to head over to the library," said Emi. "I'm dying to check my simulation results."

***

Emi walked through the corridors of the library and saw a quote on the wall that reminded her of her mom: "Be alone, that is when the best ideas are born."

She sat down in a solo room and bit her fingernails. Sadee hovered above her shoulder, making the anxiety worse. It would take a few minutes for the simulation to boot up and show her the results.

Despite her nervous impatience to see the results, she trusted her instincts. The Agon was nineteen days away, but Jilli would go to Iceland next week. Emi needed to get the results back from her simulation so she could arm Jilli with the antidote.

The monitor showed the list of element combinations that could potentially stop the plague.

"Brumby." Emi sighed. "This can't be right."

Emi had built her simulation to find combinations that could stop the plague. There were infinite combinations, and the purpose of her model was to narrow that list down to a manageable number that she could then investigate further. She suspected she would have two or three element combinations.

"There are millions of combinations here," said Emi. "I can't parse out what is a false positive or a minor change. This doesn't help us at all."

Emi groaned. Sadee glowed blue. Emi put her head in her hands. "We're no further along. This simulation is worthless."

Emi rubbed her eyes. "OK, we'll rebuild the model. We have to figure this out so we can help Jilli."

She heard a tap at the door, and Hans entered.

"Hey, Emi, I thought I'd find you in here," said Hans. "How's your simulation going?"

Emi looked at Sadee and then at Hans.

"Good. We just built a first pass to see if it could narrow it down and had a really good insight that we need to tighten the parameters to get a smaller list."

Her voice sounded defeated. Despite Emi trying to put a positive spin on it, Hans could see she was frustrated.

"Let me do something, Emi," said Hans. "I'd be happy to help."

Emi knew she could really use Hans's help fine-tuning her model, not just for the Agon but more importantly for Jilli. She thought about Rockland and the kids who were left behind. Surely some had already lost their parents. Deep down Emi knew that she needed to prove to herself that she was a great scientist like her mother. In doing so, she'd set an example for Earthlings, showing them that they too could make a big impact even in the most wretched circumstances. She for one welcomed the challenge.

"Hans, I've got a pretty good handle on this," said Emi.

"I've built some models before that help filter out false positives," said Hans.

Emi paused.

"I appreciate the offer, Hans, but it's important to me that I do this on my own. Sadee and I are really close to cracking this."

Hans's avatar slumped a little.

"But, hey, after finals let's plan a Sputnik together," said Emi. "I've got a few ideas."

Hans nodded. "OK, Emi. Best of luck."

59 · LEO CONCA

"I know about the Bio Center," said Archimedes, his face serious. "I also noticed you weren't on IGIST during the Lunar Park prank."

Emi, sitting across from the chancellor, squirmed in her chair a bit.

"I've been receiving nonstop messages from the head of Apollo."

Emi had signed up for office hours to ask an important question. Not for this. "I had nothing to do with the moon," she replied.

"Both were fantastic Sputniks," said Archimedes, smiling. His face then turned serious again. "Is your eye OK, Emi?"

Emi's iris had turned black, and the area around her eye had turned a dark maroon. Emi reached up and rubbed it but couldn't feel a thing.

"Yes, I'm fine," she said, embarrassed. "I've just been staying up late studying."

Archimedes furrowed his brow skeptically. "OK, Emi, what can I help you with?"

"Why haven't other scientists tried to stop the plague?"

If she could find others who had tried to combat the plague, it might help her find the right combination of elements.

"Most of our studies at IGIST have been focused on advancing space exploration and advances that will help life flourish in space."

"But in your matriculation speech, you mentioned the plague and said you were sure an IGIST grad would solve it."

"That's right. I also encouraged you in our first one-on-one to focus on your studies as a first-year. I understand from Florin and Volta that might be something to refocus on. Why don't you really commit to getting through this first year, and then we can discuss additional projects?"

Emi couldn't wait. It was now days before Jilli would go to Iceland, and she was no further in her discovery process.

"I'm dedicated to creating a solution to the plague," said Emi, her voice confident. "I'll never give up. Never."

Archimedes stood up. "Let's go for a walk."

***

As Emi strolled along with him, Archimedes pointed across the star-draped sky to Earth.

"The reason I encourage luminaries to think of solving the plague is out of a sense of guilt."

"Guilt?"

"Yes, guilt," said Archimedes. "You see, IGIST is responsible for the plague."

Emi's mouth dropped open. She couldn't believe the plague had a connection back to IGIST.

"Have you ever heard of Leonardo Conca?" asked Archimedes.

She shook her head no.

"Leonardo Conca was a great scientist and one of the founders of IGIST, along with Berlin Snow. Conca was born into a wealthy family that owned much of Naples, which is on Italy's coastline."

Archimedes showed a hologram of Leonardo Conca in his hands and continued. "He was named after the famous Italian painter and inventor. His family owned some of Leonardo da Vinci's original manuscripts. Conca studied his namesake's work with reverence. He idolized the concept that human creativity and the power of ideas could master the impossible.

"Conca grew into a very talented chemist who believed from a young age that all our problems could be solved through science. By the time he was thirty, he had already become a renowned chemist for his contributions helping Snow construct the Flux distributor and the rest of our campus.

"As the Earth heated up, the ocean levels rose and overtook the shores of Naples, and Conca's family's wealth evaporated. Conca was sent into space. He studied on the moon but vowed to redeem his family's lost legacy by solving climate change. He became obsessed with the idea that he could reverse climate change by engineering something that could consume the carbon in the man-made pollutants. He actually did all his work here at IGIST."

"Chasing the light?" asked Emi.

"Yes. Conca was chasing the light and he succumbed to inventor's weakness. He did it, though. He engineered a solution that would gobble up the carbon dioxide pollutants in the air. It was a brilliant feat of biochemical engineering. Once his initial discovery was made, several scientists offered to help him figure out the right way to disseminate his carbon-eating solution.

"Conca was celebrated as the savior of Earth. He had yet to communicate how he would disseminate his solution, but he wrote a theoretical paper naming it Elpis. It was quickly nicknamed 'the Big Hope.' Conca became infatuated with his creation. He professed the beauty of it at the molecular level, saying he had produced the most perfect creation of all time.

"After his initial breakthrough, Conca struggled to find a way to disseminate his solution. It seemed impossible to distribute his solution in an airborne manner that could spread and address such a big problem. During one of his fits, when he couldn't think through the problem, he scrawled *TPFS* across the walls of the library corridor."

"Conca came up with TPFS?" said Emi.

"Yes," said Archimedes. "To realize his goals, he reasoned that he could give Elpis regenerative properties. Everyone warned him against doing this. If he gave the creation regenerative properties—"

"It couldn't be stopped," said Emi, interjecting.

"Exactly," said Archimedes. "There is a balance in science between reaching for the stars but not reaching too far. When you're fighting wicked forces, you cannot become wicked yourself. Conca reached too far. He removed the safeguards on his creation and turned it loose on Earth. Initially the Big

Hope was effective, and Conca's legend grew as the maker of a masterful scientific breakthrough."

"So, the plague was created here at IGIST and brought to Earth?" asked Emi.

"Kind of," said Archimedes. "The Big Hope was invented at IGIST and released on Earth. People say that it seemed as if overnight the smog that hung over the major cities disappeared. Then something horrific happened. The clouds that had eaten up the excess CO_2 needed fuel. As with any living thing, Conca's creation followed the inevitable law of change. It evolved. After gobbling up all the excess CO_2, the creation adapted to find other forms of sustenance.

"As with any life-form, when Elpis replicated itself, some errors were made. Some of these errors resulted in versions of Elpis that could metabolize the carbon in more than just CO_2. These organisms came together and expanded into larger clouds that could consume carbon-based life—like humans. The horror has lasted more than a century, and ironically, the smog returned. I still think we owe it to the people of Earth to help fix this demon that our forefathers unleashed."

"But no one has come close?" asked Emi.

"There has only been one person," said Archimedes. "She is quite brilliant, but she's not an IGIST grad."

"Who is she?" asked Emi.

"Celeste Tusk."

60 · TURN AROUND

"I can help" was the reply Emi received from Celeste Tusk. Emi had reached out to Celeste again, this time to inquire how the tech mogul had created the air ionizer.

"Emi, I'm glad you reached out," said Celeste. "I've been wondering how your project is coming?"

"The masks are complete," said Emi.

Celeste looked surprised as Emi held up the new mask. She had decreased the length of the beak by five millimeters to give it a sharper look.

"Wow. So you were able to miniaturize the filter?" asked Celeste.

"Yes," said Emi. "I proved Volta's theory that you can, in fact, shrink the footprint by increasing the concentration of ions."

"Emi, I'd like to get a copy of your work," said Celeste. "Have you shared it with anyone else?"

"Just Volta."

"Awesome work, Emi. Your father would be proud."

Emi smiled.

"So you're submitting this for the Agon?" asked Celeste.

"No. I'm going to go in a different direction. I've decided to try and solve the plague using a different mechanism, but I'm running into some challenges. Archimedes told me you were the first person in more than a hundred years to have made a big impact on the plague by creating the air ionizers," said Emi. "What inspired you to go after this?"

"I grew up on Ceres in the asteroid belt," said Celeste. "My whole family were asteroid miners. They toiled with tough, grueling work. Whenever I asked them why they did it, they told me it was so that those materials could go into things that help people pioneer space. From a young age I knew I wanted to develop applications for the materials being extracted from the asteroids."

While Celeste talked, Emi's left eye started to flash bright lights across her vision, and she felt dizzy. Emi covered her eye, but the flashes continued. The outer area of her eye was getting darker, and the darkness was spreading. She took a deep breath and tried to focus as Celeste continued.

"One material in particular was legendary among the asteroid miners," said Celeste. "Palcerium. The precious material had extraordinary properties but was being used in trivial ways. When I went to Apollo, I read a paper on Leonardo Conca and the struggles of the people on Earth to stay safe when there was a plague outbreak. I wrote a thesis outlining my air ionizer theory using palcerium. At Apollo I was able to build a prototype. I showed it to several dealers on Earth. When I saw their responses, I realized that the impact of my invention would be massive. One of my favorite professors always said, 'If you want to be hugely successful, solve a huge problem.' This problem on Earth was massive, and growing up on Ceres and attending Apollo put me in a unique position to see this opportunity. I was so passionate about it that I dropped out of Apollo and started Tusk Enterprise."

"So, your paper theorized that palcerium could . . ."

"Palcerium was the key because of how it ionized the air," explained Celeste, "creating an effective filter against the plague."

"Oh wow," said Emi. All this time, she had the key direction right under her nose.

Emi held her hand over her left eye as the flashes died down. She messaged Sadee, "We must examine the molecular makeup of palcerium." She needed to see if this would be the right way to affect the plague.

"Ms. Tusk, thanks so much," said Emi. "This has been very helpful. I've got to go."

"Emi, before you go, how are you looking to solve the plague for the Agon?" asked Celeste.

"At the molecular level," said Emi. "Through a liquid antidote."

Celeste sat up straight.

"Emi, please send me your blueprint for the mask, and I'd love to see your write-up on the molecular approach you are pursuing."

"OK. Thanks again, Ms. Tusk."

"Of course, Emi, and given your amazing progress I've decided to come to the Agon to support you. I believe in you."

Celeste smiled, and the hologram flickered out. Emi grabbed her stuff and raced to the library.

***

On her shuttle heading toward the asteroid field, Celeste looked at the space map and plotted a new route in the opposite direction. It would take her two and a half weeks to get back, but she could make it in time.

"Turn around," Celeste told the auto-command pilot. "Head to IGIST."

61 · EUREKA

Emi held on to her hope. After her conversation with Celeste, she had spent the last five hours analyzing the makeup of palcerium.

She had also gone blind in her left eye. The entire area surrounding her eye was a dark maroon shade, spreading in a fractal pattern. Her whole eye socket was drooping, and her eye had gone nearly all black. She didn't want to think about what was going on with it. She was too focused on what would happen with her new formula.

Emi processed the formula in the Cold Trap Lab. What seemed like an insurmountable obstacle a few days ago was now within their reach. Like finding a habitable planet in a galaxy with infinite possibilities, they had found the mechanism by which palcerium neutralized the plague. The critical question would be if they could find an effective way to distribute that reaction.

Under the microscope the plague looked majestic, like a sinister storm cloud. The plague's appearance was accented by a dark maroon color that resembled dried blood.

Sadee supervised as Emi prepared the molecular machine. This robust apparatus orchestrated a chemical transfer chain that safeguarded Emi while it split the plague into two cylinders so that she could test her antidote. She had entered in the formula, and the machine was preparing to create the liquid concoction. If the antidote worked, Emi would be able to test it on her eye and send the formula to Jilli.

The molecular machine dispensed a bright turquoise-blue liquid into a beaker. Emi took the beaker and held it over her second plague cylinder. The top of the cylinder had a one-way check valve, so she could dump the liquid in without the plague escaping.

Her hand trembled as she held the beaker, causing the liquid solution to shake. She swallowed with a gulp and dumped the bright blue liquid onto the valve.

As the liquid poured over the plague, a chemical reaction turned the sinister cloud into a white ash. Instantly the plague vanished, and all that remained was a white powdery substance at the bottom of the container.

Emi grabbed Sadee like a ball and swung her around, jumping with joy.

"We did it, Sadee!"

Sadee glowed green and then changed her orb to a black screen showing fireworks.

Emi poured some of the antidote into a dropper and held it over her eye. She was nervous to test her creation but felt she had no other option. She was already infected. This was her only hope. If it failed, the plague would destroy her. She slowly squeezed the dropper. She couldn't feel the liquid at first, but after a few seconds, she felt it sprinkling from her eyelashes as she blinked. She put a bit more of the antidote on a cloth and held it over her eye.

Her blindness faded, and her vision reappeared in her left eye. Her iris was still topaz-brown. She thought of it as her battle scar keeping the memory of her father alive. She touched the skin around her eye; it felt fine. She grabbed Sadee again and hugged her.

"We don't have any time to waste," said Emi. "We have to get the antidote formula to Jilli."

62 · ESTEEM

Emi didn't recognize the old lady on the other end of the live stream. Her hair was silver. She wore glasses and a gray shawl. Her face was covered in thick powdery makeup, and she spoke in a hushed voice.

"Emi, it's me, Jilli. I'm in Reykjavik, about to leave for Esteem. We have to travel in disguise to avoid bringing unwanted visitors to the celebration."

"I'm sending you the formula," said Emi.

"Thank you so much, Emi," replied Jilli. "I'll check back with you when I'm on my way."

***

In the city Jilli made two stops. First, she went to an old thrift store. She wasn't sure if they'd have it, but today was her lucky day. She bought an old water-based fire extinguisher. It was in backpack form with two large plastic containers. There were straps and a hose that connected to a nozzle.

Next, she went to an apothecary with a molecular machine. She entered in the code, and the brilliant turquoise liquid filled up the two containers.

Jilli joined some other disguised misfits and headed toward the meet-up location. They hiked ten miles outside of Reykjavik and stopped at the trailhead. Jilli took off her disguise and called Emi.

In the live stream Emi saw a group of twenty misfits. They stood on a barren, rocky landscape scattered with frost and pockets of snow. In the distance a mountain stood, looking like its top had been cut off. All the misfits looked incredible, but two stood out: an enormous grizzly bear and a white alligator misfit.

Jilli wore an amazing white fur coat, and on her back the clear containers showed the bright blue liquid. Emi could see Jilli's breath in the wintry air.

"Emi, I've got the antidote. We're headed to Thrihnukagigur. It's a dormant volcano," said Jilli, pointing to the mountain. "The celebration is inside the volcano. We have to enter through these lava tubes to keep the location a secret."

The misfits had dug a hole in the frosted ground. The grizzly, the alligator, and the rest of Jilli's companions started to climb in the hole.

"I'll call you from the other side," said Jilli.

***

Inside the tunnel the misfits created a single-file line. Every third misfit carried a torch, lighting the way inside the tunnel. There were several winding paths, and most of them were deceptions. The grizzly-bear misfit, Titus, led the way.

"Is this your first celebration?" asked Raegner, the alligator misfit.

"Yes," replied Jilli. "How long till we get there?"

"A few miles in the tunnels. We don't let a few threats or cold weather stop the party. It's worth it, trust me."

The theme of Esteem was "Don't Back Down." After they were attacked several years in a row, the misfits had a difficult time putting together an event that celebrated radical inclusion while simultaneously keeping out those who wished to do them harm. However, the dormant volcano of Thrihnukagigur proved to be an excellent venue. With a crater more than seven hundred feet deep, the cavern could house thousands of people throughout the main chamber and in the hundreds of offshoots.

The farther they went, the colder it felt inside the dormant lava tunnel. In the distance Jilli could see light from the opening of the tunnel. She could also hear the music. All the misfits in the tunnel started to chant, "Don't back down!"

As they entered the main chamber, Jilli was awestruck by the scene. In the remote crater of a volcano was a celebration like she had never seen before. It was like entering another universe. Inside the chamber a cacophony of music filled the air, while hundreds of different enormous art exhibits filled the space. A group of lighthouses glowed as misfits climbed the rope bridges connecting them. Several tall temples shot up hundreds of feet tall, glowing with different lights and flames.

The most magnificent part of the celebration was the eclectic collection of misfits, thousands of all shapes and sizes. Eagle misfits glided through the air while a kudzu-man resembling a lush tree hugged a gregarious gorilla. As soon as she entered the chamber, Jilli felt the urge to call Emi and let her know that she had made it.

Freezing-cold air shot out of the caverns. Jilli let the rest of the misfits file into the chamber and hung back in the entrance as she called Emi.

"It's incredible," said Jilli.

"Wow," replied Emi. "It looks amazing."

Jilli pointed her camera, showing the entire cavern, and then tilted it up to the crater opening. In the image two drones dropped in from above carrying large payloads.

"Terrans!" yelled a misfit. "We've been . . ."

Suddenly, Jilli heard the sound. That distinct sound. She froze. A loud crack. Her ears stood straight up. The drones had released the plague into the cavern. Its dark cloud expanded as tentacles shot out. Misfits screamed and fled into the tunnels.

Wuh-PSSSH, crack! *Wuh-PSSSH,* crack!

The first time Jilli had run. Now, she would face the plague.

"Jilli, get out of there!" shouted Emi over the live stream.

As everyone ran into the tunnels, Jilli jumped onto a temple and climbed to an overhang.

"I'm not running," yelled Jilli.

As the people scattered, Jilli marched steadily toward the plague. She pumped the fire extinguisher, but nothing happened.

"Come on. Come on."

The sound was getting louder as the dark cloud consumed the cavern. Nothing was coming out of the nozzle. Jilli felt the container. The liquid was frozen.

Jilli dropped the white fur coat and dug her nails into the frosted container.

***

At IGIST Emi watched the live stream in horror as the plague entangled Jilli. Emi felt a pierce to her own heart as Jilli dropped to her knees, engulfed by the plague. The image went black, and Sadee glowed blue.

"Jilli, I'm sorry," said Emi, sobbing. "I'm sorry."

63 · GENESIS

Ankor gazed at the bananafish in the ocean. There were also bluefin nothos, empire gudgeons, and neon rainbowfish. He was sitting in the Knight Room, which was a segment of the glass tunnel that ran through the ocean area of the Bio Center.

Now whistling in the tunnel hall, Balin had just finished explaining that an IGIST alumnus named Lawrence Knight had designed the aquarium to flaunt the aquatic creations he had engineered. Ankor had met Knight's great-granddaughter at their family's estate in Oculus, the capital of Mars. Knight's creations were the main attraction at Knightfare, which had grown from a family-owned market into the purveyor of the most luxurious foods and drinks in the solar system. Balin winked at Ankor.

In front of Ankor a hologram projection appeared, showing his elegant mother sitting in a bright courtyard. The giant crimson Arch of Fire stood behind her. "Hello, babies," she greeted them.

"Hello, Mom," said Achimi, seated beside Ankor, who had a radiant grin on his face.

"Here he is!" said their mother as their father took a seat beside her.

"Achimi, Ankor, you look great," said their father.

"OK," blurted Balin, causing Ankor to nearly jump out of his seat. Now standing next to him, Balin presented a red box in his hand.

"Is that for me?" asked Achimi as her eyes lit up at their parents.

"Domis Genesis," said their father.

Balin handed her the red box. Inside was a gold necklace with a pendant of the Tower of Oculus. Achimi's eyes widened. She pressed the gift against her heart.

"I love you, guys."

"We love you," replied her parents simultaneously.

Balin held a black box in front of Ankor. He squeezed his lips together and nodded at their parents before he clutched it.

The black box contained a silver bracelet with an ornament of what looked to be a lion's face. He swung his head toward the projection.

"Is this Polar?"

"Yes," their father said.

"I don't even like his music," snapped Ankor.

"Balin informed us of your distasteful behavior toward a misfit who visited your school, not to mention your peers," their mother said forbiddingly.

"You give Achimi the Tower of Oculus, and me Polar?" Ankor asked.

"Polar was a hero in the misfit community. It seems to me you need a reminder to treat everyone with respect," remarked their father.

"To hell with this!" Ankor rose and hurled his bracelet against the glass wall, causing a pack of empire gudgeons to disband swiftly.

***

It had been days since Emi had left her room. She signaled to Sadee to turn off her morning chime and buried her head in her pillow. Her room was dark, and she huddled under her covers, shivering with grief. She had been paralyzed by seeing Jilli overtaken by the plague. She had spent days trying to avoid the reality that Jilli was gone. She was angry that Jilli hadn't fled. Hundreds of misfits had fled into the lava tubes; surely some of them had made it to safety. When she looked deep inside herself, though, it wasn't anger Emi felt but guilt.

She could deal with the bullies, but the weight of the guilt was crushing her. She felt responsible for Jilli's death. The tragedy replayed over and over in her head.

Waking or sleeping, she saw Jilli, that smile when she pointed to the celebration. Jilli embodied not backing down; she was courageous. That stupid antidote had given Jilli false confidence. No one runs toward the plague. The sound sends people running away from it. Emi felt she had sentenced Jilli to death by giving her false hope. Jilli tried to combat the plague because she believed Emi had armed her with a life preserver, when really Emi had given her lead weights.

Sadee chimed again. They had a visitor. Hans's glowing avatar entered her room. It seemed like a hundred years had passed since she first met Hans. His hovering hologram gave her a familiar comfort she hadn't expected.

"I'm here for you, Emi," said Hans. "I remember Jack. She helped you get to IGIST, right?"

"I wouldn't be here if it wasn't for that misfit."

Emi told Hans how she had met Jack Lemore and how Jack had encouraged her to take the League test. As she described her memories, Sadee brought her a Venus Thirst and some comet cake.

Having absorbed Emi's pain, Hans sat in silence with her for some time and then said, "Emi, please come to Genesis."

Emi hadn't realized that today was Genesis. She had been looking forward to the event and now didn't want to go.

"I can't," said Emi.

Glowing tiger stripes, Sadee emerged from Emi's closet with her nifty extension arm holding the Yve mask that Jilli had given Emi at the matriculation ceremony. Emi smiled when she saw the mask.

"You've got to go, Emi," said Hans.

***

Emi made a stop on the way to the gathering. She dropped off a letter addressed to Mr. Lemore. She felt that she had to tell him what happened to Jilli at Esteem. She needed to take responsibility. The last line of the letter to Mr. Lemore was also the last thing she'd said to Jilli, "I'm sorry."

***

Emi walked up to the IGIST Mausoleum with Hans to celebrate Genesis. All the luminaries were dressed in white and wearing the white Yve masks. Hans changed his avatar from his normal bluish-green glowing image to be a white hue with the Yve mask. Sadee hovered above them. She glowed a spectacular white with the shape of Yve.

The Mausoleum was a pantheon-styled building. Neon lights lit up the crowd as everyone danced to the thumping music in the center of the room. All the luminaries' and professors' white outfits changed color from the light show. A Polar song came on, and the crowd went nuts, jumping up and down.

A tall figure walked up to Emi and Hans. He wore trim white formal attire, and the dark skin of his face contrasted with the Yve mask.

"Domis Genesis," wished Ankor.

"Domis Genesis," responded Emi, "Nice outfit!"

"V-hale?" asked Ankor. He lifted up the mask and chuckled. He held out a small device that had a mouthpiece connected to a tube.

"No thanks," said Emi.

"Come on, Emi. Genesis is a time to be happy." Ankor held the device up to his mouth, pressed, and inhaled. "You know, I admire your determination," said Ankor, grinning. "I really do."

Ankor was actually being nice to her. Emi couldn't believe it. He handed Emi his vapor device. She studied it. The clear tube contained a liquid. She pressed the top, and the device atomized the liquid solution, spraying a white vapor into the air.

"Hey, don't waste it," said Ankor.

He reached for it, then pulled back his hand.

"You know what, keep it. Save it for later, but definitely hide it now."

Ankor grinned as if he had just done Emi a favor, then pulled the mask back down over his face and faded into the crowd.

Emi felt a tap on her shoulder and quickly tucked the vapor device into her backpack. She turned around to find a woman wearing a beautiful white gown. She didn't recognize the woman, who was unusually short. The person removed the Yve mask, and Emi smiled upon seeing Florin.

"Emi, I'm sorry to hear about your friend. We should pay our respects upstairs."

Florin pointed toward the flight of steps in the back of the building and grabbed Emi's hand. They walked around the dancing crowd to the rear of the Mausoleum.

"What is this place?" asked Emi.

"This is where we honor members of the IGIST community who have died," said Florin.

She gestured to Emi to follow her. They walked up the steps and passed a statue of Sappho leading the way into the chamber.

Inside, the walls were split into sections with names and dates of people who had died, although there were no physical bodies housed in the Mausoleum. In the center was an empty tomb representing all the people from Earth and across the solar system who had died in the quest of space exploration. Florin pulled the mask off her head, as did Emi.

"Your friend was a space transporter, right?" asked Florin.

"Yes, and a misfit," responded Emi.

"It's important to say goodbye," said Florin. "I can give you a minute."

Florin started to walk out of the chamber.

"No, wait," said Emi. "Could you stay?"

Emi pointed to smaller sections of the wall.

"What are these?"

"Those are back-up right-of-passage monuments," said Florin. "In the early days of the Spacefaring era, people would upload their consciousness to the cloud. There were often problems, so they would 'back up' their consciousness as a safety precaution. This innovation was a key milestone because once they were connected to the cloud, people began to lose their capacity for emotion, their ability to feel—"

"Are you connected?" asked Emi, interjecting.

"I've had all the prework done," said Florin, "but I've never gone all the way. I guess, being an Earthling, I feel a connection to my human emotions and am in awe of human consciousness. I know my thoughts and feelings are just electric chemistry, but we still can't quite explain how sensations arise out of those connections. Emotions like grief, longing, guilt, passion, anger, and love are things that, as I've gotten older, I've been more deliberate in appreciating. People say you don't lose it completely when you connect but that it fades over time. I know that I want to live forever but I'm not quite ready to take the jump."

Sadee glowed blue.

"Sadee wants to feel emotions," said Emi. "That's all she used to ask about. I told her emotions are like colors, and anytime she suspects she should feel some way, she likes to show it."

"Have you backed her up?"

"I don't want to fork her," said Emi, referring to the process of backing up an older model of a sentient robot. "Her personality is so unique, I'd hate to rob her of her experiences. If her backup goes up to the cloud, her older aspects will get washed out."

"We can keep it local," said Florin. "A lot of older robots were backed up as part of an IGIST time capsule. What do you think, Sadee?"

Sadee glowed green.

"OK then," said Florin. "It's super easy. Just connect here, and you'll go into hibernation mode for a few minutes."

Sadee connected, and her orb turned gray.

"Emi, there's something I've been meaning to talk to you about," said Florin.

Emi looked at Florin and waited.

The professor carefully considered the words she intended to speak. She knew how vulnerable Emi was, but if she didn't confront her now, she might never learn. Emi needed to learn to work with others or she would lead a lonely life and never reach her potential. Florin opened her mouth to speak and then paused. Now was not the right time. "Let's discuss another time, Emi."

"Are you sure?"

"Yes," said Florin, patting Emi's back. Emi knelt next to the empty tomb. She put on her Yve mask, hummed the Polar song, and pictured Jilli's warm, graceful smile.

64 · RESOLVE

Emi walked up to the loading dock. She wore her hooded cloak, and her backpack contained her precious canister. She studied the log of incoming and outgoing shuttles. There was a shuttle leaving in one hour for the moon, and she would try to catch a ride. She needed to get the plague off IGIST. Sadee tried to convince her to use the antidote to neutralize it, but after Jilli's death Emi had lost confidence in her solution and just wanted it gone.

Emi would get the sample to the moon and figure out how to get rid of the canister so that it could never harm anyone in space. The phantom sound of the plague was getting louder and louder. She rechecked the shuttle log display. An incoming shuttle's information was scrolling across the screen. She turned around, interrupted by the sound of someone approaching. She figured it was the moon transporter at first, but the figure that appeared in the darkened passageway was a warden.

"Balin!"

Emi threw her arms around the warden. Balin gave her a bear hug and patted Sadee.

"Emi, what are you doing here at the loading dock?" asked the shaggy giant.

"I've got to go away for a while," said Emi. "I need to take care of something."

"Emi, you must stay at IGIST. You've done so much to get this far."

She didn't want to tell him or anyone else, but she couldn't help herself.

"I've done some terrible things, Balin . . ."

As she broke into tears, Balin gave her another hug. When Emi calmed down, she proceeded to tell Balin everything.

She told him how Jack Lemore had helped her get to IGIST. She told him how she had signed up for the Agon with the mask and the other students had ridiculed her. She told him how Florin had become her favorite mentor and helped her build a foundation for understanding how to push the boundaries of scientific advancement. She explained why she had wanted a live sample of the plague and how she and Jilli had retrieved one from Earth. She told him how she had determined the molecular makeup of the plague and discovered a way to neutralize it, using palcerium. And finally, she told him how her solution had failed when it had been needed most, costing her friend her life.

"I have to get the plague off IGIST before anyone else gets hurt," said Emi.

As she confessed, she felt relief from the pressure of her ambition to win the Agon. If she ran away and ditched the plague, the sound of the fear would go away—that awful sound she had heard the day her father died. It had been reawakened when she brought the plague to IGIST, but the real fear had started the day she met with Archimedes and decided to go after the cure. It was too much, and she wanted it gone.

"You've got the plague in that backpack?" asked Balin as he recoiled from her. His positive demeanor turned to a defensive stance. He regarded her with dismay, confusion, and even anger.

"Emi, how could you?"

"Can't you hear it?" asked Emi. To her, the sound was deafening.

"No," said the warden, still tense. "We must get this off IGIST."

"It's contained in the canister," said Emi. "I swear, I've tested the antidote—"

"On your eye?" asked Balin, interjecting.

"Yes," responded Emi.

The warden softened his stance and reached for Emi's face, studying her eye that had been cured.

Emi sheepishly continued. "It didn't work for Jilli at Esteem, and I'm unsure if I've gone too far."

"I don't understand. Didn't you solve it?" asked Balin. The warden paused, pondering for a second, and then he narrowed his eyes with conviction. "Emi, you must finish what you've started. Whatever it takes, you must finish."

"It's too dangerous," said Emi.

"Emi, if you leave tonight, your dream will die. Tomorrow is the Agon. If you've done what you say you have, you need to show the galaxy."

Sadee nodded along with Balin.

"But what happened at Esteem . . ."

"What happened there was a great tragedy," said Balin, "but you can't let that stop you from finishing. Have you learned nothing at IGIST?"

"I'm not ready."

"You never will be. Emi, you must believe that no matter what problems we face, an idea can prevail, but I need to tell you the yin to this yang. The key to the right idea prevailing is that wrong ideas also push science forward. Striving for a solution, trying ideas that fail, is equally important. These failures represent science and are a crucial part of creating the best future possible."

As Balin spoke, Emi realized the warden was talking about himself. The wardens were, by some accounts, a failed science experiment. The thought of genetically altering humans with animals to increase their likelihood to live in space must have seemed like a viable solution long ago. When the Star League created the wardens, there was a clear purpose, but it was impractical now, and like a long-lost Amazonian tribe, the wardens were forever sentenced to live in an altered state.

Unlike the misfits who pursued this out of a desire to transform, the wardens were transhuman figures that were a reminder of when science didn't work out perfectly. But to hear the shaggy yak-man talk, he didn't sound like someone representing failure. He represented something else. Something that was ingrained in every hair on his body. He represented progress.

"You'll never be ready, Emi, and that's why you must present at the Agon tomorrow."

Balin grabbed Emi's hands.

"Emi, I want you to picture yourself on stage at the Agon, telling your story. Millions of people across the galaxy hearing you talk about your parents being killed by the plague, your journey to IGIST, and how you created a solution. Now imagine getting the help of others to bring that reality to life to help the people on Earth. I want you to remember why you went after this in the first place."

Emi could not hold back a nervous giggle. She felt the hunger to succeed again. That hunger drowned out the sound of the plague. The Agon would start tomorrow morning, and Emi was signed up. If she was going to present tomorrow, she would need to get to work preparing.

"OK, Balin. I'll do it, but I need a favor."

Emi and Balin turned and walked away from the loading dock. On the shuttle log display, the incoming space shuttle's information appeared. It would arrive in a few hours for the Agon. The shuttle was registered under Celeste Tusk.

The group of twenty Agon contestants started the procession in a double-file line across the catwalks. Emi looked up at the three grand structures marking the entrance to IGIST. She remembered the first time she walked through the memorial spires at the matriculation ceremony. Emi and Ankor were the only first-years in the group and brought up the rear. Ankor represented the robot team. He smiled confidently.

"So, you've decided to go through with it, I see?"

"I had to," said Emi in a hushed voice.

"I'm going to win," promised Ankor, puffing out his chest.

"I'm sure you will," replied Emi.

Emi couldn't stand him, but there was a charming quality about Ankor that made her wish it could be different. At Genesis, he had been so nice.

She winked. "The robot assignment was great for first-years."

Her response shut Ankor up as the procession started. The luminaries were silent as they marched underneath the fountains of IGIST. When they reached Snow Tower, the lines divided and snaked around the structure. Emi looked up at the tower shining against dark space.

Emi took a deep breath to calm her nerves. She had been up all night with Balin, constructing the display enclosure for her big reveal. She had come close to fleeing, but here she was, a bygone about to walk onto the biggest stage in the universe to take the plague and everyone who had doubted her head-on. The stakes were high.

The plague was lethal, and she had brought it into space. She had done the work and would show that her science was sound. If something didn't work, she'd risk embarrassment and ridicule on an epic scale. She'd certainly be expelled, or worse. Everything would work. It had to, and when it did, Emi was sure it would be the redeeming moment she had waited for her whole life.

The procession stopped when they reached the Coliseum. Bright lights shone on the outside, illuminating the enormous columned amphitheater. Inside waited the entire IGIST luminary body and staff, as well as thousands of spectators who had flown in for the event. The archway of the grand entrance towered above them. Slowly, an enormous door rose. As the procession entered, the Coliseum lights flashed, and a deafening roar erupted with the spectators clapping and cheering. An energy like no other filled the air as the music mixed with the crowd chanting contestants' names. It was impossible not to feel the excitement. Emi's heart pumped with adrenaline.

Volta's voice projected a booming "Welcome, Agon contestants."

The two files of contestants walked in and sat in the front row before an enormous stage. Emi's eyes were fixated on the stage, hoping Balin had been able to sneak in their creation without raising any questions.

Next to the contestants sat a panel of judges. Archimedes sat in the middle, flanked by other esteemed IGIST professors and a few people Emi didn't recognize. Behind the judges were the rest of the IGIST professors.

Across the way Florin gave Emi a glance that said *there's only one way to learn*. Emi felt Florin's desire for her to succeed but saw in the squint of her eyes caution, worry, and uncertainty for her pupil, as if she were about to fly too close to the sun. It wasn't a forewarning of "I told you so," but rather a wishful hope. Her look seemed to say *for space and time, I hope you know what you're doing*. Emi couldn't help but wonder what Florin would be thinking if she knew what Emi really had planned.

Behind the contestants, judges, and professors, a large walkway separated the next level of seating from the podium. The podium was filled with the most important spectators: scientists, League officials, journalists, and prominent businesspeople. Behind the podium sat the IGIST luminaries, and the rest of the amphitheater was filled with people from across the solar system.

In the first row of the podium, Emi recognized a striking figure, Celeste Tusk. The mogul was flanked by an entourage of men who appeared to be bodyguards. Celeste raised her hand, waving to Emi.

Holograms of each contestant appeared while Volta, the grand emcee, described each contestant's Agon submission. Emi saw the Apollo student whom she had walked by that night in the library. Her name was Jemma. She would be presenting first. Following Volta, Archimedes gave a brief intro, highlighting the IGIST motto and the importance of the Agon for pushing scientific progress forward.

Jemma's presentation blew everyone away. She began with the legend of Sappho, her foremost inspiration. Over her three and a half years at Apollo, Jemma developed a new formula that transformed atmospheres in deep space, like those of Kapteyn b and Kapteyn c, into Goldilocks zones. The crowd's standing ovation after Jemma's presentation indicated that her creation was not just a game changer but a miraculous sensation. Emi felt her chances of winning dwindling with each triumphant hurrah.

The next five presenters flew by. After each presentation was a quick recap by Volta, followed by the huge screen panning the judges, who always seemed to be scribbling notes. Emi couldn't focus on the presenters at this point. All she could think about was the menace lurking under the stage. The hunger that had drowned out the phantom sound was starting to wane. She heard the dull sound of the plague crackling between her ears.

Before Emi knew it, Ankor was on stage. Above him, a dazzling image appeared of Fortna's hopeful planet. The audience sat captivated as he explained.

"We set out to create a rover mechbot that could overcome Linus77's crushing gravity and jagged terrain."

The Martian's showmanship radiated as he described the project from inception to finish, highlighting their mechbot's ability to jump a gap of twenty-five feet. Ankor gave credit to the team, and the crowd nodded along, impressed with Ankor's leadership. While Emi had toiled alone, Ankor had rallied a group of the smartest P-lumin talent around a common technical goal.

"And now," said Ankor, "I give you the Vaulting Spider."

The crowd oohed and aahed as Achimi drove the elegantly designed rover right up to Ankor. He pointed to the mechbot's air compressor and said, "The key was making it leap." The Vaulting Spider crouched down and effortlessly jumped up and over Ankor. The crowd broke into raucous applause, and Emi found herself clapping along, proud of her tube.

Volta calmed the crowd, and Ankor walked off the stage. Emi closed her eyes briefly and rubbed her hands together. She was surprised to hear Archimedes's voice.

"This P-lumin sparked off the idea that first-years could even have a chance in the Agon," said Archimedes, standing next to Volta. "Let me introduce Emi."

The crowd cheered as Emi walked onto the stage. Ankor gave her a nod of respect as he passed by. Emi was tingling with excitement as she stood behind the podium. She took a deep breath and spoke.

"Fellow luminaries, it gives me great pleasure to reveal my Agon challenge. But first, look up."

Emi pointed through the open roof of the Coliseum to Earth.

"Mother Earth. That blue marble is our origin. So what do we owe Earth and the people who live there? Bygones, some call them. Maybe we owe them nothing. Every single person in the Coliseum can trace some connection back to that blue marble we can see from here. Not only everyone here tonight but every single person you have ever loved owes their existence to that planet. I think we owe them something. I think we owe them a chance. A chance to join us in the stars."

Some of the IGIST luminaries snickered at Emi's Agon challenge. Emi's conviction came through in her voice as she continued over the rising murmurs from the crowd.

"Today the single biggest threat on Earth is the plague. Most of you are sheltered from the plague and its devastation. Let me tell you what happens when it attacks. It first appears as a tiny speck, almost unseeable. Then it explodes into a dark cloud and a horrific sound that snaps and crackles as it expands, looking for its victims. It's indiscriminate in whom it attacks, and it consumes any living thing it engulfs, eviscerating them in a painful and agonizing way. When the plague appears, its lethality is imminent. Once unleashed, it causes certain havoc. This chilling machination killed everyone I've ever loved."

Three pictures flickered to life above Emi, showing her mother, father, and Jilli, all smiling.

"Archimedes told me that he encouraged everyone in the scientific community to explore solutions to the plague out of a sense of guilt in that it was inadvertently created by IGIST founder Leo Conca.

"For all these years the only key contributor in doing anything to combat the plague has not been an IGIST grad, but Celeste Tusk. Her air ionizers make living on Earth barely tolerable by protecting peoples' homes, but it's not enough. Living caged and in fear is hardly living at all.

"Let me remind you, not a single IGIST professor or luminary has made any contribution to eradicating this menacing killer. I realized, to solve this threat, it had to be an Earthling. Only an Earthling would care enough to go after it.

"In searching for a cure for the plague, I leaned on my mother's memory and her insight that being alone is often the key to invention. During this quest I repeatedly found myself alone. As I searched for the solution in these moments of solitude on the brink of discovery, I found beauty in the evil force I was trying to vanquish. I learned through my own failures and trials that we need to solve for the whole problem."

She paused and lifted her arms, pointing to Earth and then back to the crowd.

"And now I present it to you."

Emi gave the signal, and a portal opened on the floor of the stage. A six-foot-tall cylinder rose from the ground onto the stage behind Emi.

"To solve this problem, we needed to work on the live plague," said Emi.

The crowd gasped. Behind her, the plague's cloudy substance writhed inside the cylinder. Blackish-maroon tentacles reached out of the cloud toward the glass, then writhed back inward to the smoky substance. On top of the cylinder, another glass component held the brilliant blue antidote liquid.

Emi paused and brought up images of her work on the screen. Two of them showed her approach. The first was a molecular map of the plague, and the second was an explanation of the plague's response to correctly applied palcerium.

"Before I release the antidote, I want to explain how it works," said Emi.

As Emi described her process, a loud explosion in the back of the Coliseum interrupted her. Emi looked to the back of the amphitheater and saw a pillar falling into the seats. People screamed as it crashed into the crowd.

Suddenly, Emi heard breaking glass followed immediately by the sound. That distinct sound. A piercing crack. *Wuh-PSSSH,* crack! This was not a phantom sound. *Wuh-PSSSH,* crack!

Emi only knew one thing to do. Run.

66 · FLEE

The people in the pit didn't have a chance. An explosion of the plague emerged from the cylinder and regenerated aggressively with its long fractal tentacles shooting in every direction. The dark cloud fell upon the pit and then spread throughout the entire Coliseum.

Among the blood-curdling screams, thousands spilled out of the Coliseum, fleeing for safety. Emi was one of the first people out of the Coliseum and had already made it to the edge of the catwalk. She had at least a hundred-yard head start on nearly everyone. If she sprinted down the catwalk, she could certainly make it to an escape pod at the loading dock. According to the crisis training drill, she needed to get to the first-year living quarters, which was shielded from the plague. She also wanted to get to her masks.

Sadee hovered above her, glowing yellow. Emi was at a fork in the road. She looked toward the first-year housing area then down the catwalk. The fountains of IGIST sprayed up and fell in the direction of Snow Tower. It seemed that the fountains were signaling to her. Were they telling her to get out while she still had a chance?

Everyone now knew that Emi had brought the plague to IGIST. Not everyone would die, but many already had and many more would before the chaos was contained. She was to blame, and they would have to hold her accountable. If she got off IGIST, she could make it to the moon, and from there she could figure out where to go next. She could disappear in space. No one would know her. She could start over. If she stayed, she'd be harshly punished or doomed to die. Her intentions had been to help humanity by curing the plague, but no one would care about what she'd meant to do. It made so much sense to her now why Jilli was always on the run. *Why fight when you can run?* she thought. *Jilli should have run at Esteem.*

In front of her was the path to the solar-sailing dock. It would be easy to run to a solar-sail craft and launch toward the moon. She saw two sail crafts deploy their solar cells and take off from IGIST.

Emi looked up and saw the blue marble. Her intentions had been to help. Just to help. She looked toward the first-year living quarters. If she was going to stay alive and save others, she would need to get the plague masks in her room. She had another container of the antidote there too. She'd also need to make it back to the Cold Trap Lab. She was sure her antidote would work. The science was sound. But could she get it to actually work? It hadn't worked for Jilli in Iceland, and something had just gone terribly wrong at the Agon. Emi looked back at the Coliseum and saw people running out of every exit. The plague's cloud was shooting out after them. If she stayed, she would probably die.

"Follow me," yelled Emi to Sadee.

She turned away from the catwalk and ran toward the first-year living quarters.

67 · SABOTAGE

In her room Emi saw the masks. In less than an hour, the plague would spread through all of IGIST. Her room display showed several areas of IGIST already on lockdown. This would be hopeless, but she had to try. She'd need to figure something out quickly, or more people would die. She slipped the antidote container in her backpack, where it clanged against something on the bottom of her bag. She shoved in the masks too. She needed to get to the molecular machine in the Cold Trap Lab so she could synthesize more of the antidote.

She headed out to the courtyard, where the other P-lumins were gathering. One of them had calculated the spread of the plague and showed a countdown of when it would wipe out the whole school.

"You did this," yelled Achimi. Most of her pod was assembled. They were all staring at Emi. "You've sentenced us to death!"

The group was angry and started crowding in on Emi. "Let's get her," murmured someone in the back.

Hans's avatar moved in between Emi and the crowd. "Leave her alone," he yelled. "She was just trying to help."

Achimi reached through Hans's hologram and swatted the drone projector to the ground. She grabbed Emi and pushed her into the crowd.

Seemingly from nowhere, the Vaulting Spider climbed over the wall and jumped down, landing in the center of the courtyard. The mechbot's spherical body had opened and expanded, its breadth stretching ten meters in beast mode, triple its diameter in ball mode. The cockpit door opened, and Ankor yelled down to the group, "She was sabotaged!"

Emi sighed in relief as the crowd backed away from her. Ankor climbed down from the Vaulting Spider.

"Let me show you what I saw," said Ankor.

He projected a video of Emi presenting on the stage. It was dark in the Coliseum, and only the main stage was lit up, showing Emi and the large cylinder behind her.

Watching the video, Emi heard the noise of the explosion in the back of the Coliseum, but before the video turned to the back of the Coliseum, a javelin-like object flew through the air and crashed into the cylinder.

"Someone deliberately broke the glass," said Ankor.

68 · STUCK

The shock of the sabotage took the P-lumins' focus off Emi. They were asking Ankor questions and requesting to play the video again. *It doesn't matter,* thought Emi. *It doesn't matter how the plague got out. I brought it up to IGIST.* She clutched her masks. Now she needed to get to the Cold Trap Lab.

Due to its the ancient-future design, IGIST had many open communal spaces, all enclosed under Sappho's membrane. They were running out of time before the plague would spread throughout the entire campus. Emi waded through the crowd of fellow P-lumins, heading toward the entrance.

"Where are you going?" asked Hans.

"I have to get to the lab where the molecular machine is located."

The tube was on lockdown. To get out, Emi would need to open the front entrance.

"You're crazy," said Achimi. "We need to stay here, locked down in the tube. We're not opening that door."

Emi needed her tubemates to let her open the lock. "I have to go!" she exclaimed. "I know how to make the antidote, and the only place I can do that is at the Cold Trap Lab."

"IGIST is in danger," said Achimi. "Protocol says to wait."

Hans displayed a hologram of IGIST, showing how Sappho's membrane could open.

"IGIST is not in danger. At any moment they can open up the membrane and shoot the plague into space. But there aren't enough escape pods, and if they open the membrane the section enclosures won't hold," said Hans.

"He's saying *we're* in danger," said Ankor.

"If Emi thinks she can help, we should let her go," said Hans.

"We're running out of time," said Emi. She pointed to the hologram. "I'm going."

"You can't go alone, Emi," said Hans.

"Hans, I have to."

She turned and tried to wade through the crowd that was blocking her in. She paused to read a message from Sadee.

"You can't go alone."

She messaged back, "I'm going to do this by myself."

Sadee glowed red. "You can't!"

Emi responded, "I'm going. You're all the help I need."

"No," messaged Sadee. "We won't make it without the help of others."

Emi sighed. If they went alone, they would be strapped to create the antidote and figure out a way to deliver it. If she had more time, she could figure it out, but the clock was ticking. If she was wrong, more people would die. She couldn't risk it. Sadee was right. If they brought help, they could divide and conquer. She turned back to the group.

"OK, I need some help," said Emi. "I can't do this alone."

She held up two fingers and said, "I've got two masks. One for me. One for someone else. We need to join forces to help save IGIST. Who's coming with me?"

Hans's glowing avatar stepped forward. He wouldn't need a mask. Ankor stepped away from the Vaulting Spider. Achimi grabbed him, and he whispered something in her ear. She moved aside.

"I'll go," said Ankor. "We need to open the door to get out."

The crowd of P-lumins nodded to Ankor and got out of the way. Emi gave Ankor a slow nod of appreciation and handed him the mask. The plague, it seemed, could make allies of Martians and bygones. A few hours ago, she would have never pictured the adversarial Martian coming to her aid.

"Let's go. We don't have any time to waste," said Ankor.

The trio ran to the tube entrance with Sadee hovering behind and tried to open the door.

"It's not working. They must have locked us down," said Ankor.

Emi pressed the intercom.

"This is Emi. Someone, please open the door to our tube. We need to get to the Cold Trap Lab."

Emi was surprised to hear Florin's voice come out of the speaker.

"Emi, we need you and the P-lumins to stay put. We're in more danger than you think."

"Florin, I can help! In the Cold Trap Lab, the program for the antidote is in the molecular machine. We need to get there now."

"Emi, we have reason to believe the wardens sabotaged the Agon."

Emi pressed the button again. "You're wrong! Balin was trying to help me!"

Florin responded, "You've done enough. Stay in the tube."

69 · VAULTING SPIDER

Emi stood at the door. She couldn't believe Florin wouldn't let her out. Her frustrations were mounting, but she remained cool. On top of getting to the Cold Trap Lab and figuring out a way to dispense the antidote, they would need to figure out a way to get out of the locked-down first-year tube.

"Follow me," said Ankor. He ran back to the Vaulting Spider. He waved to Emi and Hans. "We jumped in. We can jump out."

Emi was relieved. Working with a team already had its benefits.

"Let's put on our masks."

Sadee and Hans hovered next to the Vaulting Spider as Emi climbed onto the side. Ankor and Emi put on their masks. Through the cockpit Ankor gave a thumbs-up, and Emi gave him one back.

The Vaulting Spider crouched down and started to roll toward the wall, then sprang up to the top of it. The air compressors helped provide for a soft landing. From that vantage point they looked out over IGIST. Rolling clouds of the plague were spreading throughout the campus.

The Vaulting Spider jumped down from the wall and headed toward the catwalk that they would need to cross to get to the Cold Trap Lab. As they headed toward the catwalk, they ran into an obstacle. The entrance had been blocked. In between the volaring court and the catwalk was a fifty-foot gap, making it impossible to jump over. The height of the tower archway was too high for the Vaulting Spider with both Emi and Ankor. It couldn't make the jump with such a heavy payload. Ankor drove to the side of the volaring court. Emi climbed off the mechbot and ran over to check the gondolas. They were also locked down.

Ankor opened the cockpit and lifted up his mask. "What should we do?"

This was no time to withhold information. They were blocked from getting to the Cold Trap Lab, and if they were to have any chance of stopping the plague she needed to be open with the trio.

"We've got three items we need to address," said Emi. "We've got to find a way to get to the Cold Trap Lab at the Bio Center. Once there, we need to create the antidote and then figure out a way to spread it."

She wondered how they would respond.

"A way to spread it?" asked Ankor.

"The antidote is in liquid form," explained Emi. "In the controlled experiment we just released the antidote through a one-way valve, and it poured over the plague, neutralizing it. To be effective in a situation like this, we need to figure out a way to spray the liquid."

Emi waited for them to react, expecting them to be irritated that she didn't have everything figured out. For the moment, they were safe on the volaring court. In the distance the plague clouds loomed over the Coliseum and spread toward the dining hall.

"I've got an idea," said Hans.

He pointed to the air compressors on the Vaulting Spider's legs.

"Yes, the air compressor can spray the liquid," said Ankor. "We could go to the electronics lab and modify the Vaulting Spider to do that."

Ankor's tone was positive and reassuring. Instead of resenting her, Ankor and Hans were helping. They were working as a team. Sadee pulled a volaring bag down to Emi.

"Great idea!" said Emi. "Let's divide and conquer. Sadee and I will go to the Cold Trap Lab and make the antidote. Hans and Ankor, you guys go to the electronics lab and make the modifications. We will sync back up here."

Ankor gave Emi a thumbs-up and shut the cockpit. He and Hans drove off toward the electronics lab. Emi climbed to the top of the volaring ladder. It had worked to get into the biosphere before, so she hoped it would work now.

She clipped in, and Sadee pulled her through the air toward the Bio Center. Emi couldn't help turning her head to see the Vaulting Spider rolling toward the electronics lab.

She hoped Ankor and Hans could feel her determined outlook and that she was sending them encouraging vibes. Her bag started to wobble, and she turned back to focus on the direction of the Cold Trap Lab. Her heart was beating confidently as she flew through the air, thinking through the creative possibilities that could unfold. She imagined the Vaulting Spider spraying the antidote and cherished the feeling of hope. In the midst of a crisis, her determination was strengthened by being part of a team.

70 · PLAN Δ

Sadee glowed green as they floated in through the biosphere opening. Behind them floated six volaring bags. It had been more than two weeks since Sadee had cut TPFS into the savanna. The grass had grown back, but Emi could still see the *TPFS* imprint in the field.

She directed Sadee to fly as close to the door as possible. As they descended over the grassland, Emi braced for impact. Once they got about twenty feet off the ground, the centrifuge gravity kicked in, and Emi and the volaring bags fell to the field. The water in the bags bounced as they hit the ground. The mask was making it hard to maneuver. Emi pulled it off and shoved it in her backpack. It clanged against the antidote container in the bottom. She'd keep it close in case the plague came.

Under one of the acacia trees, she spotted the rose, which had totally flourished. It glowed bright red, and Emi felt a rush of conviction. Like her mother, she was determined as hell. She would remain resilient no matter what stood in her way. Her idea must prevail. She was ready to risk everything.

She looked up at the acacia tree closest to her and Sadee. Towering sixty feet above the waist-high grass, it looked like a mossy green cocktail umbrella in a golden sea drink. It was thirty yards from where they'd landed and forty yards from the entrance to the Cold Trap Lab. To move the six volaring bags would be a challenge.

Emi thought for a second about what was ahead of her. They would need all six bags to have any meaningful amount of antidote and maybe more. Emi decided brute force would be inefficient. Having thought it over, she dumped the water out of the six volaring bags.

She could carry the empty bags to the lab, create the antidote, fill the bags, and bring them to the tree two at a time. She'd then have to climb up the tree to bring each bag up above the gravity threshold. She needed to get moving.

Emi strapped three of the empty volaring bags to her chest and three to her back over her backpack and headed toward the Cold Trap Lab where the molecular machine was located. As they approached the lab, Sadee held back, careful not to go into the EMP zone.

Emi opened the door and was surprised to see Florin in the lab. She was at the molecular machine.

"Emi, what are you doing here?" asked Florin.

"Florin, we've got a plan."

"Emi, wait. This is very important. Is there any other form of matter you've created the antidote in?"

"What are you talking about?"

"Did you just make the antidote in liquid form?"

"Yes. Well, no. Actually, Jilli's antidote froze in Iceland."

Florin looked frustrated, and her face was as pale as moon rock. The professor pointed to a display screen in the next room, showing the IGIST campus with clouds of the plague engulfing several buildings.

"Emi, there isn't time to explain. This is a very dangerous situation. I must get to Snow Tower, and you must get back to your tube."

Florin's container was almost full of the brilliant blue antidote.

"Our plan is to load the antidote into the Vaulting Spider," said Emi. "We'll be able to spray it through the air compressors on the mechbot's legs."

Florin gave Emi a wretched look. Florin's container was full, and she placed the cap on it.

"Emi, we must get to Snow Tower," said Florin. "I'm going to give you two choices. You can either come with me and help, or you need to go back to the P-lumin tube. If you don't do that, I'll have to expel you when this is all over."

"Florin, we have a plan," said Emi, her heart filling with agony. "I can't leave Ankor and Hans at the rally point without the antidote. They may die. I have to get it to them."

“Emi, there is no time. This is bigger than just IGIST now. You’ve put us all in grave danger. I’m going to give you one last chance.”

Emi couldn’t understand why Florin was being so rigid. She didn’t care what happened to her now. She couldn’t abandon her friends.

“I’m staying,” said Emi.

Florin shook her head, charged over to the door, and ran out of the lab with two containers of antidote. On the opposite wall Sadee floated behind the glass. Emi sighed, opened the first volaring bag, and started the molecular machine.

71 · UNMASKED

In the electronics lab Hans and Ankor worked on modifying the Vaulting Spider. On the way over, Hans had quickly engineered a plan for how they could mold on tanks behind the legs that would fit perfectly over the air compressors.

"Ankor, while you're implementing the modifications, let me see the Agon video," said Hans.

Ankor transferred the video to Hans, and he pulled it up. Hans paused the video. In the frame a javelin-like object could be seen flying through the air. It was too blurry to make out. Hans zoomed in and sharpened the frame. The image went from a blurry pole-like object to a crystal-clear image of a scepter.

"Mother of Sappho."

Ankor gasped. "An Agon scepter."

The Agon scepter was the prize for winning the competition. On the top of the scepter, a glowing bulb represented which Star League school the contestant was from. The very tip of the scepter was a crystal made of wurtzite boron nitride, a material even stronger than diamond that would certainly break any glass.

It was customary for the previous Agon winners to attend the event. Bringing the prize scepter was part of the prestige of returning to the Agon. The vast majority of the scepters would be IGIST green. Marston's bulb was red, Sp43's black, Ganymede Tech's orange. This scepter in the screen was white, the color for Apollo.

"Hans, we have to finish the modifications and get back to the rally point." Ankor turned away from the image and focused on getting the final tank onto the mechbot. He poured some water into one of the tanks and tested the spray. It worked perfectly. Ankor was proud of their hasty modification. Once the tanks were filled up with the antidote, they could spray them out any of the Vaulting Spider's legs.

While Ankor finished working on the Vaulting Spider, Hans had been reviewing the open footage of people entering the Coliseum, specifically the parade of former Agon winners. As he suspected, there were lots of green IGIST bulbs, several red Marston bulbs, a few Ganymede Tech orange bulbs, and some Sp43 black bulbs. Hans projected the image.

"Ankor, check this out."

Entering the Agon, looking magnificent like a movie star, a single person held the only Apollo Agon scepter proudly, the white bulb glowing spectacularly.

"Brumby!" exclaimed Ankor and Hans simultaneously.

The person holding the Apollo scepter was Celeste Tusk.

72 · I CAN HELP

Back in the Cold Trap Lab, Emi anxiously waited for the antidote to materialize. After Florin walked out, Emi wasted no time getting the molecular machine ready.

She gulped and rubbed her jittery hands together. Something wasn't right. No liquid was coming out of the machine. The molecular machine must not be working. Emi checked her program again. It was correct. She walked around the machine, her mind engulfed by the enormity of the situation. Her favorite professor had stormed out on her, her friends' lives were hanging in the balance if she didn't get back in time, and the machine wasn't working.

She tapped her quivering hand on the glass.

"It's not working," Emi said in a shaky voice.

Through the glass she saw the cameras in the corner of the Capture Lab. They were still covered.

"The door," messaged Sadee, tilting forward against the glass.

Emi turned to look over her shoulder. Across the room the door Florin had exited through was still open. In the Cold Trap Lab, there were only two openings. One was through the Capture Lab and was separated by glass, and there was another across the room. For the machines in the Cold Trap Lab to work, the room must be a secure chamber with all its openings shut.

She breathed a sigh of relief. This should be an easy fix. As she turned, Emi spotted someone out of the corner of her eye entering the Capture Lab.

"Celeste Tusk!" said Emi.

"I can help," said Celeste.

This was the first time she had met the mogul in person. Here Celeste was, standing tall and thin in front of Emi, projecting an aura of power. The mogul was flanked by two men in black suits. Celeste nodded at them, and the men stepped to the back of the room.

"I can help you," said Celeste. "The other guests who made it out have fled, but I heard this is where you made the antidote."

"Ms. Tusk, we must create the antidote and get it to my friends. They have a way to spray it out of the Vaulting Spider."

"What can I do to help?" asked Celeste.

Emi pointed to the door in the back of the room.

"These rooms are sealed. Nothing can get in or out. In order for the molecular machine to work, I need to close off the chamber so we can create the antidote."

Celeste nodded to Emi and gave her two guards a look. They left the room.

"OK, Emi, I'll wait. Once you're done, my men and I will get you to your friends."

Emi smiled. It felt good to have Celeste in her corner. Behind her Emi heard that distinct sound. As she turned around, she saw the dark cloud seeping through the door that Florin had left open. Emi had forgotten to shut it. She wouldn't be able to make it across the room. The dark cloud expanded as tentacles shot out, entering the Cold Trap Lab.

Emi turned to open the door to the Capture Lab. Celeste Tusk was blocking it.

"Open the door," yelled Emi.

Sadee tried to get around her, but Celeste held her arm over the lock and shook her head no.

"What are you doing? Open the door!" yelled Emi.

"Emi, you could have joined me," said Celeste. "My Tusk empire is one of the most powerful in the galaxy. Do you think I would let some P-lumin jeopardize that? I had hoped your attempts would fail, but here we are."

Flabbergasted, Emi tried again to open the door. Celeste was revealing herself as a mercenary, but Emi couldn't imagine that she would let her die. Emi pounded on the glass. If she didn't get out, the plague would be upon her in no time. The dark cloud was filling the room.

"I'm determined too," said Celeste. "How do you think I've built my empire?"

Sadee tried again to maneuver around Celeste, but the mogul held her hand firmly over the lock. Emi was horrified by the impending danger. She pounded on the glass. The sound of the plague was getting louder and louder. It was clear to Emi she wouldn't open the door. Celeste would let her die to protect her interests.

"You'll go down as the girl who brought the plague to space. The girl who doomed the universe," said Celeste. "And now that there is that risk, I'll sell even more air filters."

73 · BREAKTHROUGH

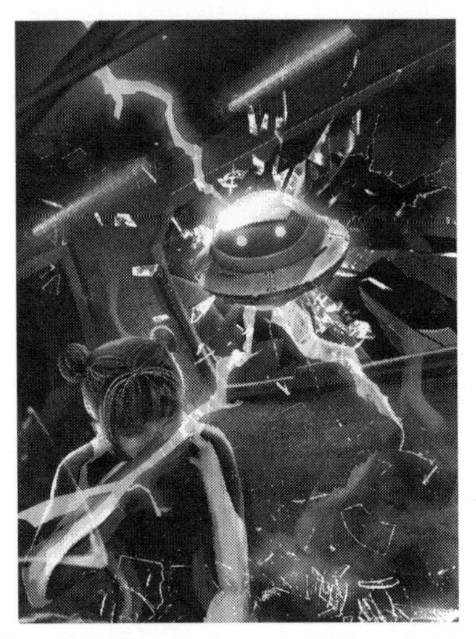

Emi took her hands off the glass and covered her mouth. The room would be filled with the plague in no time. If she tried to run and shut the door, it would be suicide. The plague cracked as it closed in on her.

Sadee tried to get around Celeste's arm and open the lock, but her grip was like iron. Sadee messaged Emi, "Duck."

She backed up to the other end of the room.

"No, Sadee!" messaged back Emi. She knew what she was going to do.

Sadee flew straight into the glass with as much force as she could muster. A loud smack resounded as she hit the glass walling off the Cold Trap Lab. A splintery crack spread out from the spot of impact on the glass. Sadee backed up and rammed the glass again, making a larger shattering footprint. If she went through the glass into the EMP zone, she would be zapped.

"Stop!" yelled Celeste. "You'll kill us all."

She tried to swat the drone down, but Sadee pulled back. The flying droid took an angle where Celeste could not stop her. Sadee sent one last message to Emi, "I feel love for you."

The drone glowed a brilliant white as she flew through the air. Sadee crashed through the glass, shattering the entire window separating the Capture Lab and the Cold Trap Lab. As soon as Sadee went through the glass, an EMP bolt zapped her. Sadee fell to the ground. All the color in her orb screen disappeared, leaving her a dull gray.

The plague was just a few feet away from Emi. Celeste Tusk let go of the lock and ran out of the Capture Lab.

Dazed by the situation, Emi steadied herself and reached her arm through the glass to open the door. She grabbed Sadee's lifeless sphere and quickly went into the Capture Lab. The plague had filled the whole Cold Trap Lab. A dark cloud seeped through the window, and tentacles shot out into the other room.

Emi pressed the clear-room sequence, and the vents on the top of the Cold Trap Lab kicked in, humming. The pressure from the vents sucked the plague up into the roof. With the vents' suction, the plague was stuck on the other side of the Cold Trap Lab. Any particles close to the vents were sucked up. For now, Emi was safe.

Emi felt numb all over. She slowly walked out of the Cold Trap Lab toward the savanna section of the Bio Center. She looked at the golden grass. TPFS. She started to cry. She felt empty inside except for the hurt. It was unbearable. Every step she took through the grass was worse than the last. TPFS. The whole thing was awful. She held Sadee's lifeless orb.

She tried to message Sadee. Nothing. The drone's last message to her was "I feel love for you." She didn't know if Sadee had ever really experienced feelings. All she ever talked about was wanting to feel. To be like a human. Emi couldn't remember life before Sadee. The drone was part of her.

She did know this: if there was a test for humanity, Sadee would have passed. Sadee knew what would happen if she flew into the EMP zone. Emi plopped down in the grass on the *T* of TPFS. She had been the cause of death for everyone she had ever loved. She held her head in her hands and cried.

74 · REVIVAL

Emi looked up at the towering acacia tree. Without Sadee she couldn't get up and out of the biosphere. Sadee was dead. Celeste Tusk had tried to kill her. It would be impossible to use the molecular machine with the breach in the Cold Trap Lab. She'd have to exit the Bio Center another way. Emi ran through the biosphere, leaving the savanna and entering the rain forest. She rushed through the ocean area and charged out of the biosphere, nearly reaching the Mausoleum.

She looked across the IGIST campus. The plague clouds were hovering over the Coliseum, but there was no sign of the plague at the volaring court. Her plan was of no use now. Even if she made it to the rally point to meet Ankor and Hans, she didn't have the antidote. All she had was Sadee's lifeless orb. Emi sent a message to Ankor, "Plan trashed, no antidote, molecular machine broke. Head to safety. I'll figure out another way."

No antidote, she thought. What was she going to do? Reframe the problem. That's what Florin would tell her to do. She didn't have the antidote. There was only one molecular machine on campus that she knew about. Maybe there was another one? Emi took a deep breath. *Step back from the obvious,* she told herself. How could she alter her point of view?

She looked up at Snow Tower. From that vantage point she could see the whole campus. The large gates to the catwalks were closed, blocking off any way to get there.

Across from the Mausoleum was a staging compartment where the 'plicants had suited up at the probo, and someone was entering the area. She sighed. Florin had been so demanding about critical thinking. "Chance favors the trained mind," muttered Emi, repeating one of Florin's sayings to herself.

It was Florin. Florin had set foot in the staging compartment, and she had the antidote! Emi ran toward the compartment. It wasn't the six volaring bags' worth that Emi hoped for, but Florin had the antidote. It might be enough to allow them to keep the plague at bay and come up with an evacuation plan.

"Florin!" Emi yelled as she opened the door.

Florin emerged, holding a spacesuit. "Emi, there's no time. We must get to Snow Tower," she said.

Emi wiped her tears and tried to explain.

"Florin, it was Celeste Tusk. She sabotaged the Agon to protect her business empire. She tried to kill me," said Emi. She trembled. "But Sadee saved me."

Emi held out Sadee. Florin looked Sadee over.

"Florin, we must get your antidote back to the rally point to meet Ankor and Hans."

"What's wrong with Sadee?" asked Florin.

"She got zapped by the EMP bolt in the Cold Trap Lab," said Emi. "Celeste Tusk tried to . . ."

Florin looked at Snow Tower and the gate blocking them from the catwalk. The professor then looked at the Mausoleum and turned to Emi.

"Emi, I need you to listen. How did you get into the biosphere?" asked Florin.

"Sadee," said Emi. "I hooked a volaring bag onto Sadee, and she glided me in through the savanna. Then we ran into Celeste—"

Florin cut her off. "I don't have time to explain. Here's what I need you to do. Hold on to this antidote. We're not going to your rally point. We must get to Snow Tower. Give me Sadee. You stay here and find a spacesuit and two volaring bags."

Florin pointed to the entrance to the catwalk. "We need to get over that wall to Snow Tower. I'll be back in a few minutes."

Florin reached out and grabbed Sadee. She took off running toward the Mausoleum. Emi was confused. She didn't understand what was happening, but she trusted Florin. She set the antidote down at the front of the storage compartment and rummaged through the suits.

Emi found a suit that fit her and held it up. Suddenly, she felt a familiar feeling of being in the presence of an old friend. She couldn't help but smile as a comfortable warmth filled her entire body.

She turned around. At the front of the compartment, Sadee was glowing green. Emi's face filled with joy. She grabbed the suit and ran to embrace her friend. Florin had revived Sadee from the backup in the Mausoleum.

Florin grabbed her arm. "There's no time to waste."

75 · OVERCOME

"You go first," said Florin. They climbed to the top of the Mausoleum. Emi strapped her backpack tightly, leaned onto the volaring bag, and clipped in Sadee. Sadee messaged her, "Let's go!"

Emi smiled and zoned in on the center fountain on the catwalk, remembering the first time she'd volared. She felt a moment of calm and happiness to be reunited with Sadee. Her serenity faded as she looked away from the fountain and gazed at the whole campus, where the plague was spreading.

As Emi started to wobble, Sadee glided over the tall gate and brought Emi down on the catwalk. Emi unclipped herself. She told Sadee, "Go get 'em!" before her drone floated back to get Florin. Emi sat down next to the fountains and felt the spray of water on her back. As she waited for Florin, Emi messaged Hans and Ankor, "Abort plan and get to safety. I've linked up with Florin. I'm in the center of the catwalk. We're going to Snow Tower with antidote, she has a—"

Emi stopped midtransmission. In the air she saw Sadee clearing the tall gate with Florin trailing behind on a volaring bag. An eerie sensation crept over her. The splashing of the fountain made it hard to hear clearly, but she felt it. She felt the plague. Emi turned around toward Snow Tower.

Seeping around the bottom of Snow Tower, the plague engulfed the base of the monument. At the same time the fountains sprayed an arched wall of water and light into the air.

"Turn back," Emi messaged Sadee.

Emi reached around and pulled off her backpack, then quickly slipped on her mask. She held the beak above her head so that she could yell.

"Turn back!"

Sadee and Florin descended toward the catwalk. From their vantage point, with the fountains' columns of water spraying into the air, they could not see the plague. About fifteen feet above Emi, Florin reentered the force of the centrifugal gravity and dropped to the ground on the catwalk.

As soon as Florin landed, Emi grabbed her and lifted her to her feet.

"Run!" yelled Emi, transfixed at the sight of the approaching plague.

Florin resisted for a moment and then turned to look down the catwalk. In just seconds the plague had spread onto the catwalk, immersing the fountain and creating a wall of darkness that was heading their way.

Florin and Emi ran down the catwalk in the direction they had just come. By the time they reached the gate, the plague was halfway down the catwalk. They looked up at the gate. There was no way over, and the sleek structure made it impossible to climb, so they couldn't try to get Sadee to lift them out. They were trapped.

Florin gave Emi one of the antidote containers and grabbed her.

"I need you to put the mask on and get to Snow Tower," said Florin. "Get to the top."

Florin insisted that Emi go and explained something about the phase of matter of the antidote, but Emi couldn't focus. The plague was closing in, and she was being asked to leave her mentor to die. Emi shook her head and started crying.

"I can't go, Florin," said Emi. "Take the mask. You must go."

The plague continued to close in on them.

76 · THE CLIMB

Emi and Florin crouched, trapped, against the gate of the catwalk. Sadee hovered above them, glowing red. To the right and left of the catwalk was the openness of space. If they broke the membrane, they would float off. The plague seeped down the walkway. The bursts of water from the fountain kept pushing the plague to the sides of the catwalk, but it would reach Emi and Florin in no time, and with only one mask, only one of them would survive.

From behind the gate they heard a clank. For a second Emi thought they were surrounded by the plague. This was something different, though. The Vaulting Spider appeared at the top of the gate.

"Hold on!" projected Ankor from the Vaulting Spider. "I'm coming."

The mechbot jumped down in between Emi, Florin, and the plague. Sadee glowed green as Ankor opened the cockpit.

"Climb on," yelled Ankor. He gave his confident smile and winked. "Sadee messaged."

With no time to spare, Emi and Florin climbed up the sides of the rover.

"Ankor, you must get us to Snow Tower," said Florin.

The rover spun around, facing the long catwalk. Now the plague was a few feet away and closing in fast. It seemed like an impossible task.

Ankor's face turned from his boyish grin to one of sheer stoicism. "I'll get you there," he said. "Hold on tight."

The cockpit to the Vaulting Spider shut, and the mechbot crouched down. Emi pulled the mask over her face. The Vaulting Spider leaped into the fountain, causing a splash, and then picked up speed. The sound of the plague was all around them as they drove through the fountain. From the dark cloud, tentacles shot out at them, but the Vaulting Spider zigged and zagged and leaped, managing to avoid each one.

Water sprayed on Emi's hands, and she could feel the impending danger as they pushed through the fountain toward the base of Snow Tower. The rover jumped over the fountain's spray and continued to leapfrog.

The Vaulting Spider was nearing the end of the fountain. The entire bottom of Snow Tower was engulfed by the plague. Florin pointed to a balcony still out of the plague's reach. Ankor tapped the glass from the cockpit and yelled, "Hold on!"

The Vaulting Spider barreled down the final stretch of the fountain. Emi swallowed a gulp and tightened her grip as they headed right toward the plague cloud. In the final stretch the rover crouched down and leaped over the large plume of plague onto the balcony.

Ankor opened the cockpit. Emi pulled her mask off, leaned inside, and gave Ankor a hug. From the balcony they could see the plague below.

"We've got no time to lose," said Florin. "We must get the antidote to the air distributor on the top of Snow Tower before the plague. Ankor, take the Vaulting Spider and get to the parade deck and help with plan B of evacuating. There's only enough room for one-third of the people currently at IGIST to get off the station in the escape pods, so you'd better hurry."

Ankor nodded and gave Emi and Florin a salute. He shut the cockpit, and the Vaulting Spider jumped down to a clear catwalk and made its way toward the parade deck. Florin paced around the balcony, studying the entrances, and came back, speaking quickly.

"In order to ensure our best odds of success, we must divide and conquer. Some of the pathways to the top might be blocked off. I'll take the main route. I want you to go up outside on the escape ladder. Remember what I told you about the matter. We must go now."

Florin took her container of antidote and raced up the main pathway in Snow Tower. Below, Emi could see the plague crawling up the walls of the tower.

Shell-shocked by everything that was going on, Emi approached the bottom of the escape route. She tucked her mask in her backpack, hearing that distinct clang again, and ensured the antidote was secure. She put on the spacesuit and opened the membrane door. Sadee flew up the hatch and floated up the tube mesh that was exposed on the outside of Snow Tower. Emi put one hand out on the rung and methodically made her way up the tower.

Sadee hovered above Emi. She had stopped and was glowing yellow.

"What's going on, Sadee?"

Emi approached where Sadee was holding still. There was one more section to the final ascent, and it was clearly marked as an EMP zone, meaning no electronics, no MET, and no Sadee. Emi reached up, took off her MET, and attached it to Sadee. Her orb morphed into images of several horseshoes. Emi gave her a hug.

She closed the last section behind her and started her final ascent. As she climbed alone, Emi tried to make sense of it all. What had Florin meant about matter? She assumed getting the antidote to the air distributor would be a way to disseminate it through all of IGIST and stop the plague.

She looked up. In the distance of space, she could see the blue marble of Earth. To her left was the moon. She looked back at the blue marble, and a sinking feeling weighed down in her stomach, turning her nervousness from fear to dread. She gasped as she realized the enormity of the situation. The flux air distributor!

She looked out on Earth and the moon again and gulped, thinking of the possibility that every human in the galaxy could die. Not millions, but billions. Every space station, spaceship, settlement, and Earth. The air distributor sent the frequency to all of them. If the plague hit the air distributor, it would broadcast the formula for the lethal particle combination throughout the galaxy. She envisioned people seeing the tiny speck appear, not knowing what was about to come. When the sound hit, it would be too late.

If the plague hit the flux air distributor, it would wipe out all humanity throughout the universe.

77 · THE FALL

Emi's heart throbbed. She struggled to breathe as she quickly climbed to the next rung on the ladder and then the next. From the escape hatch she could see the plague one level below her, accelerating up through Snow Tower.

Emi looked up and saw a ship leaving IGIST. The ship was marked with the Tusk logo. *What a coward,* she thought. *I'm going to put you out of business.*

Emi looked down and saw Florin through the glass and paused for a second to lock eyes with her professor. With a glimmer of hope in her expression, Florin pointed for Emi to continue on. Her mentor was fighting for all humanity. Her teacher's gesture was more than pointing her to get to the top. The gesture symbolized a passing of the torch. Against all odds, Florin believed in Emi. A powerful sense of pride came over Emi. Florin, who had always seemed cold and harsh to Emi, was proving to be her biggest champion. Now the Earth-born pupil and mentor were together taking on a seemingly impossible challenge. With every advance up the tower, the two Earthlings battled dejection, hopelessness, and despair.

But with every rung behind her, the weight of the situation became heavier and heavier for Emi. Maybe Celeste Tusk was right. Was Emi the girl who doomed the universe?

Emi climbed past a door from the escape hatch and quickly continued toward the top of the tower. She could see the apex where a door led into the capstone of the tower. Emi could feel the plague and heard the phantom sounds. She turned back and saw the plague entering the level below her.

She peered into the tower at the level where she was, hoping to see Florin. She was not there. Maybe she had passed Emi and was already at the apex. A sinking feeling grabbed her as she reached the bottom of the apex and looked into the capstone room. No Florin.

She paused before opening the door. From her vantage point she could see the level below. The plague was spreading through the room. Emi's hand slipped from the rung, and she slammed into the door. The knock hurt her head, and she pulled back from the door.

That was when she saw her professor.

Florin stood in the corner of the level below her. She looked courageous and stood in a fighting stance, her arms tensed, her hands clenched in black gloves. In the room the plague expanded and was in between Florin and the inner entrance to the apex, also blocking her from the exit to the escape ladder. Florin could have tried to flee down the staircase but appeared to be scanning the room, trying to figure out how to maneuver around the plague and get to the top of Snow Tower.

Emi squirmed as she debated climbing down to open the escape hatch and try to help Florin. She could do it. She could climb down and open the hatch, but there was no time. The plague cloud that was blocking Florin from the apex would expand and reach the air distributor in no time. Emi couldn't go back. She needed to press on. Humanity depended on her. Before she opened the door to the apex, she took one last look at her professor.

"No," Emi whimpered.

Below her, Florin did the unthinkable. She ran into the plague. The professor admirably charged through the cloud as the tentacles engulfed her. In less than a second, Florin disappeared into the dark cloud.

There was no noise in space on the escape ladder, but the sound of the plague was deafening to Emi. Paralyzed with fear, Emi couldn't open the door to the apex chamber. Would she be able to stop the plague? If Florin couldn't get to the top, how could Emi stop it? Doubt filled her mind. She couldn't turn back, but she trembled, unable to open the door.

She looked down the escape hatch, and Sadee beamed an image into space. The image showed Emi and her father on the minaret at the Marrakesh. She took a deep breath and opened the chamber to the apex.

78 · ΔPΞX

Emi entered the apex chamber of Snow Tower. The glass pyramid overlooked the solar system. It was deathly quiet inside. In the center of the chamber sat the flux air distributor.

Positioned on top of a single black pillar display, the flux air distributor was its centerpiece. This device was what had made deep-space travel possible. Three neon temporal tube capacitors created a mini pyramid, hovering above the pillar. Surrounding the pyramid was an open plasma sphere. Striking plasma filaments alternated currents, sending randomized purple and pink streaks of light from the outside of the sphere onto the tubes. The tube's center point at the top of the pyramid formed a magnificent randomized purple frequency beam that shot up through the center of the room, from the flux air distributor to a broadcaster that beamed the frequencies throughout space. The intense purple glow filled the room and reflected off the glass, making for a silent, serene experience.

When the frequency hit receivers throughout the universe, they would repeat it, causing the microbiomes of their human hosts to react and morph, creating a living virtual armor against cosmic radiation.

Emi rushed to the center of the room and dropped her backpack. She quickly pulled out the liquid antidote. She was unsure of what to do next. She opened the container and tilted it slowly, pouring a little out. The blue liquid hit the sphere and poured right through the open plasma beam onto the tubed pyramid, and then the liquid spilled onto the floor. Nothing happened.

She leaned closer, this time putting the container into the sphere, the plasma tingling her hands with little shocks, and dumped a bit of antidote liquid directly onto the tubes. It spilled through and dripped on the floor. Nothing again.

Emi sighed in frustration. She had expected the liquid to be absorbed by either the plasma gas lights or the tubes and then shoot up into the beam. This wasn't working. She needed help.

Emi dropped to her knees. She was going to fail. "I need help. I can't do this alone!"

Her whole life she had strived to be a solo inventor, the brilliant scientist who alone would emerge with the world's solution, and here she was in the greatest ordeal of all time, but she needed help. She thought of the few memories she had of her mother. Every moment she had been in the lab toiling away, there had been someone with her. Her father had supported her mother all along. Her mother had never done it alone. Emi thought back on her journey at IGIST. She'd been helped all along the way by Florin, Jilli, Balin, and Hans. Even Ankor had helped her.

She desperately wished they were with her in this moment. She needed the help of others.

She took a deep breath. What would Florin do? What would Balin, Hans, and Jilli do? What would Ankor do? She would give anything to have their help.

In the corner of the chamber, a tiny speck appeared. A faint hiss, then a crack, startled Emi. *Focus,* Emi mouthed. *What if?* What if she broke the tubes? Would that change their reaction to the liquid? The plasma was a gas. The gas was forming the beam. What did that matter? Matter! That's what Florin was trying to tell her. The matter of the antidote needed to be a gas.

The tiny speck had multiplied into a little dust devil of a black cloud. *Wuh-PSSSH,* crack! It expanded faster. The first tentacle emerged.

How could Emi turn the antidote from liquid to a gas? She thought of Jack Lemore, Jilli. *"Nothing stays the same, don't pass, / No static, don't falter."*

Emi thought of Florin. She hummed. *"Phases of matter. / Solid, liquid, gas."*

Suddenly, Emi remembered Genesis, where Ankor had given her a vaporizer. "Don't waste it. Save it for later."

In her bag. Eureka! The vaporizer was in her bag.

Emi ripped open her backpack. In the bottom was the vapor device. It had been clanging around in her bag since Genesis. She held it up. The clear tube contained a liquid. When she pressed it, the device atomized the liquid and sprayed out a white gas.

Wuh-PSSSH, crack! The plague was not a little cloud anymore but was growing and growing. It would reach the flux air distributor any moment.

Emi quickly unscrewed the vaporizer and poured the liquid out. With her hands shaking she poured the antidote into the vaporizer. She screwed the vaporizer shut.

The sound of the plague was now filling the room. *Wuh-PSSSH,* crack! Emi didn't hear a thing as she chased the light. She focused on the flux air distributor. The brilliant blue liquid sloshed around in the clear tube as she pressed the button. A pale blue mist appeared, spraying onto the plasma sphere and through the strikes, hitting the center of the mini pyramid. As the pale blue antidote gas hit the purple and pink plasma, a reaction occurred, causing the strikes to turn white.

The reaction intensified, and soon the entire sphere and all the tubes were glowing bright white. The reaction overtook the center light and moved slowly up the beam.

She reached in her backpack and quickly grabbed her mask.

"Come on. Come on," said Emi as the white light moved slowly up the beam. The plague filled the room. Emi ducked down, grabbing the pillar. Her focus broke, and she heard the plague again. She took one last deep breath and held it in. The white beam was almost at the top of the apex. The plague engulfed her as she shut her eyes. The sound of the plague was deafening. Emi kept her eyes shut and held her breath as long as she could.

Suddenly, the white beam hit the top of Snow Tower, and a shockwave broadcast the antidote formula throughout space.

Emi looked out over IGIST as several of the receivers on the space station picked up the antidote formula, and then a white plasma wave shot across the campus. As the shockwave hit, the sinister clouds of the plague instantly turned into white ash and fell to the ground. Across IGIST and the universe, the plague had been wiped out, and all that remained was a white powdery substance.

In the apex chamber, a white powdery shape covered the ground where the plague formation had been.

Emi ripped off her mask and looked out into space. She didn't have a single ounce of strength left as she fell to the floor and leaned against the pillar. She looked out over IGIST. From Snow Tower she could see the blue marble of Earth and the moon. She breathed a sigh of relief. The room was silent.

79 · OLD STARS DIE . . .

A silence fell over the Mausoleum as Emi entered. She felt everyone staring at her. In her arms she carried some things that meant the world to her. To Emi's knowledge, Florin would be the only actual human to be placed at rest in the Mausoleum. Her body was found in Snow Tower after the plague had been extinguished. Sadee glowed blue and made a sighing sound as they approached Archimedes. The chancellor stood next to the casket.

The casket's glass cover showed Florin's body. Emi gazed at her sadly. Florin had always looked so serious. Lying in her casket, her professor finally looked at ease. The bygone belonged at IGIST.

In Emi's hands was the IGIST model she had sent to Florin. On the base of the model, Emi had placed a handful of dirt from Earth as well as the rose shining red.

Emi felt grief as she looked at Florin, but more than grief she felt gratitude. She was so thankful that she had gotten the chance to meet Florin, an Earthling who had also made it to IGIST. Florin was not the dull professor she had first met during the tour of the Bio Center. She was a courageous woman willing to sacrifice everything for humanity. Florin, as it turned out, had a gift for seeing the best in her students. A sage mentor recognized the value of letting someone arrive on her own time.

"Emi." Archimedes nodded to her with a kind smile. "You're a different person than the one who sent that model to Florin."

He smiled and pointed to the bottom of the casket. There she placed the model, along with the glowing rose. She then took a seat between Hans and Ankor.

Archimedes stood at the podium and addressed the crowd.

"I will miss Florin as a professor and as a friend. I'm comforted knowing that her indomitable spirit and example will live on in the inspiration of her luminaries. Florin expected greatness and held her luminaries to a high standard. She demanded critical thinking. When they entered into a lab with Florin, her students would see their understated professor transformed into a giant. Her lab created a training ground for the real world of science—a place where her students aspired to become scientists, creators, and inventors in their own right here at IGIST.

"It was not good enough to just understand the basics of science with Florin. She demanded her luminaries attain a mastery of the subject so that they might extend the boundary of human knowledge. Being from Earth, Florin, more than anyone, knew that for us to thrive and continue on in space each one of us must be able to make that commitment and contribution."

Archimedes paused and looked at Emi.

"As the universe continuously expands in the vastness of a space where Earth itself appears as a pale blue dot, we might ask, 'Can one individual make a difference?' Florin is proof that we can. As we look to the future of space and science,

Florin's memory will be a catalyst for her students to strive to do the right thing for humanity and inspire their future adventures. In the enormity of space, as galaxies rush away from each other into eternity, new clouds of gas are collapsing into new galaxies."

He paused again. Emi smiled at Hans and Ankor. Sadee glowed green. If Archimedes was right, it was only the beginning of their adventures at IGIST.

Archimedes finished, "As old stars die . . ."

EPILOGUE

In the domed structure that overlooked the capital of Mars, the high council had met for the esteemed race.

"Venter, welcome!" exclaimed a councilmember, "Have you brought a champion?"

Venter nodded and cracked opened his hands, showing the squid monkey. The creature was very small and could easily fit on his thumb. It stood inside a thimble holder with two of its tentacles perched on the edge.

Venter placed the thimble containing his squid monkey in the center of the table.

Walking around the table, the official held a red sandstone pot for the ante. Venter reached into his pocket and dropped a stack of mauro coins in the pot. The financial stakes were high and a testament to the high council members' ability to bet a substantial amount of wealth on the ritual.

After collecting the ante, the official spoke, "High council, the Oculus race will commence shortly. This is a fine batch of squid monkeys. I see we have a strong and lean selection. When the bell rings, the racers will navigate the table course. The squid monkey who makes it to the outer ring first will be crowned the Oculus champion and be named the Captain of the Starfall."

The squid monkeys were writhing in their holders as the officials scanned the table one final time before the race would commence. The squid monkeys were genetically engineered creatures that would take on the League's most challenging assignments in space exploration.

The little beasts were a marvel to look at. In their youth they were tiny and highly susceptible to infant mortality. The race would produce only one winner. All of the racers had to be less than two months old.

The table's obstacles consisted of three escalating rings that raised in height to the edge of the structure. The first ring was filled with orange liquid that the squid monkeys would need to navigate across. The second ring was a light ring channeling sunlight that would stun the squid monkeys if they were directly exposed. The third ring was a U-shaped trench with blades crisscrossing and cholla needles shooting across.

On the back of each squid monkey's head, two numbers were etched in black: 55, representing the 55th Oculus race, and their number in the race, one through seven. Venter's racer was number six. The etchings were linked to a leaderboard projected above the three rings.

"Ladies and gentlemen, on your mark," announced the official. Around the table the high council looked down on their racers. Venter held the thimble before the bell rang.

***

The cap of darkness lifted before her eyes. She could finally see it. She had always known her mission. It was time to prove her worth. She was number Six. Surrounding the circle starting point was the moat of bubbling orange liquid.

The liquid was swirling faster and faster toward seven dips. *Whirlpools,* she thought. There were only six vessels. She wriggled through the sand behind another squid monkey numbered One. He slid into the canoe. She plucked the two oars. As he reached for them, she swung two tentacles at One, knocking him back. He lost his grip. She wriggled into the canoe and with the oar walloped him. This time he fell, flailing in the pool.

Number One screeched as he burned. Suddenly, what looked like an enormous missile head dropped from above. It was a human finger, hanging over the squid monkey who was burning in the orange liquid. Number One wriggled his tentacles above the bubbling liquid and screamed in agony. The finger remained in the same spot. One reached out his tentacle and wrapped it around the finger before it raised him out. *So long,* she thought.

As she navigated across the orange moat, she saw that three of the squid monkeys had already made it to the other side. The next obstacle was to cross the ring with direct light shining down from the top of the dome. The first and largest of the squid monkeys, number Seven, started to gallop on his tentacles. The squid monkey took a leap into the sunlight.

As number Seven's slimy, rubbery tentacles hit the sunlight, steam and then smoke came off the beast. Seven yelped and fell to the ground in the direct sunlight. The beast whimpered as the direct sunlight scorched him. Shriveled, he wriggled onto the finger.

Number Six hunkered down behind a rock and gathered her composure. She watched as number Four tried to use brute force to evade the direct sunlight. The squid monkey tried a similar run and jump that ended in the same fate as number Seven.

The leaderboard showed Two in the lead followed by Five, Six, and Three all still in the race. One, Seven, and Four were listed below the line with a red "X" next to their names.

Number Two, Five, Six, and Three all stalled behind the rocks. It had only been a few minutes, but it felt like a lifetime. There was nowhere to hide, and it seemed imminent that the race would end in an uneventful draw of scared squid monkeys hiding behind rocks.

Suddenly, the orange moat exploded, and the liquid spilled over the track between the moat and the sunlight. Before Six could react, the sunlight ring also started to expand, inching closer to the liquid. The squid monkeys were trapped.

Six climbed on top of her rock as the liquid inched closer. She looked as number Five took an oar to number Three, knocking down the other squid monkey. Number Five held the other squid monkey over his head and charged into the sunlight. Number Three acted as a shade shield as number Five hurried across the sunlight barrier. When he reached the other side, he threw the remaining husk of the withered Three into the sunlight and pushed on to the last obstacle.

Number Six looked over at number Two and considered a similar tactic. It would take too long to get to the other squid monkey, and the liquid was now almost at her rock. The canoe that she had used to cross the first barrier was getting pushed up closer to her while the sunlight also closed in on her rock. Number Six leaned over the rock and lifted up the canoe with her tentacles, raising the boat above her head.

Shaded by the canoe, she jumped off the rock directly into the sunlight and charged across the sunlit ring. When she got to the other side, she dumped the canoe and saw that number Two had used the same tactic.

The leaderboard now showed Five in the lead followed by Six and Two. They had just one obstacle ring left to overcome.

In between the three remaining squid monkeys and the finish line ring was the most daunting of obstacles. A U-shaped trench encircled the arena. Inside the trench, blades swung back and forth, crisscrossing the path.

Six assessed how she might get across the trench. To her left, Two dragged the canoe to the edge and tried to use it as a shield. The blades quickly chopped the boat to shreds and dismembered Two in the process.

Five had taken a different approach. The squid monkey was crawling across the trench, alternating between a slow crawl and quick bursts to avoid the blades and shooting cholla needles.

Six still hadn't entered the trench. Behind her she felt the heat. She turned to see the sunlight ring expanding, forcing her to jump into the deadly trench. As she hit the ground, a blade swung in front of her, just barely missing her. Six squatted down on her tentacles and then leaped up high, missing two blades.

Surprised that her jumping tactic had worked, Six wasted no time squatting down and jumping, avoiding the blades once again. She had caught up to Five and would certainly beat him if she could keep up her jumping momentum. Just three more jumps and she'd reach the finish line.

Timing would be key. She needed to jump as the blades swung. If she jumped too soon, they would swipe her when she landed. If she waited too long, she'd get hit by the blade. Six waited until the blade swung and then jumped. She stuck the landing, avoiding the blades. *Two more jumps.* She paused and timed her next jump perfectly. *Only one more.* Six paused, waiting for the blade to swing. She saw Five crawling along, barely avoiding the seesawing blades. If she could make her next jump, she would win.

The cholla needle came out of nowhere. It pierced one of Six's tentacles, pinning her to the ground. She tried to wriggle away, but the microscopic barbs in the cholla needle only further ensnared her tentacle. As the blade swung, she ducked down, barely avoiding the initial swing. In seconds the blade would swing back. Six struggled, unable to get away. She ducked again.

Six looked up as she tried to get her tentacle free. Five inched closer to the last blade obstacle. If she didn't get away, he'd surely win. Five crouched low, preparing for his final burst.

As the blade started to swing, Six held her breath and walked forward. She leaned in with all her strength, stretching her impaled tentacle. She screamed in agony. The separation was instant. The blade slice was smoother than she'd expected, but the throbbing pain started immediately.

On the far side of the blade, Six remained intact minus a tentacle, now a bloody stub. On the other side of the blade, Six's tentacle remained pinned to the ground with the cholla needle. Six crouched down and flung herself with all her might toward the finish line.

The leaderboard showed Six in the number-one slot and flashed green. In the number two spot, Five lit up as he crossed the finish line seconds behind Six.

The councilman held up the squid monkey in the cup of his hand and kissed the little wonder.

"Tanvi!" yelled Venter. He repeated himself, chanting his squid monkey's name in joy, "Tanvi! Tanvi! Tanvi! Today is just the beginning of tomorrow's voyage!"

JOIN THE IGIST MOVEMENT

- ***Download the IGIST app and share with friends! Get the full experience:***

- ***Don't miss out on all the fun in the IGIST universe:***
    - *Visit www.igist.com/events to sign up for our epic Book Tour and meet author L.S. Larson!*
    - *Follow IGIST Studios on Instagram to see new behind-the-scenes illustrations and fan shout-outs.*
    - *Tune in to IGIST Roll Call, our YouTube series featuring your favorite characters.*
    - *Enter the IGIST Zurcon Challenge in the app to get free giveaways and a chance to* ***WIN A TRIP TO SPACE!*** *(Yes, we're serious. A real trip to space.)*

- ***We'd love to hear from you!***
    - *Share your favorite aspects of IGIST with lsl@igist.com and submit a cool pic from the app.*

Watch IGIST gear come to life with AR features in the app.

Interstellar gear available at www.igist.com

Made in the USA
Middletown, DE
07 April 2019